Frankly, Madame

I Don't Give a Dear

H.L. Ford

PublishAmerica
Baltimore

First printing

ISBN: 1-60563-086-1
PUBLISHED BY PUBLISHAMERICA, LLLP
www.publishamerica.com
Baltimore

Printed in the United States of America

Chapter 1

Ghosts Are My Business

Run!

My mind screamed at me to flee from this evil place. I had to restrain my feet from taking off without the rest of me.

Something was coming.

And there was no place to hide.

Sleep paralysis during a nightmare. That's the feeling that overwhelmed me.

Get hold of yourself, Kaytie, I scolded inwardly. *You're a grown woman with a sound mind, even if you do forget to use it at times.*

That little lecture did not stop me from searching the shadows of the ruined sanctuary for a route of escape. The only exit was the double doorway at the entrance to the long and narrow hall. Once a place of consecration it was now a site used to celebrate unholy things.

Unholy spirits.

Ghosts are my business, but the self-named Count Ribaldo was a flesh-and-blood man and probably far more dangerous than any so-called spook I'd ever encountered.

I'd recognized his words: *ta muid anseo leis na deith a adhradh*. "We are here to honor the gods…to open the gates between the worlds and to allow the power to flow."

Until that moment, I had been merely curious. Now I was crawling with tension. He lifted his robed arms and tilted his head back, staring upward into the dark recesses of the temple. Forty cult members imitated his posture, a few faces exposed as cowled hoods fell back on their shoulders. I did not recognize any of them, except one man who could have been my dentist. Surely I was mistaken.

Lit only by candlelight, the cavernous room moved with flickering shadows. I couldn't help glancing upward toward the high ceiling, hoping I would not see whatever it was they were calling on to appear. Nothing was visible in the swirling darkness, but I sensed such a malevolent presence that my instinct to flee switched to overdrive. My skin literally sparked with tension. The musty odor and the dampness added to my discomfort.

An eerie blue flame leapt up from the center of chalk markings, symbols from an ancient book of sorcery, traced on the worn stone floor. All chanting ceased. An expectant hush filled the room. I could detect a pungent odor somewhat like ozone after a lightning strike. The candles flickered weakly as the scent grew stronger.

The cult leader was clever. He had attracted media attention by claiming he had predicted the terrorist attack on the twin towers after contacting the spirit of an ancient Druid. Skeptical reporters such as myself challenged his claim, coming as it did years after the attack. In rebuttal, Ribaldo had invited selected journalists to witness his next contact with the spirit world.

It was a bold move. He had to produce a show for his guests. Something *would* happen. He would see to it that five members of the press were not disappointed.

Darkness seemed to gather in the highest rafters at the apex of the neglected sanctuary. A small blue flame appeared as if to reflect the fire burning on the dusty floor.

Mirrored light?

A column of black smoke snaked downward and circled Count Ribaldo like an eager hound before appearing to enter his nostrils and all but disappearing. The count threw back his head and uttered a long howl unlike any wolf I'd ever heard. The eerie sound was feral, wolfish yes, but with a hollow quality, almost an echo, as if projected from a far distance.

Glancing toward the reporters standing on either side of me, I could see my own doubts reflected on their faces. So far, what we had seen could be cleverly staged effects. Good showmanship. Nothing really supernatural; however the presence of evil was palpable. I wanted nothing more than to leave the hall at once.

Then the voice spoke, curiously different from the count's normal tones.

The language sounded similar to Gaelic at first, becoming English as the figure turned toward me.

Ribaldo raised a draped arm theatrically.

He pointed me out and announced, "You are not who you think you are."

Goose bumps pimpled my arms. I wanted to pipe back, *And just who do you think you are?* but I couldn't find my voice.

After several unintelligible utterances, the count spoke of a coming fire in California. Of course anybody could make that prediction and be correct, eventually.

He continued to make non-specific forecasts until finally the blue flames died. The stillness of the room remained eerie, as if filled with unseen presence. The count seemed to come to himself, blinking and staring. He chanted a recitation of sorts to unwind and conclude the ceremony. His voice was decidedly different.

As the group began to disperse he approached the knot of reporters who were eager to ask questions and jot down notes.

Finally it was my turn.

"What did you mean when you said I'm not who I think I am?"

The count's eyes fixed on mine and blazed with a peculiar fire. "The spirit guide singled you out. You have a peculiar destiny."

His voice was deep and resonant, not at all the same voice which had spoken through him earlier during the performance.

I wanted to inquire further, but he turned to another news hound, leaving me with unanswered questions.

Later, driving back to my Chicago residence, I was aware of a sense of foreboding, of unknown danger ahead. I had the prickly sensation that I was being followed and turned to glance over my shoulder several times.

A hot shower and a few pages of reading would cure this case of jitters.

I was wrong. I ended up reading most of the night, unable to sleep.

* * *

My story on Count Ribaldo's cult involved researching the group's funds. By the time my editor ran it, the count was already charged with sexual misconduct involving members and fraudulent use of donations for luxury vacations and lavish personal expenditures. He would be locked up for a long while.

I hoped to lock him out of my mind as well, but the curious words he had uttered kept echoing in my mind.

Not who you think you are.

The vague feeling of unease became so strong I actually thought of calling my mom in Baton Rouge to ask her if I was adopted, then laughed at the preposterous notion.

No way. I looked in the mirror.

Yep, it was me alright. I had Mom's green eyes and Dad's unmistakable auburn hair. They were my parents without doubt. I was their one and only daughter, Kaytie Flame O'Reilly, named for a flamboyant character from the pages of my mother's favorite Civil War novel and movie.

My name earned me lots of teasing from classmates over the years, but it also helped me develop a sense of humor. However, I saw nothing humorous in Ribaldo's strange prediction for me.

No matter how I tried to shake it off, the foreboding persisted. The count had been dabbling in serious occult practices, dangerous stuff. Could he cause some *thing* to come after me? Some wicked spirit eager to pounce on me?

You're just letting your imagination run away with you, I told myself.

Like that time at age seven when I dreamed wild chickens were underneath my bed waiting to flog me. The dream was so vivid I refused to sleep there again for a week. To this day, I don't let my hands or feet hang off the mattress.

If my editor noted my jittery nerves, he didn't mention it. Instead, he asked me to cover the story of a haunting in a famous New Orleans hotel and to uncover any possible fakery involved. I jumped at the chance, thinking a change of scenery might be just what I needed.

Briefcase in the overhead bin and seatbelt buckled, my plan was to nap during the flight, but sleep avoided me. I hadn't really slept well since observing Count Ribaldo's cult activity. That's bad for the people around me. I'm a real grouch when I don't get enough sleep.

The flight was uneventful until we approached the runway of Louis Armstrong International Airport. Then it got bumpy.

I could see thunderheads rolling ominously across the night-blackened sky, their bellies hanging low reflecting city lights in muted colors. It was a breathtaking sight before the plane touched down and bumped to that sudden forward-propelling stop that always makes me want to jam my foot on imaginary brakes.

As soon as the pilot turned off the seat-belt sign, I hurried to retrieve my bag at the baggage carousel and headed for Ground Transportation, hoping to grab a taxi before the clouds split. I was not fast enough. Whisks of rain began sweeping the tarmac, and I could see two of the three remaining cabs already pulling away.

If he had been the romantic hero of one of those adventure novels, the famed Mr. Dax Larue never would have jumped into the last taxi without offering to share it. He would have lifted me in those strong arms, carried me over the curb-side flood and placed me gently inside the cab, where overcome by my beauty, he would have been compelled to kiss me tenderly.

Whoa. What was I thinking? Overactive imagination indeed.

I would have settled for staying dry. I must have been invisible, or he simply pretended not to see me standing there, drenched in the downpour. In either case, he was no romantic hero and I was no beauty.

Before he could close the door, I grabbed it and tossed my bag inside.

"Move over, mister, I'm getting wet out here." Dripping raindrops the size of dimes, I climbed inside.

"Where y'all going?" the cabby asked.

"The Lafitte Hotel in New Orleans," we answered simultaneously. That's when Larue first looked at me. Feeling totally bedraggled at that moment, I half wished I were invisible. Instead, I lifted my chin and decided it was lucky for him that we were going to the same place.

"Ahhh, the *haunted* hotel," the driver replied with a very southern Texas drawl. He pronounced the word in three syllables, *hotayal*.

"Betcha you're both reporters. They've been coming in from all over. Some of the biggies from Discovery Channel and *Haunted Houses of History*. Even that Jeremy guy from *Scientific American*. Ain't none of 'em found a ghost out there yet, so far as I know. But tonight's supposed to be the big night, huh?"

He pulled away from the curb, to my great relief. I was certain the rising water would flood the vehicle and drown us any minute.

Well, maybe it wasn't exactly a torrent yet, but it had potential. Rain sluiced down the windshield so hard the wiper blades couldn't clear it.

That didn't bother the cabby. He drove as if he could navigate the area blindfolded.

"You guessed right. Dax Larue from the *Supernatural Seeker* out of Chicago." My companion nodded toward the driver's reflection in the visor mirror.

I'd recognized him immediately at the airport's baggage claim. Mister Crackerjack Reporter, the heartthrob of every woman who has ever viewed one of the *Seeker's* TV specials or followed his adventures in the magazine. My heart did *not* throb over him that night. It was pounding from irritation at his lack of chivalry.

Of course he hadn't recognized me. Unlike Larue, I'm never on TV except when a cameraman accidentally pans my way during a press conference. I work for a less sensational but more solidly researched magazine.

My job is just the opposite of Larue's—to take the mystery out of the mysterious, explain the unexplained and put the natural back into false claims of the supernatural.

Working for competitive publications with opposing points of view, I knew our paths as well as our words were bound to cross sooner or later. I just hadn't expected it to be when I was dripping wet. I'd wanted to be at my best when I crossed word swords with Dax Larue.

Robbed of the chance to make a good first impression, I decided to speak up.

"I'm from *Beyond Fantasy* magazine, also based in Chicago, and I'm not here just to do a story on the haunted hotel."

Actually I was, but I figured I'd think up some other reason for being in New Orleans. After all, I didn't want the famous Mr. Larue to feel threatened by my superior career status.

"*Beyond Fantasy*? Isn't that the freebie with a shopping guide and garage sale addresses?"

"You have my journal mixed up with *Beyond Bargains*," I corrected icily.

Larue had named the leaflet listing all the blue-light specials in Chicago, and no self-respecting journalist works for a shopper's guide. He was being snobbish. Either that or my lack of sleep was making me extra snarly.

"So your paper's not just an ad flyer?"

"It's a quarterly journal. We don't do television specials like the kind you host for the *Seeker*, but we do have an international reading audience. We do investigative reporting all over the world."

That sounded braggadocios, but the words just slipped out.

"Oh, yes. I think I read one of your magazines once. The story on the UFO sighting caught my eye. Some wacky woman claiming she saw something shaped like a gigantic garbage can hanging over the treetops. Was she on drugs or something?"

I considered a snappy comeback, but checked my sleep-deprived temper instead, saying with a smile, "You happen to be talking to the wacky woman who saw it, and I wasn't on anything but a morning cup of coffee."

I looked him straight in the eye—actually straight in the ear since he wasn't facing me at that moment. He turned to look at me a second time, and this time I had his attention.

"You really saw that thing you wrote about?"

"With my own two eyes. And if I'm wacky, I'm not alone. The late Peter Jennings once reported that over 40 million people worldwide have seen mysterious things in the sky. UFOs are no big deal anymore."

Being a veteran reporter with the *Seeker*, Larue probably knew a lot more about these things than I did, but I was determined not to let him intimidate me.

"That's true," he agreed. "But usually witnesses describe an object that at least looks like it can fly. A garbage-can shape suspended over a tree. Now that's unusual. However, I do apologize for using the term *wacky*, Miss…?"

So he wanted to know my name. Debating whether to accept his apology, I decided to keep things formal.

"It's O'Reilly."

"Well, Miss O'Reilly, I'll try to find a copy of your magazine and read it more carefully next time."

I considered offering him a copy from my briefcase. The lead story was mine, and I was proud of it.

No, I thought, *he probably doesn't know good writing when he sees it.*

Just then a huge clap of thunder shattered the night as well as my eardrums. Lightning blinded me momentarily. We rode in silence most of the eleven miles from Kenner into the Crescent City with only the sound of the wipers swishing vainly.

I peered out the window thinking to see some of the remaining devastation from Hurricane Katrina. There was little evidence on our route. The Superdome looked completely restored.

Finally Tex spoke up.

"Hey, I'm thinking y'all will be lucky if they have any rooms at the Lafitte. It's not a big place and like I said, reporters have been coming in for two days. If you want, I'll drop you at the Bourbon Orleans or some other hotel to check in for the night, and then you can catch a cab over to the Lafitte."

"I have a reservation, thanks," said Dax.

"Me too," I echoed.

I didn't have one, but I wasn't about to take a chance on missing the event. Even if the ghost didn't show up, there would be plenty of mysterious stories to cover.

This year's spectral appearance fell on a Friday the thirteenth. The New Orleans police were dealing with a rash of reports on weird happenings. Some witnesses even swore they saw zombies walking about the city. Probably roaming Bourbon Street if I had to guess. You can see most anything on Bourbon Street if you hang out there a minute or two.

The famed Lafitte Hotel is located in an area rumored to be a hot spot for psychic energy. Every witch in the area would be trying to get her broom off the ground. Every voodoo do-er would be sticking pins in dolls, and every New Orleans medium would be trying to contact the "other side."

My guess was that a few visitors at the Lafitte might tip a glass too many and see the apparition, or hear the legendary organ music which is said to accompany her appearances. I briefly wondered if the ghost played Dixieland tunes. Maybe jazz. We could even wind up snapping our fingers and tapping our toes.

That might be fun.

Of course, if all the guests were reporters, we might just have a bunch of cameras on tripods filming quietly while everybody sat still for hours in the gloom. Ghost lady might be camera shy and stay away.

That could be very dull.

Fun or dull, I wasn't going to miss the evening if I had to sleep on top of the haunted organ itself.

We split the cab fare. Dax offered to help me with my bag, but I refused, thinking I'd do just as well without his belated chivalry. Fortunately, there was a canvas awning over the entrance to the Lafitte. It kept the rain from further soaking me to the skin.

I lugged the suitcase—now I know why it's called luggage—inside and headed for the reservations desk.

The foyer was not overly large, lit by charming antique gaslights, which made it seem quaint and cozy. Furnishings were French provincial period pieces, Louis XIV and Queen Anne. The concierge's desk of carved mahogany looked impressively antique and very ornate. A middle-aged lady lifted wire-rimmed glasses from the tip of her pointy nose and raised her penciled eyebrows at me.

"You have a reservation for Dax Larue from *Supernatural Seeker* magazine?"

Larue had pushed ahead of me.

What a gentleman.

She glanced down at the registry a moment, then nodded. "Ah, yes, Mr. Larue. We have you in the Pirate Suite, room 311 upstairs." Her smile broadened when she looked up to see him standing there, and she actually fluttered her skimpy eyelashes.

"It's a good thing you placed your reservations early. There's not a room left in the place. Not so much as a chaise lounge in a corner." She cast a frosty glance in my direction with her last remark.

I groaned inwardly. Outwardly, I smiled and turned to Larue.

"Well, dear, it certainly is a good thing you booked our room early," then breezed past him, nodding to the bellhop. "My husband and I are in the Pirate Suite, room 311 upstairs," I notified him without waiting to see how Dax was going to respond.

I didn't see an elevator so I just forged up the stairs. Dax followed me. By the time we reached the third-floor landing, I was breathless and he was laughing.

"Well, *Mrs.* Larue, that was one of the smoothest con jobs I ever saw. You certainly aren't shy about sharing cabs. Or hotel rooms."

He used the old-fashioned turnkey and opened the door to the Pirate Suite, then turned toward me with a slightly wicked grin.

"Shall I carry you over the threshold, my dear?"

What was I doing? I had spoken without thinking, which my mother always says is one of my worst faults. She wouldn't approve of course. Not until I reminded her of Clark Gable and Claudette Colbert in *It Happened One Night*, one of her favorites. Then she'd probably laugh.

Ignoring his grin and his remark, I walked in and surveyed the rooms.

"Mr. Larue, this suite looks large enough to accommodate two persons nicely."

Actually it did have the appearance of a honeymoon suite. The sitting area was elegant. A bowl of fresh fruit sat on a low marble table in front of the brocade davenport, and cut flowers were arranged in an alabaster vase on a desk. Cream-colored carpet with a dusty rose motif felt cushy under my feet.

Curtained French doors opened to the bedroom. A king-sized bed draped with a diaphanous canopy stood in the center on a raised and carpeted dais.

The bath opened off the bedroom, where I glimpsed an old-fashioned claw-foot tub.

It looked very deep. In Miss Flame's day, the maid would have had to pour several kettles of hot water to warm it.

"Yes, this will do nicely," I announced as the bellhop entered the room with our luggage.

Dax tipped the man and he promptly disappeared.

I reached for my bag and immediately dragged it into the bedroom.

"I'll take this room and you can sleep on the chaise lounge," I directed, thinking I should return his wicked grin with that declaration.

Instead, I merely smiled cheerfully.

"Ahem, Miss O'Reilly," Dax began. "My employer paid for this suite. Now I'm not going to turn you out in the storm, but I should at least have the bed."

He looked more disgruntled than gruntled, assuming *gruntled* means pleased.

"If you will excuse me," I used a very matter-of-fact tone. "I'm soaked to the skin. I haven't wept a slink in what feels like a week, and I need a hot bath and some dry clothes before the evening's activities begin."

I closed the French doors in his face, wondering why his expression had changed from mild irritation to one of complete amusement.

The bath was marvelous.

Forty minutes later I stepped out of the bedroom, dry, combed and fluffed, wearing a slim white skirt and matching jacket over an emerald green blouse.

With just a little eyeliner, I felt ready for the challenge of both the ghost and Dax Larue. Not that I wanted to impress him, and the ghost lady would hardly care if I wore eyeliner. However, self-confidence boosters are important to any woman.

I tilted my chin up once more and assumed a professional air.

Larue had changed into gray slacks and a red turtleneck. He cut a dashing figure there in the Pirate Suite.

Red was his color, I had to admit. It set off his dark hair and darker eyes the color of a moonless midnight sky. I didn't have to wonder how many women would give up their favorite hairstylist to be in my place—in a Pirate Suite with Larue—ghost or no ghost.

He was studying the screen of his laptop, but he glanced up as I entered and his eyes registered instant approval for my no-longer-bedraggled appearance.

My confidence level jumped up several notches, and my petulant mood disappeared.

"Well, well, well, Miss O'Reilly! Or should I continue calling you *Mrs. Larue* since you're posing as my wife? You look charming either way."

"Just call me Kaytie," I answered, suddenly feeling a little disconcerted that I'd actually bamboozled my way into sharing his suite.

"Kaytie O'Reilly. And is there a Mr. O'Reilly?" His eyebrows rose inquisitively.

"No, but I *am* engaged," I blurted. I didn't want him to assume I was a member of the throngs of adoring female fans who would do anything to get his attention.

Oh great. Now I had an imaginary fiancé.

"Engaged?" he asked as if the concept eluded him.

"Yes. His name is Ashton Wilson."

The name jumped off my tongue: Flame's beloved hero in the Civil War novel. It was the first thing that came to mind. I should have known it sounded very contrived. Especially if he had known my middle name is Flame, but I wasn't about to tell him.

He glanced at my ring finger.

I was glad I had chosen to wear my grandmother's emerald ring that night. It went well with my green silk blouse. Eyes too. People always tell me my eyes are as green as the grass of Ireland.

Looking at his watch, he suggested we head downstairs.

It was already past ten o'clock. The ghost was scheduled to show up at midnight.

Of course. What self-respecting ghost appears at any other time? Midnight to four a.m. Those are considered the witching hours.

Why those hours, I don't know. I suppose that's when most mischief occurs.

Larue offered me his arm, and we started for the downstairs ballroom.

It had once been the grand ballroom of an old sugar plantation manor situated on the outskirts of a rapidly growing New Orleans in the 1800s. Renovations had narrowed the room over the last hundred years, but the elegant and gracefully curving staircase remained its charming centerpiece.

A chandelier hung slightly off center overhead. Softly glowing candles cast dancing shadows in various places throughout the room. Perfect ambience for spectral appearances.

TV camera crews were setting up tripods and doing their visual checks. Five rows of folding chairs had been set up, and most were already occupied by newspaper, radio and television reporters.

Discovery Channel TV cameras from the program *America's Most Haunted Places* were stationed on either side of the staircase. The crew also had a third camera located on the balcony above.

The ghost had drawn a bigger turnout than the governor's last press conference. I briefly wondered if she had been a Democrat or a Republican.

Of course not.

She was a Confederate!

Silly me.

Dax and I found a couple of chairs in the third row.

"Where's your camera crew?" I asked in a low tone.

The atmosphere of the room begged for hushed conversation.

"We've got a cameraman here somewhere. Oh yeah, he's over there." He pointed to a *Supernatural Seeker TV* camera stationed near the grand staircase on the floor of the ballroom.

I opened my purse and pulled out a small digital camera. It looked very unworthy in the presence of all the high-tech equipment surrounding me, but it would do the trick. I might write for an obscure journal, but I was here on the job just the same as all the big corporate-owned newspaper and network journalists.

"How long have you been at *Beyond Fantasy*?" Dax asked. "Do you like it?"

"About a year, and yes, I actually enjoy debunking urban legends. Modern myths. The kind of supernatural junk that a certain part of the population is always so willing to believe—some of it harmless enough. Some of it not."

I knew I shouldn't be taking jabs at his journal, which did not concern itself with truth so much as sensationalism, but I wanted to get even with him for his snobbish remarks in the cab.

He nodded.

"Ah yes. Deceived people and dangerous behavior definitely go together. Like the San Diego Heaven's Gate cult's mass suicide in 1997. I'm guessing that's a good example of what you're talking about."

Slightly surprised that we were on the same page, I answered, "Exactly. How do you suppose that happens? Almost forty misguided fools apparently believed they would wake up and sail away to bliss on the passing Hale Bopp comet. Did you ever see the Heaven's Gate cult leader on television? That guy had a spark of insanity in his eyes. Who in his right mind would follow a man like that?"

Dax shrugged his shoulders.

"Right-minded is the operative term. Sane people *wouldn't* follow him. Then you also have the opposite types. Guys like David Koresh or Jim Jones, handsome and charismatic. It's not hard to believe Jones could attract large numbers to his People's Temple, or that they would follow him to Guyana to build his Jonestown paradise."

"Yes, Jones was an attractive man," I conceded. "I can understand why people might follow him to Guyana, but all the way to mass suicide? Over nine hundred victims. Nearly three hundred of them children! I just don't get it. Mothers and fathers deliberately poisoning their own children. Man, if I went to a church where the leader started rehearsing the congregation for mass suicide, I'd be saying, see you later guys. I think I'll go find a church where you don't have to kill your kids as an act of faith."

Dax looked amused.

"Me too. Maybe there's a place for martyrdom, but I don't want to blow myself up, or a whole lot of other innocent people along with me, just to show my devotion." He turned toward me with a disarming grin.

"I think your magazine will do a great service if you can warn people to stay away from the Heaven's Gates and Jim Joneses of the world."

Pleasantly surprised, I blurted, "Of course, we can't expose the weirdoes unless we can verify exactly how they're off the elevator. Even then, some people will continue to believe regardless of the facts. I've come to realize there are groups who just plain *want* to believe weird stuff. That's up to them. My job is to present the truth."

I thought that remark might trigger a rise out of him, a writer who specializes in stories on telekinesis, mediums, psychic healers and other spooky subjects with fraudulent potential. When he didn't respond, my curiosity got the upper hand.

"What about you? Do you enjoy working for the *Seeker*?"

"It's interesting. The money is good." He nodded and shrugged nonchalantly.

I didn't sense any of the passion for his subject that most journalists have. Was he really just about fame and fortune?

"I like the travel. Guess I'm just an adventurer at heart."

I immediately pictured him in an Indiana Jones role with a hat and whip in hand and decided he looked the part.

Someone passed a tray of shrimp-filled canapés, and I realized I was hungry.

"Maybe we should get a late supper somewhere after the event is over?" Dax suggested as if reading my mind.

Either that or my stomach was growling too loudly. I nodded, thinking this time he'd better pay for the cab.

And the dinner.

A pendulum clock near the entrance hall chimed the eleventh hour. Cameramen ran visual checks and others jotted down notes.

We passed the time making brief introductions and getting acquainted with news hounds we didn't already know. Some of the female variety kept glancing at Dax.

If you're a female TV anchor or reporter, it's an unwritten rule that you have to be young and cute, and they were. They must have assumed we were a couple, because they kept their distance.

Too bad for Larue.

The haunting hour approached.

Quiet chatter dwindled to a murmur. All remaining gaslights were extinguished. Only the flickering candles cast a soft amber glow in the lower room, leaving the grand staircase shrouded in shadow.

An antique grandfather clock began to chime. At the somber tone of each gong, anticipation mounted.

Nobody moved or spoke.

What would we see?

By the eleventh chime I was lightly gripping the edge of my seat in anticipation. The twelfth gong sounded, faded, and a melodic echo hung in the expectant hush.

Nothing happened.

No one moved.

I realized I was holding my breath and wanted to release it, but feared I might sneeze and break the spell. Thunder grumbled, a timely sound effect.

I needed to sneeze.

Lightning briefly silvered the room, and candles flickered, casting giant shadows of misshapen beings on the walls.

I stifled the sneeze and dared to release my breath slowly, glancing at Dax. He was cool as a card player holding all the aces.

My eyes riveted on the shadowy stairs once more.

That's when I saw it.

A misty, whitish figure began to materialize at the top of the staircase.

There were no discernible features, but the shimmering figure was definitely a female wearing a long, flowing white gown. She faded in and out for a moment and then dissolved.

A moment later she materialized on the second stair, wispy and ethereal.

I struggled to stifle the insistent sneeze. What if I couldn't keep it back and scared her away? I'd be the object of everyone's wrath if the wraith vanished because of me.

The wrath of the wraith crossed my mind as a great title for a story.

Funny what pops into my mind during the most intense moments.

Not exactly a gasp but a kind of collective intake of breath could be heard around the room. We remained frozen in our chairs, not daring to make a sound as we watched the figure re-materialize on a lower stair.

No one moved to flash a camera.

The phantom female floated haltingly down the graceful staircase.

I have to admit the hair on the back of my neck prickled, although I had no sense of the presence of evil such as I'd experienced in Count Ribaldo's meeting.

As she neared the last step, the figure paused, appearing uncertain. She hovered there, transparent in the candlelight, as if made of vapor. Then she began to dissolve slowly.

Aware that this might be my last chance, I flashed my little camera just before she disappeared completely.

The room erupted in gasps and exclamations. Lights blinked on. Cameras turned toward various anchormen who began commentary on the spot. If the ghost had managed to play a haunting melody on the organ, it was drowned out by the commotion in the room.

Dax picked up a microphone.

"This is *Supernatural Seeker* Anchor Dax Larue broadcasting from the old Lafitte plantation house in New Orleans. What you have just seen, assuming our camera captured it, is the legendary apparition said to appear every September thirteenth on these very stairs."

He made his voice dramatic with barely controlled excitement.

"For well over a hundred years, guests and staff members have been claiming to see the female apparition. Various guesses as to the ghost's identity have been offered, the popular theory being that she was the manor's former mistress who died during the Civil War."

The drama in his voice drew me into the story and made me want to hear more than what I had just seen with my own eyes.

"Her appearance every September thirteenth has been so regular that it has become a spectator event in the last several years. The Lafitte's ghost has made the list of New Orleans' most haunted places, rivaling even the site of the former historic Royal Street mansion, a place where screams and groans are still said to be heard, voices of slaves owned by the sadistic Madame Delphine LaLaurie—the very slaves she tortured and mutilated in the early 1830s."

Someone stuck a microphone in my face, and Dax turned to me with a serious expression.

"With me tonight is Miss Kaytie O'Reilly from *Beyond Fantasy* magazine based in Chicago. Miss O'Reilly, can you describe for us what you just witnessed?"

Cheese and crackers. He was interviewing me to get his story.

"I saw the same thing everyone else in this room presumably saw. The misty image of a woman appearing to float down the grand-ballroom staircase," I answered. "And a bunch of reporters with their mouths dropping open and their eyes popping out of their heads."

Dax kept a straight face.

"Tell me, Miss O'Reilly. Did you believe in ghosts before you came here tonight?"

"Not really. Not ghosts in the sense of the word that most people understand it," I piped.

"And do you believe in ghosts now?"

His lips had just the slightest hint of a mischievous smile.

"My beliefs have not been changed by what I saw."

Now Dax looked plainly amused.

"But you do agree that there was a spectral image which appeared and disappeared on the stairs?"

I nodded. "Yes, there was an image."

"Do you have an explanation for what you saw?"

"No. But I'm willing to bet there is one. What do you think?" I fired back.

"Miss O'Reilly, you sound very skeptical. How do you feel about sightings of unexplained floating objects in the sky?"

The scoundrel.

He was trying to provoke me by bringing up my floating garbage-can thing. I spoke confidently.

"I think there are unexplained things happening in our world all the time, and there are reasonable explanations waiting to be discovered."

"Spoken like a true representative of the magazine you write for. So are you saying you don't believe in the supernatural?"

"That is not what I'm saying. Not at all. I believe very much in the supernatural. The Bible is filled with examples."

I had plenty more to say on the subject but he cut me off.

"Thank you, Miss O'Reilly."

He quickly turned to another person to get more commentary. While the rest of the room whirred with cameras, lights and broadcasters interviewing each other, I started up the stairway.

The oaken stairs sported a cream-colored runner with muted splashes of mauve flowers. I ran my hand over the wood first. It was dry. The carpet, however, had a hint of dampness to the touch.

Higher up the stairs it was definitely damp. Of course this might be explained by the passage of rain-splashed guests. A faint white powder clung to my fingers.

What was this?

If there was more of this stuff I wanted a large enough sample to test. I ran my hand over a few more stairs, collected a dusting of powder and brushed it into a plastic bag from my purse.

No one seemed to notice me. On the way down I ran my hand over the walls. There appeared to be sprinkler-system valves at close intervals, following the descent of the stairs, added in recent years no doubt to pass the building code inspection.

This only made sense. In the event of fire, the stairs would need even more protection from flames since guests would not be able to use the elevators.

I'm no expert on building codes, but it seemed there were more sprinkler jets than normal.

Forget that late supper with Dax. I wanted to get these samples to a friend of mine, a chemist.

Would it be too late to visit after midnight? In the French Quarter many doors remain open all night, so I decided to give it a try.

I hurried out into the dripping night and hailed one of four taxis waiting, the drivers obviously expecting an exodus of reporters who hadn't been able to get lodging at the Lafitte.

No doubt they had tuned in their radios to hear reports of the famous Lafitte apparition. Giving the cabby the address on Chartres Street, I was pleasantly surprised to see Tex again behind the wheel.

"Howdy, Miz O'Reilly. Told ya you wouldn't get a room tonight, ma'am," he drawled pleasantly.

"Thought I'd better come back and make sure you didn't have to hoof it anywhere. Rain's stopped at the moment, but it could come a downpour again at the drop of a Stetson."

"Thanks," I said, grateful for his concern.

He chattered pleasantly, curious about what I had seen, as he drove through the French Quarter.

One block off Jackson Square, we pulled up to Ye Olde Alchemy Shoppe, which was actually a modern chemist's laboratory. My friend, Jean Claude, had taken over the business and upgraded it from perfumes, voodoo powders and witchcraft potions after the death of an eccentric aunt. He was now doing some independent research for a couple of pharmaceutical companies. Private investigators and New Orleans detectives also frequented his lab.

Jean Claude shook his head in surprise to see me at the door.

"Kaytie Flame O'Reilly! What are you doing in New Orleans? And what brings you here at this time of dark?"

He gave me a bear hug that nearly cracked a rib and would have made me faint if I'd been wearing a drawstring corset. No wonder those southern belles were always fainting, laced up so tightly they couldn't breathe and wearing all those layers of petticoats over pantaloons in the sweltering Louisiana heat.

"I'm here covering the ghost story at the Lafitte Hotel," I explained. "And I need your professional services."

Jean Claude and I had graduated high school together in Baton Rouge. He'd proposed to me in the seventh grade. He'd also proposed to eighteen other girls before his sophomore year. They all said *yes*.

To my knowledge, he was still unmarried.

After exchanging a little small talk—how's your family, your job, your life—I showed him my sample of white powder.

"You think somebody was selling cocaine at the Lafitte?" He raised an eyebrow and studied the contents.

"No, silly boy. This stuff was on the stairs after the phantom floated down. It may be nothing, but I wanted to check it out."

Jean Claude sniffed the baggie.

"I don't have to run any tests to tell you what this is. Talcum powder. My mother used to wear the same brand. I'd recognize that scent anywhere."

"Talcum powder!" I was truly surprised. A woman had dabbed it on so liberally that she left a trail of it all the way down the stairs? No. There had to be something more.

"Couldn't you please check it anyway? Maybe there's something mixed in with the powder," I suggested.

"Anything for you, Miss Flame," he agreed and gave me a wink.

Of course all my classmates had known my full name. Most of them let me forget it. Some of them, like Jean Claude, still call me *Miss Flame* today, with the exaggerated southern accent used by the movie characters, but only when they want to tease me.

He scraped up a sample with a small spatula and walked back to the lab.

A few minutes later he emerged, holding a glass beaker. "Sorry, sweetheart. It's just talcum powder…and…" he teased.

"And what?"

"Minute particles of a specially developed foil."

"Foil? What kind of special foil? I collected this stuff on the stairs."

Jean Claude shrugged his shoulders.

I noticed the reflective qualities of the substance on his hands, even in the dim glow of the lantern's light. Of course, his lab was state of the art, but he still used old-fashioned lanterns for the front office in keeping with the block's antique atmosphere. The soft glow bounced off the powder with an eerie glow.

"Would large enough volumes of this powder reflect an image? Supposing it was spewed from sprinkler jets and a small projector was installed nearby?

He nodded.

"You're talking about a hologram. It's entirely possible. With steering optics and small moving mirrors you could get an image. You'd need two small laser beams of light intersecting to reflect the image projected on the foil particles. Those would have to be blown into the air from something."

"Something like a sprinkler valve!"

Jean Claude's eyes lit up. "You think that's where your ghost lady came from?"

"I'm willing to bet on it!" I exclaimed, slapping one hand on the counter.

Clever. The ghostly apparition had managed to attract lots of business over the past several years. Hotel competition was fierce, especially since Hurricane Katrina.

Of course, that didn't explain the sightings of more than a hundred years ago, but who knew if there really were any ghostly appearances way back then? Maybe the whole story had been fabricated in more recent years.

We exchanged a few more updates. Who got divorced and who didn't. One of our classmates had run for state senator and lost. Another was an astronaut in training.

When I said I needed to get back to the hotel, Jean Claude insisted, "You aren't walking anywhere at this time of dark. Let me drive you."

I leaned down to glance out the low-set, latticed windows. Groups of enthusiastic revelers still filled the street, walking from bar to bar, clubs or restaurants.

"No, thanks. I have a cab waiting right outside your door." I smiled, touched by his concern.

Jean Claude leaned down and glanced out to see the yellow taxi through the latticed pane. Apparently satisfied, he grinned.

"Okay. But stop by tomorrow and let me take you out for some real N'awlins cuisine. Pat O'Brien's or The Court of Two Sisters?"

"Why Jean Claude, you handsome old thing," I said in my best imitation of Flame's flirtatious voice, "I'd truly love to, but I've got a plane to catch tomorrow."

He grinned and kissed my cheek, and I promised to stay in touch. Then I was out the door and into the taxi.

"Just so you know, I *did* manage to get a room at the Lafitte," I babbled, climbing into the taxi and replacing my sample inside my purse without bothering to look at Tex. When he didn't respond, I glanced up and realized my Texas cabby was *not* at the wheel. Instead there was a swarthy-looking man who could have passed for a buccaneer just off the meanest pirate ship in the dock. He wore a scarf tied over his head and multiple earrings. The tattoo of a black skull grinned wickedly on the back of his neck.

I was certain he probably wore a black patch over one eye and carried one of those large, curve-bladed rapiers as well.

To my horror, I was not alone in the back seat either.

Next to me sat a large woman dressed in a flowing caftan, gold bracelets up to her chubby elbows, earrings dangling to her shoulders, and an old-fashioned *tignon*, a madras kerchief tied over braided hair—the typical garb of a New Orleans gypsy fortuneteller, strangely menacing in the darkened interior.

"You know where to go, *mon petit chien*," she spoke to the driver in a calm voice.

"Oops! I'm in the wrong cab," I said, reaching for the door handle.

The woman clenched my arm with a steely grip. I'd have had to be Wonder Woman to free myself from her, a female with the shape and strength of a sumo wrestler.

What was going on here?

Where was Tex?

For the second time that night, the hair stood up on the back of my neck. This had to be some mistake.

Chapter 2

Madame Chevalier

"Excuse me. I have a room at the Lafitte Hotel, and if you'll just let me out—" I stammered.

Her grip on my arm tightened painfully.

"Or you could just drop me by there if it's on your way?" I suggested lamely.

The pair ignored me. Instead the driver began a circuitous route through narrow streets.

"Where are you taking me?" I asked, not really expecting an answer.

"If this is a robbery I don't carry more than fifty dollars with me. You can have it. Just take me to back to the hotel. Or let me out right here. I'll be glad to walk."

Neither spoke a word. We drove down Decatur, passed Jackson Square and turned right on North Peters.

I recognized the historic old U.S. Mint building and the Esplanade Station streetcar terminal. Then we took a darker road. And a darker one still.

The cab finally pulled up to an old, abandoned warehouse along a battered wharf, dark and sinister in the rain-washed night. Mist floated low on the ground, adding to the gloom of the place and fueling my imagination with unwanted possibilities.

"Look, lady, I don't know who you think I am," I began, still hoping this was a case of mistaken identity.

She raised a ringed finger to her lips in a gesture indicating silence. Even if I screamed at the top of my lungs, who would be anywhere near this lonely place to hear my cry?

"At least tell me who you are and why you brought me here," I demanded as the cab driver climbed out and opened the rear door.

Inclining her braided head, she announced in an imperial and deeply toned voice, "I am Madame Chevalier," surprising me by her willingness to identify herself.

Her next words startled me.

"But you, my dear, are not who you think you are."

Huh?

Oh boy.

These were the very words spoken to me by Count Ribaldo. No other phrase could she have spoken to cause such a chill to grip my entire being.

Stunned but not speechless I began groping for logic.

"Obviously you have me mixed up with someone else. I'm Kaytie O'Reilly, a reporter for *Beyond Fantasy* out of Chicago."

"You *are not*!" Her words were emphatic, laced with a theatrical quality probably reserved for enthralled clients eager to know their futures.

Madame Chevalier would have been more aptly named *Cheval,* a true workhorse of a woman in size.

If she made her living as a medium, then mediums also come in size extra large, I decided wryly. Yet she managed to roll her lumbering frame out of the cab with some degree of queenly grace.

Pirate Man walked to the rear of the cab, opened the trunk and out scrambled a figure.

"Tex!" I exclaimed, dumbfounded.

He looked at me, mystified but unharmed, his hands tied behind his back. Our captors directed us to follow them.

We walked single file along the rickety wharf, Pirate Man in front followed by Tex, then me and the gargantuan gypsy behind. A motorized watercraft bobbed gently on the water, and we clambered aboard, the boat listing heavily to one side under Madame Chevalier's weight.

Damp, heavy bayou air wrapped around me, clinging like a steamed towel.

"What in a Texas tornado have I gotten myself into now?" Tex muttered, echoing my thoughts.

Pirate Man revved the engine to life.

Soon we were slicing through the water, moving away from the rapidly dimming city lights. The sound of the engine blocked out all noise except a sudden clap of thunder.

I was grateful the boat had a canopy of sorts to protect us from the threat of more rain. I was also extremely anxious to know what this pair of creeps wanted with a New Orleans taxi driver and a Chicago reporter.

Minutes later we slipped beneath a canopy of live oaks and cypress trees, their branches draped with Spanish moss that hung in ghostly folds. Intermittent spears of lightning scarcely penetrated the thick darkness beneath towering branches. The boat's running lights bounced off swirling mists, adding an ethereal quality to the night.

A look of alarm in Tex's eyes mirrored my own.

Were they going to slit our throats and dump our bodies out here in the swamp for the alligators to feast on?

For what possible reason?

Between the two of us, we probably had no more than a few hundred bucks. Hardly enough money for committing a double homicide.

The woman was out of her mind, or she really had mistaken me for someone else. When she realized her mistake, what would happen?

My mind raced with frightening possibilities.

What if this had something to do with Ribaldo? I couldn't see a possible link between him and the gypsy.

Cheese and crackers! I should have been enjoying a candlelight dinner with Larue in a classy restaurant, at his expense. Instead, here I was, the victim of a kidnapping.

While that thought was worthy of alarm, my curious mind wondered to the terminology. There really ought to be another word for it. *Kid*napping sounds so juvenile.

Adult-grabbing maybe?

Nope. Guys would probably think it a new form of erotic thrill and try to sign up for it.

Too bad the "adult" label gets associated with things other than maturity.

I was surprised to see lanterns hung at intervals in the trees, marking a channel through the swamp with a soft amber glow. After a short time of drifting through the mist, we tied up at a clapboard shanty supported on stilts above the black waters. A set of steep, rickety planks offered a shaky climb to the platform above. Incredibly, Madame Chevalier hoisted her heaviness up those steps with apparent ease.

Tex climbed up next. Then me. It was tricky in my pencil-slim skirt, but I managed after kicking off my heels.

Barefoot is best when climbing rickety stairs over a swamp.

You never know when you're going to need that helpful little bit of information. I wouldn't have guessed I'd ever be in such a position.

To my relief, Pirate Man stayed in the boat.

Aglow with candlelight, the shanty clapboard cabin's interior was unexpectedly charming. Huge satin pillows in a rainbow of vibrant colors—turquoise, cranberry, emerald and amethyst—offered inviting places to plop on the carpeted floor. Curtains of multi-colored glass beads served as room dividers and cast turquoise and cranberry pinpoints of reflected candlelight on the clapboard walls. The only window apparent was curtained by the same colors reflecting tiny pinpoints of light from beaded fabric.

A pot-bellied cast-iron stove stood in the center of the single room. Wooden shelves and cabinets, a low table made of rough planks and the suggestion of a sleeping couch behind a wispy curtain were the only other furnishings. Sweet, spicy fragrances drifted through the heavy air. Incense maybe.

The whole effect, surreal and enchanting, made me think of a fairy's lair or the home of a bayou mermaid.

It was definitely *not* the Cookin' Cajun's fishing shack.

"Okay, lady, what's your scheme?" I demanded, a little braver now that Pirate Man was out of sight.

The very sight of him would raise the hair on an alligator's back, if an alligator had hair. I didn't know and didn't want to get close enough to find out.

The gypsy moved through the room, her silky caftan swirling around heavy ankles. Candlelight flickered across her facial skin, the color of *café-au-lait*, and pirouetted off dangling earrings. She looked like a heftier version of Queen Latiffah.

Was she going to tell us why she had brought us to this colorful hideaway?

Madame reached through a beaded curtain and pulled out a well-worn, leather-bound volume from a rough, plank shelf. Opening it to an earmarked page, she picked up a candle and placed both book and candle on the low table, motioning for us to draw near.

A book and candle. Now where's the bell?

I tried not to roll my eyes, thinking of Mom's favorite Kim Novak movie, *Bell, Book and Candle*. The entire scene was just too contrived.

Too theatrical.

It felt like the set of a fantasy movie. However, this was no fantasy.

Tex's eyes met mine in silent consternation. We moved toward the gypsy and stared at the well-worn page she was indicating, her fat finger tapping a photo. It was a photo of a woman.

"Well I'll be horse whipped," Tex exclaimed. "It's *you*!"

He pointed to me with an expression of genuine curiosity.

In fact, the woman in the photograph strongly resembled me. She had the same eyes, same-shaped mouth. Her jaw line was mine. Even her hairline was the same, except it was ribboned back from her face, and her costume was from the 1800s Civil War era.

I stared, uncomprehending.

"You see, you are not who you *think* you are," Madame Chevalier announced, her painted eyebrows lifted in a knowing expression.

Then she gestured to the pillows on the floor.

"Sit."

Tex and I pulled up a cushion. He sat with his ankles crossed, a feat I could not manage in my slim white skirt, so I folded my knees to one side.

This was going to be interesting, I thought as Madame lowered her enormous frame to a cushion and began her story.

"I be waiting for you to come for a long, *long* time, my little friend. Let me tell you why. The woman you see in the photo was the mistress of a big sugar plantation on the outskirts of New Orleans before the Civil War. Her fine manor is now known as the Lafitte Hotel."

She paused, than announced dramatically, "Her name was Elizabeth O'Brien."

The irony of another name from the novel was not lost on me. It seems I was linked to the book and the character of Flame, no matter how hard I tried to escape it.

Madame continued in a storyteller's dramatic voice.

"When the war began, Elizabeth's husband was one of the first to join the Confederate army. He was killed—not in battle but because of a fall from his horse later on in war. At that time, Miss Elizabeth released all the slaves from the plantation.

"They scattered. All but Magnolia, who had been Elizabeth's personal maid. Magnolia stayed with her beloved mistress. They had a chest filled with pearls, rubies and diamonds. The jewelry belonged to Elizabeth's English grandmother and also to her husband's Irish family. The two women buried it somewhere on the plantation.

"At that time, Major General Benjamin F. Butler was in command of the Yankee army and had taken possession of New Orleans. Butler the Beast they called him. He took what he wanted. The slaves and the whites both hated him. Elizabeth and Magnolia were nearly arrested because they pulled their skirts away if a Yankee soldier sat next to them on street cars. Once Magnolia even emptied a tinkle-pot on the heads of some Yankees passing below an upper window. I bet those fellas were mighty pissed."

The woman chuckled at the story, but her smile faded quickly.

"A band of Yankees took up residence at the house, probably found it more comfortable than Camp Parapet. Elizabeth had to open her smokehouse and vegetable cellar to feed the soldiers—if they *were* soldiers. Some say they were just raiders dressed in uniforms they had stolen from dead soldiers. Anyway, after a couple of days, one of the men took a fancy to Magnolia. She fought and screamed...until Miss Elizabeth shot him dead."

Madame paused for effect.

Tex and I waited for her to explain how this long-ago crime affected us.

"They hanged Elizabeth from a beam over the grand ballroom stairwell...hanged her on September 13, 1862."

Her dramatic voice announced the date with theatrical emphasis.

Ahhh. I made the connection between the date and the apparition.

She paused, then assuming we were properly astounded, she continued.

"Magnolia escaped with her life, but she promised to avenge her mistress. She vowed that Elizabeth's spirit would return to the O'Brien plantation on a future anniversary of her death and the two of them would reclaim all that the Yankees had stolen from the South."

The words fell from convinced lips. Madame's eager eyes watched us for impact.

"Now, Miss O'Reilly. I been watching for you every September thirteenth for a long time. Yesterday you finally arrived. You be the reincarnation of Elizabeth O'Brien as sure I'm Magnolia's great-great-great-granddaughter!"

Madame looked at me with victorious glee in her eyes.

"You and me, we're going to find that buried chest as sure as there's stars in the midnight sky. And we're gonna be rich, you and me, girl!"

I had listened in silence, watching the animation in Madame's face as she related the story in perfect English, only slipping back into a Cajun accent as she ended it, her eyes, black as the velvet of a livery man's jacket, filled with fire.

I could almost see the loyal slave girl, Magnolia, behind the plump cheeks and well-formed mouth.

Almost beautiful. Until greed lit her expression. Greed bordering on madness.

"Look, I admit that woman in the photograph looks a lot like me, but I'm not related to any O'Briens that I know of, even though I am part Irish," I began, hoping I could convince her.

"First, I don't believe in reincarnation. And second, even if I *were* somehow related to Elizabeth, I don't have the slightest idea where to find her buried treasure."

"But you will. The tea leaves and tarot cards have predicted it for years."

"The tea leaves and tarot cards are wrong," I declared.

"It will happen."

She spoke emphatically and folded her arms across her ample midriff with an air of having settled the entire matter.

"Madame Chevalier has spoken."

I folded my arms across my chest, imitating her gesture, and declared in my best imitation of Clark Gable's voice:

"Frankly Ma*dame,* I don't give a *dear*."

(My mother taught me not to use swear words; she always had a hard time forgiving Clark Gable for that one.)

Madame Chevalier grunted. Then she moved to the door of the cabin, where she paused, and turned.

"I have business to take care of, but I will come back for you. You gonna be glad to cooperate with me, girl. Very glad."

I didn't like the sound of that.

Tex scrambled to his feet.

"Hey, wait a minute, Miss Chevrolay! I got nothin' to do with this. You don't need me. Take me back to N'awlins in the boat with you now. My dispatcher is going to be looking for me, and I've got a wife and four kids. The twins, Monica and Unica, are just babies. They gotta have their daddy to survive. "

My eyes darted toward Tex in dismay. Would he really leave me here alone?

Madame didn't bother to answer Tex. She was already clambering ponderously down the ladder.

We could feel the vibrations of each heavy foot on the steps, hear the boat motor revving up as Pirate Man pulled away from the fairytale house on stilts.

"Monica and Unica?" I raised a skeptical eyebrow.

"I know that sounds dumb. I got no children. Never been married to anyone. Not even close."

Tex looked forlorn and genuinely chagrined.

"I'm sorry I got you into this mess, Tex. But were you really going to get yourself out of it without me?"

"I was gonna come back for you," he answered sheepishly.

I could see that he meant it.

We stood at the doorway peering out into the rain-drenched night. The faint glow from a few of the lantern markers was visible ahead in the trees. Beyond those small beacons, all was blacker than the bottom of a deep well on a starless night. A hungry blackness, it seemed, eager to devour us in one great ravenous gulp.

The sound of the boat's engine quickly faded as if swallowed up by the night beast.

Turning toward me, Tex spoke in his soft Texas drawl.

"Way I see it, we can wade ourselves outta here by following those lanterns, or wait till Madame Chevrolay comes back with that thug and does us in."

I stared at him in disbelief.

"Wade? Wade you say? In the swamp water? There are alligators and mosquitoes and water moccasins and who knows what else out there? We need a boat, Tex."

"Look at it this way, ma'am. Which would you rather face? A few swamp critters, or that crazy woman and her tattooed creep? She's plumb loco if you ask me. The worst kind of loco. She's convinced and there's no changing her mind!"

He had a point.

Still the thought of wading in swamp water filled with slimy, slithery things made my skin crawl. "But I don't like spiders and snakes."

The words of an old Jim Stafford song came to mind. Funny how even in the most stressful of circumstances, a song can pop into my head. "Why don't we just call someone for help?" I suggested, fishing my cell phone out of my jacket pocket.

Tex's eyes widened. "You got a cell phone with you?" Then he grinned and slapped his leg. "Durn, girl, let's get to it! Call the cavalry. Get John Wayne to the rescue."

I pondered the tiny phone.

"Let's see. Who do I know in New Orleans? Or better yet, who do you know?"

"I know lots of people, but none of them would be willing to motor out here in the middle of the day, let alone the dark of the night. We're in Rainy Bay Bayou. I can feel it in my bones. Most folks think this place is haunted."

From a haunted hotel to a haunted swamp, I had certainly found my way to some weird places on this night of surprises.

Except Madame Chevalier was no ghost. She was ample flesh and bone, some three hundred pounds of it, and definitely *off* her broad beam as well.

I didn't know what to expect from her.

That unnerved me.

"You mean your friends wouldn't risk facing a few ghosts to save your hide?"

"It's not ghosts out here, ma'am. More like the Bigfoot of the swamps. Probably a skunk ape. It's been seen around this area for years by Cajun fishermen. Not many folks ever venture out here."

"Bigfoot of the swamps? You're sure it wasn't just Big Madame Chevalier they saw?"

With sudden inspiration, I punched in the number for information and asked for Jean Claude's Alchemy Shoppe. Soon enough the line was ringing.

No answer.

"Where could he be? I was just there a couple of hours ago."

Tex pulled the beaded curtain aside from the window which instantly mirrored our reflections.

"It's going to be morning soon. Think your friend might have gone home to catch some sleep? Some people do that you know."

He had a point. Jean Claude's laboratory probably didn't stay open all night. He probably was home where he should be, snoozing away at this ungodly hour, but his residence was an unlisted number. I had no idea how to reach him there.

"Why don't we just call the police?" I suggested with yet another inspiration. "Don't they have a river-patrol boat or something?"

Tex slapped his hand across his knee, a gleam of hope in his eyes.

"Of course! Why didn't I think of that? Call 'em."

I had to dial for information again, and just as the number connected to the New Orleans Police Department, my cell phone bleeped that irritating signal that means it's time to recharge the batteries.

"Oh no!"

I tried redialing, hoping against hope, but there was no juice left to reconnect me. Tex looked disheartened.

"How do you know we're in Rainy Bay Bayou?" I asked.

"We passed Jackson Square and took a right. I knew the minute we passed the old mint by the sound of the pavement. I knew approximately where we were at the boat landing. And we didn't take the expected turns for Cane Bayou or Manchac Swamps."

My amazement showed on my face.

Tex shrugged his shoulders.

"I know the city streets like the back of my hand. I've been up and down the rivah on the *Creole Queen*, and even been on the swamp tours a few times. We're in Rainy Bay wetlands alright."

"Okay. So now what? The phone's deader than a drowned duck."

"Guess we climb down that ladder and start wading."

"I'm not getting my feet in that slimy muck! What if we sink in quicksand?"

"Then I'll carry you on my back. Look, it can't be that long till daylight. That Chevrolay woman could come back here any minute and her hired thug with her. I say let's make a run for it."

He had a point. The thought of facing the tattooed man was enough to make me agreeable.

"Wait! Maybe we can find something in here to use for a float." I glanced around the room again. Satiny beaded pillows. Candles. No inflatable rafts in sight. Not even an inner tube.

What I wouldn't give for an air mattress at that moment.

Tex was poking through cabinets and kitchen items. He found a wicked-looking knife that might have been used to filet fish and handed me a table knife. Then he found a flashlight, candles, matches and insect repellent.

"Good, this will keep the skeeters away," he muttered as he sprayed us down.

"What about snakes and alligators? Or leeches!" My voice quivered slightly.

He didn't answer.

Somehow, I'd rather face a skunk-ape monster, maybe even Madame Chevalier and her tattooed thug, than deal with snakes or alligators, but I supposed Tex was right. Perhaps the wetland creatures were the lesser threat.

"Okay, I'll go first," Tex rolled up his pant legs.

I followed him down the ladder, promising myself I'd never again let my phone batteries run down. He slid into the waist-high water and motioned for me to climb on his back.

I groaned, but obeyed, hiking my skirt up above my knees.

"Turn on the flashlight," I urged.

"Huh, uh. It would just draw the critters." He started sloshing through the muck.

Ugh!

I kept my feet turned up to avoid the water, suddenly very thankful for Tex's long legs. He was almost too thin. I could feel his shoulder blades jutting sharply through his shirt, but his leggy height assured me of a dry piggyback ride.

We slogged along toward the channel markers.

"Tex, if those critters are drawn to light, what makes you think they won't be lurking around the lanterns?"

"They will be. But we'll give them a wide berth."

I wasn't reassured.

We hadn't walked twenty steps when Tex stumbled, lost his footing and went down, dumping me in the water. I came up sputtering, my toes sinking in the gooey mud as I scrambled to upright myself.

"Stand back!" Tex ordered. "I'm caught up in something."

"What?"

I was suddenly more concerned about him than my ruined white skirt and jacket.

"Some kind of fishing line maybe. Hold on. I've got to dive down and see if I can cut myself free."

Chapter 3

Cajun Jack

I shivered, longing to turn on the flashlight, but the blackness of the night was fading to gray, the first hint of dawn. I waited, counting the seconds.

What was taking so long? Come on, Tex, don't leave me now!

Amazingly, I counted to sixty-eight before he broke the surface, gasping for breath.

"Dang!" he spewed. "I dropped the knife and it musta sunk in the bog. Can't find it nowhere. I'm tangled in a mess of fishing lines and wires."

I started slogging toward him.

"Here, I've got the kitchen knife."

"That thing's worthless. I might as well try cutting through steel with a matchstick."

"Give me your flashlight. I'll dive down and see if I can find the knife."

Ordinarily I wouldn't have dared to dive underneath that black, mucky water, but I was already standing in it up to my waist.

The bayou air felt hot and sticky, even though the water was cold. I had been vaguely aware of the night sounds a few moments before—frogs singing, crickets, and jar flies—suddenly conspicuous by their silence.

Tex handed the flashlight over and I dived. I couldn't see much but from the feel of it, a wiry tangle of fishing cords was hopelessly snarled around his legs from knees to ankles.

How did he ever get into such a trap?

We had stirred up so much silty mud that I couldn't begin to see where the knife had fallen.

Breaking the surface I moaned, "It's impossible to see anything down there. You're trapped until the mud settles, and then maybe I can find the knife."

Tex wasn't listening. He was staring at something over my left shoulder. I could tell by the look in his eyes that I wasn't going to like it.

"You're going to have to move away from me real slow and easy." Tex kept his voice calm though his eyes were frantic.

"Don't turn around. Just keep going and don't look back."

Of course I looked back.

I didn't see it at first. But then it moved. A big alligator, some thirty yards away, gliding through the water straight towards us, no doubt attracted by our thrashing movements.

On it came. Slowly at first.

Then more rapidly, propelled by its long tail rippling the water from side to side.

"Move away from me, girl!" Tex exclaimed.

"I c-can't leave you!" I stammered, desperately searching our surroundings for some kind of help, hoping for some Tarzan figure to miraculously appear and rescue us.

Tex dived under the water, trying vainly to extricate his legs from the hopeless snarl of tangled lines.

I froze in horror.

Visions of vicious razor-sharp teeth filled my mind. Scenes from Mom's old movie *Jaws*. The approaching, armor-plated creature was no great white shark, but his grinning, wicked snout looked every bit as deadly.

Alligators have the strongest bite in the animal kingdom. They seize their prey in powerful jaws and hold the hapless creature under water until it drowns. Somehow that seemed slightly less horrifying than being chomped, chewed and eaten alive, although certainly no less final. You're dead either way.

Tex hadn't come up for air again.

The beast was ten yards away and closing fast.

I had to do something. But what?

I flailed for something to use as a weapon.

The flashlight? Maybe I could whomp the beast on the nose hard enough to dissuade it.

It was a desperately frantic hope.

Five yards.

Hurry, Tex. Find the knife!

Tex broke water, gulping air, the whites of his eyes stark against his terror-filled face.

My mind reeled with the awful fate in store for both of us if I couldn't do something to stop it. Alligator wrestling has never been one of my hobbies. I had to find that knife!

The rifle report split the air and sent a ripple of shock waves through the heavy bayou mist. A second blast, and the gator sank beneath the surface, a dark patch staining the water where its ugly, grinning head had been, barely a foot away.

My knees quivered and my teeth started chattering. Someone shined a bright light in my eyes.

"*Mes amis*. What you tink you be doing *ici*? You tink you can wade around in deese place?"

Behind the sudden beam of a high-powered flashlight, a pirogue floated into view.

"Mister, I shore am glad to see you!" Tex gushed gratefully. "I'm hung up in a tangle of fishing line."

Standing spread legged and using a pole to move the boat forward, the fellow pulled up next to Tex and handed him a fishing knife.

While he was busy cutting himself free, I climbed up into the shallow, hollowed cypress craft without waiting for an invitation, the fisherman steadying it as it dipped under my weight.

"Hurry, Tex. That thing might just be wounded. It may still want to take a bite outta you."

"Ol' Jack done killed dat critter deader than a rabbit on a roasting spit," said the boatman reassuringly, his voice somehow familiar in a reassuring way.

He reached a strong, gnarled hand toward Tex and helped him aboard. Again we wobbled in the water for a moment as Jack balanced it expertly with his own weight.

Tex collapsed on the floor of the craft, lifted his hands and breathed a prayer of thanks.

"What kind of ting dis be? I go out looking for crawfish and catch me a couple of swamp rabbits." He lifted his lantern toward us. "*What you was doing* besides becoming dat gator's dinner?"

"We're in need of a ride outta here," said Tex weakly.

I suspected he was shaking even worse than I was at the moment.

"Could we hire you to take us back to the city?"

"You wanna tell ol' Jack *what you was doing* out here before daylight?"

Ol' Jack was a typical Cajun bayou fisherman if ever there was one, probably a true descendant of exiles from the French colony of Acadia who had left their homeland in 1755 and found refuge in southern Louisiana. I'd never expected to meet one in the swamps near New Orleans.

Cajun country includes the wetlands along Bayou Lafourche and Bayou Teche where they've harvested crawfish, shrimp, crabs and oysters, fished, trapped, raised cotton and corn and even planted rice over the years.

Like his ancestors, Jack spoke a mixture of French and English.

Our rescuer wore suspenders over a striped shirt, and a red bandanna tied rakishly around his swarthy neck. His beard was tousled and his eyebrows formed a heavy shelf of thick gray above dark eyes that seemed to dance with amusement.

"Oh, we were just out picking palmetto blossoms," I babbled in answer to his question, "and we took a wrong turn somewhere."

He harrumphed at me with a sort of growl.

"You was lost alright if you wandered dis far. You be clients of Madame Chevalier?"

"You know Madame Chevalier? Why would she bring anyone out to this place?" I asked, hoping he could shed some light on the woman's motives.

"She brings her high-paying clients out here sometimes to tell their fortunes. I tink she drugs 'em into believing they've had a genuine supernatural experience. Dat be her business. They're willing to pay her. Me, I don't say nothing. She don't bother me. I don't bother her."

He stared at us as if he couldn't decide what to do with us.

"That's right, we were coming to get our fortunes told, and we got lost," Tex blurted. "Now we just want to get back to New Orleans. We can pay you when we get there. Don't have any money with us now."

I thought that admission was wise of Tex. After all, who knew whether old Jack might want to rob us and dump us back in the swamp?

"Fortunes huh," Jack started poling the pirogue once more.

I could see that he didn't believe our lame story. After all, how would we have paid Madame if we had no money with us?

As we glided through the waters, the eyes of alligators reflected red in the lantern light now and then. For a moment I could hardly catch my breath, thinking of what might have happened. I had to shove the grisly images to the back of my excited imagination.

"I'm beholden to you, Miz O'Reilly. You were really going to stay with me to the bitter end." Tex's voice choked with emotion.

"Think nothing of it," I answered breezily.

My voice sounded stronger than I felt.

"Unlike some people, I wouldn't leave a person alone in a sticky situation."

I couldn't help jabbing Tex just a little.

"Now hold on. I said I'd come back for you, and I would've too. I figured one of us had to go find help."

Jack spoke up.

"I'm gonna take you to my place."

Then he started humming an old Hank Williams tune, "Jambalaya." He kept it up until Tex surprised me by joining in on the chorus. He must have felt like singing from sheer gladness at being alive.

So here I was on the first night of my adventures in the swamp, riding in a pirogue with a Texas cab driver and a Cajun fisherman singing "Jambalaya" at the top of their lungs.

Mom used to say my middle name should have been "Trouble" instead of Flame. Maybe she was right. However, I'd managed to escape the worst of the trouble.

At least I was in the boat instead of the gator's stomach!

So far, so good.

"Goodbye Joe, me gotta go" I joined the singing duo. "Me oh my oh."

* * *

The Louisiana swamp is forbidding and deadly. It's also beautiful in a primal way as the first pink wands of morning light slice through the swirling mists.

I'd heard of the famous Louisiana irises. I didn't see any. The owls were silent, but the marsh birds had started their ritual songs to welcome the day, and there were other sounds to indicate the animal kingdom had roused. A great blue heron stood motionless, visible near a large palmetto fan.

Ever hear the bellowing of a bull alligator? Me neither. I'm told it's something you feel vibrating through the water, even more than you hear the unique sound. I don't want to be anywhere near the water when it happens.

Jack's fishing cabin, like Madame's secret shanty, also was a half-timbered house built on stilts, equipped with a mud chimney and every convenience except electricity.

Soon enough, the inviting smell of chicory coffee boiling on a wood cook stove filled the single room.

Our host served up hot grits, biscuits, sausage and gravy.

Delicious!

That's when it dawned on me why his voice sounded familiar. He spoke like the Cookin' Cajun on TV, another favorite of Mom's.

He offered me a plaid cotton shirt and some baggy cotton pants with a drawstring waist. Not exactly fashionable, but it felt good to get out of my soggy clothes. I changed behind a makeshift curtain held up by Tex who kept his eyes averted.

"I don't tink my shoes fit your small feet," he observed. "Maybe I call up my daughter and she bring you shoes."

"Jack! You have a telephone?" My eyes darted eagerly around the neatly kept cabin.

"*Mais* no. My daughter, she insists I keep a cell phone charged in my boat. She tink I can't live alone in Rainy Bay Bayou without it. Says to keep it charged just in case of emergency."

Jack swallowed the last of his coffee.

"I been living here some forty years now. Been through hurricanes. Swamp fever. Got bit by a water moccasin once. Made me so mad I bit dat critter right in two."

The thought of anyone biting a snake in two made me start shivering all over again.

Jack leaned his cane-back chair against the cabin wall and lit up a pipe.

"But she tinks I need a cell phone ever since her mother died twelve years ago. She likes to call me up in the evenings to check on me."

"Jack! Can I use your cell phone?"

He raised his bushy eyebrows.

For a moment I thought he was going to say no. Then he stood up and walked out onto a deck at the rear of the cabin. Through the doorway, I could see an outboard craft bobbing gently on a tether. Jack reached into the boat and returned with the cell phone. He handed it to me with a grin.

"Well, go for it, girl," said Tex eagerly.

I punched in the number of the Lafitte and asked for the Pirate Suite.

After a few rings, Dax answered. I was almost giddy with relief on hearing his voice.

"Hello, Dax."

"Kaytie!" He stammered out my name in a half whisper.

I couldn't help teasing him.

"Yes, it's me. And you'll *never* guess where I am."

He spoke with an intensity in his voice I had not heard before.

"And you'll *never* guess who's looking for *you*."

"Oprah Winfrey wants me to appear on her talk show?"

"Don't I wish. Hold onto your hat, girl. You're wanted by the New Orleans Police!"

"Come on, Dax, this is no time to be kidding around," I rolled my eyes impatiently. "I need your help."

"You certainly do. You're wanted for questioning in a murder case."

Murder?

"Dax. Be serious."

"I'm absolutely serious."

There was no hint of teasing in his voice. "You disappeared right after the midnight spook show and just before the maid found a body in our room. You were last seen on the stairs heading up to the Pirate Suite. You're the only guest unaccounted for at that time. That makes you a prime suspect."

I couldn't believe my ears. A body? In our room?

Finding my voice, I blurted out, "How can that be? *Whose* body?"

"Some over-sized gypsy woman. The police identified her as a New Orleans fortune teller known around Jackson Square as Madame Chevalier."

His words set my head spinning even more.

Madame Chevalier? How many gypsy fortunetellers could there be in New Orleans with that same description and that exact name?

Tex and Jack sat quietly, sensing my consternation.

"The maid found her slumped over your bed when she went in to turn down the spread and leave those little pralines on the pillow. Most of the reporters were still packing up their gear in the ballroom. We heard this blood-curdling scream. Everyone must have thought it could be more ghost action, because we grabbed our cameras and ran upstairs."

I could visualize that scene alright. All the reporters bursting into the Pirate Suite, hoping to get a scoop or a front-page story.

"A CSI team has been here in our room most of the night. The coroner had to call in extra hands to move the corpse. Madame was extremely obese, too heavy for a two-man stretcher."

"Are they certain she was murdered? Maybe she had a heart attack or something."

"There was a bullet in the back of her head, Kaytie. It was definitely murder."

I sat there speechless, unable to wrap my mind around this bizarre turn of events.

Dax started questioning me.

"Okay, now it's your turn. Where did you disappear to after the ghost show? We were supposed to have a late supper together."

"You're not going to believe this. I was *kidnapped* by a very large gypsy woman calling herself Madame Chevalier. And she was very much alive last night, long after the midnight hour."

Silence.

I could imagine Dax trying to digest this bit of impossible information.

"Kaytie, what you're telling me makes absolutely no sense at all."

"I could say the same to you," I countered.

Tex and Jack were listening, riveted by my side of the conversation. I could hear Dax mumbling something over his shoulder to someone else in the room.

The police?

If this call was being traced, they were going to have a heckuva time trying to find me. As far as I knew, New Orleans didn't have Phase One cell phones which could pinpoint my location from a satellite.

Besides, I had Tex for an airtight alibi during the time of the murder. I felt doubly thankful he had not ended up in the alligator's stomach.

"Okay, first things first," Dax returned to our conversation. "Where the Sam Beauregard Hill are you!?"

"You wouldn't believe me, so I'm not going to tell you."

"Will you at least give me your cell phone number?"

"No."

"Then I'll give you mine."

I turned to Jack for writing material. All he had was an old-fashioned quill dipped in a half-empty inkwell. Not a scrap of paper, so I jotted the number on the back of my hand.

"Look, the police have confined all the guests and employees to the hotel until they get everyone's statements. As soon as they clear me to go, I have to catch the flight back to Chicago. Stay in touch, you hear?"

"Yeah, right."

I hung up.

Here I was, a damsel in serious distress if ever there was one.

This was far worse than being left out in the rain at the airport.

I'd been kidnapped by a gypsy woman and her pirate thug. I'd barely escaped from being an alligator's supper. Been lost in a swamp with a Cajun fisherman who could bite a snake in two and a Texas cab driver who couldn't carry a tune.

To top it off, now I was wanted for murder!

And my hero was leaving town?

If I hadn't jotted his cell number on the back of my hand in indelible ink, I would have tossed it in the bayou at that moment. The number was there to stay for a few days anyway.

Oh well.

See you around, Dax.

Tex was itching for an explanation.

"Well Tex, it looks like I'm wanted as a suspect in a homicide investigation."

He listened, slack jawed with disbelief as I repeated the incredible story.

"You mean to tell me we got ourselves kidnapped by a *dead* woman. Dang!"

Cajun Jack exclaimed, "*Mon Dieu*, we done got ourselves a real live zombie!"

The oxymoron escaped him.

My editor at the *Beyond Fantasy* was going to love this story. I tried dialing him at the office, but Jack's cell phone wouldn't make the connection from the bayou to Chicago.

"So what do we do now, Miz O'Reilly?" Tex asked, mistakenly thinking I had some answers.

"Call me Kaytie. I think we're passed the formalities here."

"Okay, Miz O'Reilly. I mean Miz Kaytie."

"Just plain Kaytie is fine."

I sat down, suddenly exhausted.

"We have to find Madame Chevalier. She's the key to this whole thing."

"You can't mean we just go back to her cabin and wait for her and that tattooed creep to show up again? What's going to stop her from shooting us?"

"She wants me alive, Tex. She thinks I'm the reincarnation of her ancestress's dead mistress and that we're going to find buried treasure together."

"You maybe. But what about me? Who am I the reincarnation of? She needs me like she needs a crack in her crystal ball!" Tex exclaimed.

Jack spoke up.

"She don't be coming to her place but maybe once a month. She say she brings special clients out here for added mystique. They tink she has greater psychic powers when she's in Rainy Bay Bayou. You say she kidnapped you?"

Tex and I blurted out the entire story and Jack listened, nodding his head. When we described Pirate Man, Jack exclaimed, "Um! I know dis man. Bad Leroy. Very wicked. Madame is up to bad beezness, I tink."

"Yeah, well I wish I could *tink* up a way outta this *beezness* without ever seeing Bad Leroy again," I muttered, wondering if Bad Leroy was from the south side of Chicago and if his last name was Brown.

After last night's events, I thought nothing could surprise me.

Then I yawned.

"Maybe you need to sleep on it," Jack suggested.

"I'm so tired I'd rather eat a dead spider than get up again at the moment."

He nodded.

"You rest. I take you back to New Orleans after I finish my fishing."

Tex curled up with a pillow on the rug. Gentleman Jack offered me the iron-framed bed. I crawled under a patchwork sheet of green and yellow, smelling of sunshine and bayou breezes, and dropped off like a falling star into nothingness.

* * *

Six hours later, rested and refreshed, I climbed out of Jack's boat with Tex and Cajun Jack at a dock near the Nichols Street wharf.

Jack's daughter, Jacqueline, and her husband, Bruce Boudreau, lived conveniently near the river's edge. The young couple made a living by selling crafts and tourist gifts at the Farmer's French Market on 900 Decatur Street. They also relied on Jack to provide them with plenty of fresh fish.

Jacqueline was as lovely as her father was crusty, and certainly as hospitable. She didn't ask about our curious circumstances. Instead she loaned me some sandals and a pretty pink sundress with straps that tied over the shoulders. It came with a loose-weave sweater for draping over the shoulders in air-conditioned rooms.

"I don't know how to repay your kindness," I told her.

"You're a friend of my father's. That makes you my friend too." She smiled as I gave her a thank-you hug.

Tex opted to wear his own clothes since he was taller and leaner than Bruce. I freshened up in the bathroom, feeling almost human again after a hot shower.

Jacqueline kissed her father's chiseled cheek and sent us on our way with a smile. We followed Jack on foot to catch the riverfront trolley and ride to Toulouse Station. From there it was only a short walk to the famed Pat O'Brien's restaurant. He left us there, planning to rejoin us after a stop at a smaller café nearby where Jack hoped to deliver an ice chest filled with his fresh catch of the day, even though the restaurants usually buy commercially raised crawfish from Cajun Prairie.

I would have eaten most anything at the moment *except* a dead spider. I was famished.

Tex wasn't exactly looking his best in muddied trousers, and his borrowed shoes were ill fitting, however the hostess seated us in the courtyard without raising an eyebrow. Jack entered a back entrance to the kitchen, promising to rejoin us later. Dinner, he insisted, was on him by arrangement with the chef.

That was fine with us because Jack's billfold was wet and my purse was probably still in his taxi.

In his taxi!

"Tex! What if the police have located your taxi at the wharf? Because if they have—and if they found my purse—they'll be convinced that I really am on the run!"

"Just stay calm now, little lady. If they do find my cab and your purse, then they'll know I'm missing too," Tex began. "Besides, the police know very well that N'awlins is a city where plenty of peculiar things are going on."

"What peculiar things?" I asked. "I mean besides haunted hotels and murdered fortune tellers who turn up alive and kidnap people."

Tex had a knowing look in his eye.

"Ever read any of those Dean Koontz or Anne Rice books? There's Frankenstein monsters and vampires running around all over this town," he said confidentially. "Why couldn't there be zombies too?"

I started to hoot and then pretended to cough instead, just in case Tex was actually serious. I stole a glance at him to see if he was laughing.

Did he really believe all that vampire-Frankenstein stuff? From the unchanged expression on his face, I couldn't tell. I was about to ask him when the waitress arrived, asking if we'd like to order a hurricane.

"No thanks. If I ever took a drink, my tee-totaling daddy would turn over in his grave," said Tex.

"Mine too." I nodded and ordered coffee and red snapper with red beans and rice. Tex ordered filet gumbo.

I had just lifted my cup to my lips when I saw him. Dax Larue sitting off to himself in the courtyard with a personal computer on his lap.

"Excuse me a minute, Tex, I have to see a man about a murder."

Dax wasn't expecting me, but he was definitely glad to see me. I could see the appreciation in his eyes, a look that made me glad to be wearing Jacqueline's pink sundress instead of Jack's flannel shirt and baggy trousers.

"Well, well, well, if it isn't my beautiful Mrs. Larue. I see you're not in hiding. Sit down." He was all smiles. "What in the world are you doing out in public? Don't you know the police are looking everywhere for you."

"Yeah, well let them find me. I have an airtight alibi." I took a chair. "Why didn't you catch that flight back to Chicago today? Did they keep you so long that you missed your flight?"

"Actually, I stayed in New Orleans hoping to find you. You may have guessed that the crime scene investigators were still in our suite when you called. And they were all ears. Just so you know, they, uh—they're aware that we aren't married."

His concern was out of awareness that I might be embarrassed at the roommate thing.

Actually I was slightly embarrassed, even though the police didn't know me from the man in the moon—*woman* in the moon if there is one.

"Yes, go on. I would expect you to tell the truth about the sleeping arrangements."

"I tried to play along with them, make them think I was trying to flush you out of your hiding place. I mentioned catching my plane back to Chicago, hoping they wouldn't bother following me."

"Why, Dax," I smiled my most dazzling, "you stayed in town because of *me*?" That thought was as pleasing as his admiring glances.

"I couldn't fly away and leave a lady in distress now could I? Especially the beautiful Miss Kaytie who invited herself to share my taxi and my room, and then stood me up for our dinner date."

I felt even more pleased. He hadn't abandoned me after all.

Dax was still wearing the same red pullover—the one that looked so good on him. That meant he probably hadn't been to bed all night either.

Of course not. Not with a CSI team and a dead gypsy woman in his room.

"So the police released you and you checked out of the Lafitte?"

"Not long after you called. I came here and got busy on my laptop, pulling up parish records and old newspaper stories about the Lafitte Hotel. I found an abstract from the Recorder of Deeds office, and I think you're going to find it very interesting."

He motioned for me to move to his side of the table so I could view his PC screen.

"The place was originally a sugar plantation built by an Irish couple, Michael and Elizabeth O'Brien in the early 1800s."

Madame Chevalier had not made up that part. Maybe she was telling the entire truth, at least as she perceived it.

"Elizabeth died after an unfortunate incident with a Yankee patrol. Her husband was killed in the war. The couple had no heirs, so a distant cousin, Patrick O'Brien, inherited the property. He never bothered to maintain it and the manor fell into disrepair. Finally, Patrick's brother, a seafaring man, Captain Rex O'Brien, paid the back taxes and began working to restore the place.

"He added on to the place and eventually opened it as an inn under the name Maison Belle in the early 1900s. The Belle was successful into the late 1940s when the two aging brothers quarreled over the title.

"According to a brief series of articles I found in the *New Orleans Times* archives, it seems Patrick was married to a much younger Mulatto woman, Maggie, who wanted her name on the title along with her husband's. Maggie claimed her mother was a former slave in the O'Brien plantation house who had been promised a portion of the O'Brien wealth during Civil War years."

Here she was, Magnolia's daughter. The link to Madame Chevalier showing up in the story.

"Captain Rex violently disagreed. He was the one who had put his money into the place and made it a profitable business. He wanted the title free and clear and the hotel to go to his wife alone. The couple had a son who'd been killed in a brawl of some kind. No other heirs.

"Now here's where it gets interesting."

Dax gave me one of those wait-till-you-hear-this looks.

"Captain Rex died in a fire that damaged part of the Maison Belle. At the time, people suspected Maggie of arson, but it was never proved. Pat took over the place and left it to Maggie after he died.

"By this time, building codes were more stringent in New Orleans and Maggie had a financial struggle to repair the fire damage. She began telling fortunes and developed quite a following of wealthy New Orleans patrons. Soon she was able to reopen the Belle, renaming it the Lafitte. That's when the story of the ghost lady first began gaining attention. I suspect Maggie spread the tale to draw business. It worked. The place was profitable again."

She invented a ghost to draw guests, I concluded, thinking how the city of New Orleans has always attracted supernatural-thrill seekers. Voodoo practitioners. Hoodoo, and who knew? As Tex had noted, both past and contemporary writers certainly find the Crescent City a great setting for stories of the supernatural.

"Now here's the amazing part. Before old Maggie died in 1969, she drew up a will leaving the place to three persons as joint heirs. Two were her own children—and the third was a child yet to be born to unknown parents. . .a child by the name of . . .*Kaytie Flame O'Reilly."* He emphasized the name with his dramatic and suspenseful Rod-Serling voice.

My name? In the will?

This statement threw me for a loop.

After a speechless moment, I stammered denials. "How could she know my name? It's a weird coincidence. It's too bizarre—it's—not *me!*"

Dax only raised his eyebrows at my surprised expressions of disbelief.

"You've got to admit, your name is somewhat unique. Your middle name is Flame, huh."

He looked straight into my eyes, and I couldn't help noticing that his were very dark. Like the velvet of a starless midnight sky.

"An unusual name and a very unusual coincidence, wouldn't you agree?"

Chapter 4

Tex

He was right of course. I had never met a single person with my exact same name. Never expected to.

"Tell me more about the abstract," I urged, riveted by the tale.

Dax turned back to the PC.

"Maggie's will stipulated that the Lafitte be held in a trust by all three of the persons named. In the event that the third party never claimed the inheritance, it would revert to her daughters to be jointly shared. But she wanted the Kaytie-Flame name to remain in the will for at least three more generations."

"Are Maggie O'Brien's heirs running the place now?"

Dax shook his head.

"Apparently, neither of the daughters wanted the business. One died of some mysterious disease. The other disappeared from New Orleans in the 1970s, leaving a son, Maurice St. James, to manage the Lafitte. He updated old Maggie's will, naming his two daughters and the third party, Kaytie Flame O'Reilly, once again as inheritors of the place on his death."

I stared at the abstract on the PC with unbelieving eyes. There was my name listed as a future owner of the property in the event of Maurice St. James' death.

"How can a will be drawn up to include someone the family doesn't even know? Someone not even born yet? Or who may not even exist?" I asked incredulously.

"Wills can include anyone," Dax took a sip of his hurricane. "Cats. Dogs. Neighbors. And apparently people who are yet to be born. Of course you were probably a little cutie toddling around in your diapers by the mid 1980s."

I ignored the image that comment brought to mind.

"So my name's been on the will for some years now? And they don't even know who this Kaytie Flame person is, or if she's ever going to show up and claim her inheritance."

I reached for his hurricane glass and took a sip, coughed and made a face.

Dax laughed. "Maybe you should stick with iced tea."

"Excuse me," a male voice interrupted.

I looked up to see a tall, slender man wearing a dark suit. He held up a New Orleans Police badge.

"New Orleans Detective Alex Broussard. Miss Kaytie O'Reilly, I'd like you to come with me, please. We need to ask you a few questions." His mustached mouth did not smile in a friendly greeting.

Not at all.

Cheese and crackers! They had followed Dax, and by chance I had to show up at his table of all places in New Orleans.

"Alright, Officer," I stammered, "but I'd like for you to please talk with my taxi driver as well. He can vouch for my whereabouts last night."

I looked toward Tex's table, dismayed to see he was not there.

"Tex?" I called out, hoping he was nearby. "Tex!"

"Come with me, please, ma'am," the officer insisted.

"Wait a minute," I faltered. "Cajun Jack! He can tell you where I've been."

Detective Broussard had taken hold of my elbow and was lifting me firmly out of the chair. I was being treated as a suspect in a murder case!

"Hold on, Officer," Dax interjected. "Maybe you should hear what her friends have to say before you take her to the station."

"Come with me please," the officer repeated, firmly escorting me toward the door.

"Dax, you've got to find the taxi driver and Cajun Jack!"

I tossed the words anxiously over my shoulder as Detective Broussard deftly guided me out of the restaurant.

"Look, Detective," I tried to explain as he dragged me along, "this is all a mistake. I left the hotel in a taxi right after the ghost's appearance on the stairs."

Then it hit me. Jean Claude!

"You can drive me to the old Alchemy Shoppe at Chartres and Bienville. My friend, Jean Claude the chemist—he's right next to Mike's used book store—he will tell you I was there."

Did I dare mention being kidnapped by Madame Chevalier, who was supposed to be dead, and her thug Bad Leroy the pirate man?

Right.

He would probably lock me up in the psych ward on the spot.

"You know Jean Claude?"

Apparently the name rang a bell with him.

"Yes, sir. We're both originally from Baton Rouge. We graduated high school together."

I didn't tell him about Jean Claude's proposals. That was more than he needed to know, but I did want to convince him I was not some evil creature who went around murdering women in my hotel room for no reason at all.

The detective turned to look at me as he opened the passenger door of his squad car.

"Jean Claude is a very good friend of the New Orleans Police Department," he stated. "Maybe I will drive you over there."

Relief drained the tension out of me like water from an unplugged bath. It was going to be all right. Jean Claude could tell him—

The blow to the detective's head came from behind. His knees buckled and he hit the pavement like a collapsing wall.

Before I could scream, a hand clapped a rag over my mouth, filled with the odor of chloroform, and shoved it tightly over my nose as well.

I fought like a wildcat with all the strength of a newborn kitten before the dizziness overwhelmed me.

* * *

My head hurt.

My eyes felt blurry.

My body ached.

I managed to open my right eye slightly and promptly closed it again, not wanting to see unfamiliar surroundings.

By the time I moaned and groaned a few more times, my head began to clear. Then I heard a familiar Texas drawl.

"Kaytie? Kaytie, wake up. Durned if we aren't a pair of prisoners again!"

"Tex? Is that you?"

Of course I knew his voice. Funny how we ask the stupidest questions with the most obvious answers when we're desperately hoping things are not as they appear to be.

As if Tex might answer, "No it's not me. It's Dax Larue coming to rescue the beautiful and talented Kaytie O'Reilly."

Instead, Tex muttered, "How the heck did they get hold of you so fast?"

"I guess they clubbed the detective and grabbed me," I answered, recalling the sound of the thud as the investigator hit the sidewalk.

"What about you?"

Tex was quiet for a moment before speaking.

"I was in the men's room at Pat O'Brien's after you left the table. Someone just knocked me in the back of the head. When I woke up, it was that old *déjà-vu* thing all over again. Here I was with Bad Leroy driving me to that same rickety pier. Only when we got there, the boat was gone. That's when he brought me here. I must have been out of it when they brought you in, cuz I don't remember it. Next thing I know, I wake up and see you lying there trussed up like a wild brush hawg."

Tex paused a moment before continuing in a voice of quiet amazement.

"Whatever they want from you, they want it *bad.* I know that for sure. But what the heck do they want from me?"

"You know as much as I do." I half shrugged while pulling myself into a sitting position. "Any idea where we are?"

"Well Dorothy, we're definitely not in Kansas anymore. We're in a rambling old three-story. It's near the Garden District I think. I could tell by the sound of the pavement. Maybe we're actually in the Garden District, but I doubt it. This place is too run down."

"You think it's Madame Chevalier's place?"

"Probably. I can't picture that Leroy guy living here."

Tex was situated not far from me. We had been deposited on a scarred and beaten hardwood floor in a room empty of furniture. A few dusty pictures hung on the wall, an astrological chart, a pyramid with a single staring eye. It would have been dark except for large bay window where diffused street lamplight weakly shown through dusty window panes.

I began to scoot my way toward Tex, unable to stand because my ankles were tied.

"We're on the third floor," Tex continued.

"Are you able to move your fingers?"

"A little. They're just about gone plumb numb from the ropes being so tight."

By this time I had managed to scoot over, sit up and turn my back against his.

"Okay, I'm going to try to untie you."

My fingers strained at the knots on his rope, which seemed much tighter than my own bindings. After fumbling for several minutes, my fingers trembling from the exertion, I was unable to loosen the knot.

"Tex, this isn't working."

Tex sagged against me with a hopeless sigh. Then he straightened.

"Hey, I've got a matchbook from Pat O'Brien's place. It's in my right shirt pocket. Maybe you could wriggle it out and we could burn the rope off."

I was willing to try. We both bent into unnatural positions, and I barely managed to slide my hands into the pocket."

"You feel the matchbook?"

"Barely, with my fingertips, but I can't grasp it." I panted straining to reach deeper into the pocket.

A very unmanly giggle exploded from Tex. "Sorry, ma'am," he sputtered between hoots. "You're ticklin' my ribs."

This was no time for hilarity, but the ridiculousness of our situation immediately struck me funny too. Here we were, practically in each other's faces on the floor of a dilapidated old house, in who knew what kind of danger, and Tex was giggling like a schoolgirl. Impossibly, I started giggling too. It was a tension reliever.

We both laughed uproariously together until tears ran down our faces. If anyone had been looking on, we might have appeared to be a pair of idiots. I didn't care. It did us both good to laugh for the moment, a medicinal dose of hilarity in a crazy situation.

Finally I managed to think of Bad Leroy once more.

"Hold still a minute, will you, I've almost got it!"

Tex couldn't control his laughter or his squirming, but his spasms of hilarity actually worked the matchbook into my grasping fingers. I withdrew it immediately, leaving Tex to regain his self-control.

Instantly serious once more, I barked, "I've got the matches! Now turn around."

Obediently, he scooted so that we were back to back.

"I'm gonna try to strike a match and hold it at the right place. You tell me if it gets too hot."

"Just don't catch my shirt on fire," Tex warned uneasily.

The first few matches were impossible to strike. Finally in desperation, I managed to rake five of them across the uneven floor. Yipping with pain, I dropped the entire flaming bunch. They sizzled and extinguished themselves.

"Dang!" Tex muttered.

"Okay, hold on. I'll try again."

This time I managed to grasp the matches in such a way that only two ignited. Now the challenge was to hold them to the rope without burning Tex or myself.

He moved his hands toward the heat, and we sat there hoping we had the flames in the right place.

"It's getting hot!" Tex exclaimed.

"Can you pull your hands apart?" I strained to keep the fire on the rope, but I was also feeling the white-hot heat.

"Ouch!" I couldn't stand the pain anymore and dropped the matches.

"We've got to try it one more time," Tex urged. "I think it's working. The rope seems a bit looser."

We repeated the entire process a second time, ending once more in cries of pain. Tears streamed from my eyes and Tex's chest was heaving.

He strained with all his might to pull his wrists apart. "It's no use," he muttered hopelessly.

"Catch your breath a minute. Then let me feel the cord. Maybe at least it's stretched a little and I can loosen it."

We sat there miserably, both in pain, both wondering what crazy Madame Chevalier had planned for us. She obviously wanted us badly enough to risk going to jail for kidnapping, a serious offense. So serious she might not be willing to let us go once she achieved her purpose. I didn't want to think our lives could be in danger, but the possibility seemed very real.

We had to get out of here.

I tried again to burn through Tex's bindings.

When I was down to our last three matches, I burned the cord through enough that Tex managed to break free.

"Praise the Lord!" he exclaimed in relief, working his raw hands together and rubbing his chafed wrists before he went to work untying mine.

Moments later we stood up, panting with the exertion and relief. We examined our hands and found our burns were superficial, no real harm done.

Tex went for the door and found it securely locked from the outside.

"Do you think there's anyone in the house?" I asked, lowering my voice, which was silly considering I had been hooting with laughter only a few moments ago.

"Don't think so. It has the feel of emptiness. I haven't heard a sound since you've been awake."

"The window!"

I ran to the bay windows. They weren't locked. They could be cranked open on rusty hinges, and they were large. Almost the height of a man.

I peered out on a dimly lit scene, a tree-lined residential street filled with two- and three-story French and Spanish colonial houses in various states of ill repair. This place was nowhere near the Garden District, not even the low-rent end, I thought.

No traffic. No lighted windows. No people about.

The block had the appearance of abandonment. Some of the houses were boarded up. Others had yawning windows with shattered panes, somehow sinister in the faint light, perhaps victims of Katrina.

A single street lamp cast a murky amber glow that seemed to gather in a small pool at the base rather than penetrate the darkness.

Far away, I could see city lights reflecting off the clouded night sky. We were on the outskirts of the residential districts.

Tex looked out on the scene and rubbed his eyes.

"I was mistaken. This isn't the Garden District," he muttered. "I musta dreamed it. Musta been out from the chloroform just like you."

At that moment we saw the headlights of a car turning onto the street. We froze, hoping it would pass.

"Let's get out of here," I urged.

A decorative gingerbread trim and a ledge ran underneath the bay windows, perhaps wide enough to step on. The yard seemed incredibly far below. Dizzyingly far as it disappeared into the darkness.

"Maybe we can climb our way out," I muttered, thinking aloud.

Tex was silent. Then he gulped.

"I hate to tell you at a time like this, but I'm afraid of heights, Miss Kaytie." His voice was sheepish.

"I hate to tell you, but a time like this is when you get over it," I announced firmly. "Do you see another way out of here?"

He glanced helplessly around the room and shook his head.

"But how do we know this ledge leads anywhere? We might inch our way all around the house and then end up back where we started."

He had a point. I kicked off Jacqueline's sandals.

"Okay, I'll go first. Wait here." Stepping barefooted over the low windowsill, I climbed out onto the narrow ledge and into the humid night air. *Don't look down*, I told myself. There was nothing to hold onto. I flattened myself against the wall and began to inch my way slowly along the ledge, hoping it was solid enough to support my weight.

Who knew how much water damage this structure had suffered?

The ledge was never meant for feet.

Would it collapse and send me falling to break myself on something three stories below?

I managed to move ever so slowly and eventually arrived at a second alcove of windows, dark and vacant, mirroring only the reflection of the street lamp below. The ledge jutted outward under the alcove in the same pattern as the one I had left behind.

How could I open these windows from the outside without breaking them? I had hoped for an upper balcony with wrought-iron railing around a veranda, the kind so common in the French Quarter, where generations of city dwellers have looked down on Mardi Gras revelers, paraders and street performers over the decades.

No such luck. At least not yet.

It was then I heard it. A kind of querulous bird sound—a pigeon, obviously unhappy that I was disturbing his roosting place.

"Move over, bird!" I ordered.

A cacophony of sound erupted from an entire flock of irritated pigeons. The noise seemed ear-splitting to me at the moment since I desperately did not want to draw any attention.

"Okay, alright, already. Sh-sh-sh-sh! Be quiet," I ordered in my sternest whisper.

The birds settled themselves for the moment, clearly unwilling to move from their comfortable ledge. I inched my foot toward the closest bird.

It did the most brazen thing. It pecked my foot!

"Ouch! Bad pigeon. Bad pigeon!" I scolded.

"Who are you talking to?"

Tex asked, leaning out very slightly through the alcove windows.

"There's a flock of pigeons roosting up here. They don't like me," I whispered back.

The bad pigeon boldly pecked my naked foot again. "Ouch!"

Enough of that.

I started back toward Tex, announcing, "I'm going to try the other direction."

"Please don't fall," he pleaded in a shaky voice. "Seeing you out there makes me as nervous as a kangaroo with a porcupine in its pouch."

I chuckled at the image that brought to mind, moved past Tex and stepped toward the darker side of the house.

It was there I found our path to the ground, an ancient live oak tree spreading thick branches over the roof. Perhaps we could climb our way down one of them, at least far enough to drop without risking serious injury. The older the tree, the greater the likelihood that its branches drooped downward to the ground, like those at the Oak Alley Plantation house. If we were in luck, this tree's branches could be the perfect escape route.

"Tex, this way."

"I hear you...but I can't do it," Tex groaned.

"I'm coming back for you. You CAN do it."

My feet felt sure enough on the ledge by now. I was certain Tex also could manage the Spiderman thing too. After all, he was even thinner than I was.

When I reached the alcove, he had withdrawn from the window and shrunk back into the room.

"What are you doing? Get over here!"

He didn't budge.

"Tex, we can't waste time. We need to get away from this place. *Now*."

He nodded his head in agreement, but he didn't budge.

"Okay. I'm coming in," I said as I climbed through the open window.

Standing barefooted on the floor, I held out my hand toward him.

"I'm not leaving you here alone. There's a huge oak tree only a few feet from here around the corner. Its branches are thick and wide, and it's going to be an easy climb down."

I hoped what I was saying was true.

Tex didn't budge.

I could see his face had turned a whiter shade of pale, another song title crossing the back of my mind.

That happens to me all the time, a song for every occasion. I guess it's stress relief.

I scolded myself inwardly, but I can't ever quite turn off the music channel in my brain.

"Come on, Tex, I'll hold your hand. We can do this together."

I wanna hold your haaaaand...shut up, Paul McCartney.

He took a hesitant step toward me. Then another.

"I'm sorry, Kaytie. But I'd almost rather face old Bad Leroy or a swamp gator than climb out that window."

"Look, Tex. These people aren't fooling around. They're risking federal kidnapping charges. Do you really think they're just going to let us go when they're done with us?"

Tex swallowed again, his large Adam's apple bobbing up and down.

I appealed to his bravery.

"You were willing to wade the swamps and risk the water moccasins and alligators to get away from Leroy. Do you think he's any less dangerous now?"

He moved slowly to the window.

"I reckon not."

"Take off your shoes."

Obediently he removed them.

"Okay, here goes."

With a deep breath, he threw one long leg over the sill and placed his foot on the ledge. Then he sat there, unable to bring himself to step out.

"Just don't look down. Keep your chest against the wall and *deep breathely*, You'll be fine," I tried to assure him.

He grinned weakly. "You mean breathe deeply."

"See? I'm a little rattled too. C'mon, c'mon."

Still he hesitated, sweat popping out on his forehead and his Adam's apple working up and down. He looked miserable.

That's when we heard the sound of a car door slamming. The slight but distinct shudder in the walls as a door to the house opened and closed somewhere below us.

"Come on, Tex. I hear footsteps. You can do this!" I coaxed in an anxious whisper.

He groaned and lifted the other foot over the sill. Then he began to inch along. I could hear his ragged breathing.

I threw my leg over the window ledge and was horrified to see Tex losing his balance. He teetered dangerously over the long drop, scrambling and grasping for something to hold onto.

"Tex!"

I cried out, reaching toward him.

He grasped my hand with a yelp of terror, flailing as his lanky frame tilted even farther outward from the wall.

In that heart-pounding, slow-motion instant I knew full well that my weight was not going to anchor both of us. Tex was falling and dragging me out the window with him.

His flailing motion jerked me even farther through the window ledge.

Just as I felt my body sliding over it, strong arms wrapped my waist and jerked me back inside.

My hand slipped out of Tex's desperate grip.

"Tex!"

I screamed, hearing his descending cry of terror.

Then silence.

I wrestled with steely tattooed arms on my waist, anxiously trying to peer out the window. The familiar smell of chloroform covered my nose once again. "No! Tex! We've got to help him. Let me go!"

"He's beyond help now, lady."

Those were the last words I heard.

* * *

How much time passed before I came to my senses once more on my next night in Rainy Bay Bayou is anyone's guess. I should have been getting used to the routine. This time I found myself lying on some kind of woven floor mat, my hands tied in front of me, a gag stuffed in my mouth.

"Mmm!" I tried to scream.

I could hear noises.

Drums beating a slow, sinister rhythm, definitely not a dance beat. More like a funeral march.

The dank air was heavy with bayou humidity, cloying and damp as if a wet towel were wrapped around my body.

I struggled to a sitting position and pulled the gag out of my mouth. This time the cords binding my wrists were loose enough that I managed to wriggle free after a few moments. I was inside some kind of shack. No furniture. Just a dirt floor.

Orange firelight filtered between wide chinks in the wall. The smell of burning wood filled my nostrils. Rising slowly, my eyes adjusting to the gloom, I made my way to one of the wider gaps in the clapboard wall and peered through.

Before me was a scene right out of a Hollywood horror movie—natives performing a ritual to soothe the beastly King Kong on a primordial island. Only this was chilling reality in the swamps of Louisiana, not Hollywood.

A leaping fire flickered over the shadowy figures appearing in and out of the night. Bare shoulders and arms glistened with sweat. Women wore the old-fashioned *tignon* tied around their heads. I had the feeling I was viewing a scene right out of the past.

Placed beside the fire were shallow baskets filled with weeds or herbs. Around the baskets were small piles of white beans and corn, and a number of small bones. Whether the bones were human, I could not tell from my vantage point.

An ancient, wrinkled Negress began scraping on a two-stringed sort of fiddle with a long neck, its body covered with a brightly mottled snake skin. Two younger women beat with small sheep shank bones on drums made of gourds which gave forth peculiar, hollow sounds, fitting accompaniments with the primitive fiddle.

They were chanting the words, "Who is there who can resist me."

I heard ferocity in every word, saw defiance in every gesture as the unhallowed rites proceeded.

A half-naked man held an immense and writhing snake in the air with one hand. Brandishing it wildly overhead, he talked and whispered to it. The reptile undulated, its body twisting and writhing and its tongue flickering. The evil creature seemed to acknowledge his dominion over it.

Participants formed a crescent around him, and he made cabalistic signs over them while sprinkling a liquid substance from a calabash, or Louisiana gourd over their bodies. He also passed the snake over their heads, repeating the words, "*Voudou Magnian*."

Each person held a baked clay vessel with a small spout and a capacious, rounded belly. The old woman poured into the vessels from a flask. My guess was that the liquid could be *tafia* or sugar-cane rum, a brew the slaves of yesteryear had favored.

They drank.

Next, they began to dance and as the drum beat quickened, their gyrations grew wilder. Eyes began to roll in a wild frenzy.

I must be hearing the savage music of darkest Africa brought to Louisiana on the slave ships. It was both fascinating and repugnant.

The snake charmer placed the serpent on a low surface and compelled it to lift about twelve inches of its length upright where it paused, motionless. Then he lifted it once more and the entire group again chanted *"Voudou Magnian."*

He twirled the writhing reptile and suddenly, with one dexterous motion, cast it into the blazing fire which leaped up hungrily to receive the offering with a sudden sizzle. A long, deep, exultant howl erupted from the nefarious group. The rhythm of the tam-tam increased.

I saw a magnificent and savagely beautiful black woman move lithely into the firelight, her body waving and undulating in an eerie imitation of the serpent's movements.

She tore off the white kerchief from her head and shouted, "Dance *Calinda*," then continued the undulating motion from hips to her ankles.

The whole scene drew me in with such a macabre fascination, but it was distinctly, primitively evil.

The tam-tam beating swelled even more. Men and women tore off outer garments and danced—no, not danced—they wriggled and writhed like snakes.

If I have ever been aware of the tangible presence of evil, it was that night. Something inside me recoiled, repulsed, felt contaminated.

Then, I saw a familiar figure. Madame Chevalier, dressed in a flowing white gown that might have been two bed sheets tied together her over expansive shoulders. She strode regally into the circle and raised her beefy arms.

All chanting ceased. The drums stopped. The group waited in a complete hush.

The large woman uttered the words, "*Loa* Marie*!* *Loa* Marie*! Commencez!*"

She glanced toward something I had not noticed before. A crude wooden coffin.

An *open* coffin.

Three men entered the circle of firelight carrying what appeared to be a body. A body that looked very much like...

Oh no!

An involuntary groan escaped my lips. Horrified, I slapped my hands over my mouth. No one appeared to notice the sound.

The pale body of a very lifeless Texas cab driver was carried to the firelight and placed inside the wooden box.

Dismayed, I watched as they closed the lid and nailed it shut. Naked shoulder muscles glistened in the firelight as they lifted brush and leafy branches to cover the coffin, which might have been buried underground, except coffins tend to float around if they're buried in southern Louisiana.

My mind did not want to believe what I was seeing.

Tex, dead.

The fall from that third-story alcove must have killed him, and it was all my fault for insisting that he climb out the window. I stuffed my fist in my mouth to keep from crying aloud.

What were they going to do with *me* now?

Drums started beating once more, and the chanting. Slowly at first, then faster and faster. Bodies whirled and leaped in wild contortions. Dark skin glistened like black satin in the fire's orange glow.

I stifled my sobs and lowered my head. When at last I dared to peek out through the cracks again, I could see faces in the muddy firelight.

Some were ordinary enough. Bayou dwellers who looked like they might have fished and survived on whatever they could find in the swamplands. More than a few seemed to have disfiguring features, distorted limbs, and odd facial defects.

What a scurvy lot of followers. Did the voodoo priestess deliberately choose them because they were misfits, or were these simply the kind of people who were drawn into such a wanton activity?

I glanced around my temporary jail, wondering if I could find a way out. Maybe one of the walls had some loose boards and I could wiggle through to the outside.

Before I could move, the shack's only door opened and two men entered. They lifted me to my feet by each arm and dragged me out into the night. At this point, there wasn't much fight left in me.

I was hauled before Madame Chevalier, who eyed me impassively. All I could think about was poor Tex. She lifted my chin and forced me to look into her glittering eyes.

* * *

I must have fainted because the next thing I remember, I was lying on satiny pillows underneath a canopy of gauze mosquito netting. The perfume of scented candles and incense filled my nostrils.

My head swam. Madame Chevalier's bayou cabin? Had I been dreaming? Was Tex's death and burial only a macabre nightmare?

Sitting up made my head spin and my stomach lurch. I groaned, panting a moment until my eyes cleared and the dizziness passed. Had the gypsy drugged me?

"So you wake up now, *ma petite.*" The voice was velvety. It was Madame Chevalier's voice. I glanced up to see her sitting on cushions at her low plank table.

"Come sit. I make you some chicory coffee." She had a pan of water boiling on a small camp stove.

Coffee sounded marvelous.

I didn't have anything better to do at the moment.

Chapter 5

Magnolia

The coffee and a piece of fry bread helped to settle my queasy stomach. I ate it without worrying that Madame might be drugging me again. After all, I was in her grasp now. She could inject me with sedatives or toss me to the alligators if she liked.

How could I stop her?

"You think you can escape your destiny." It was more of a statement than a question. She sipped from her cup, eyeing me with dark, mysterious eyes.

"So we're back to that again. I told you I'm not the reincarnation of Elizabeth O'Brien." I tried reasoning with her.

"I admit it's strangely coincidental that my name is the same as your predicted person's name, but that's all. And speaking of strange coincidences, someone with *your* name was murdered in my hotel room!"

Madame didn't blink an eye. She ignored my remark completely.

"You are Kaytie Flame O'Reilly. My ancestress named you in her will. She said you would come. Now you are here."

"Look, Madame, I'd like to help you. I really would. If I knew the location of any buried treasure, I'd take you to it and you could have it all. But I don't know anything. My mother is a retired nurse who loves Clark Gable flicks and old movies. My dad was a doctor who didn't resemble Clark at all. In fact he looked more like Don Knots, but she married him anyway so it must have been real love. He's been dead since I was thirteen, and we both still miss him every day."

The woman continued staring at me with inscrutable calm. Was I getting through to her at all?

"I was born in Baton Rouge, grew up there, landed a reporting job in Chicago, and here I am. Just plain ol' me. I can't help you."

Her velvet black eyes glittered with determination.

"I have rescued you from the police. You will lead me to the treasure." She announced the words with perfect confidence.

"You let Tex die!" I accused. "Why would I want to lead you anywhere?"

"You will. Perhaps you would like to see your friend alive again?"

Alive?

What was she suggesting?

I'd seen Tex's body with my own two eyes. He was very much dead at the time.

She had to be out of her gourd, crazier than a Bessie bug, which is definitely crazy according to my aunt Nan. Sane people don't kidnap cab drivers and reporters and try to force them into a treasure hunt just because of a crazy family legend. Not unless they're unhinged, and if she thought she could raise the dead, she was crazier than I originally thought.

That's what scared me.

Madame Chevalier pulled a heavy gold chain from around her neck and dangled it in front of me. The pendant was made of polished black obsidian cut into the likeness of a cruelly handsome face surrounded by black pearls. It swung from side to side, appearing to leer at me with a malevolent grin. Rubies blazed wickedly from the eye sockets, flashing red wands of light. For a moment I was spellbound, unable to turn my gaze away.

"You are very tired. Relax, *ma petite*. You will rest. You will sleep." Her voice all silk and honey, purred like a mother soothing a tired child.

I merely shook my head no.

Inwardly I resisted her by praying silently.

Did I dare ask God for help?

Not until I asked Him to forgive me for lying about why I came to New Orleans in the first place and also about being Mrs. Larue and about being engaged. I felt suddenly and deeply convicted. How could I have blurted out such untruths so easily? I began to whisper a heartfelt prayer.

The witch woman took no note, so intent was her concentration.

She continued to swing the pendant. "Look at it," she crooned. "Isn't it lovely? An exquisite work of art."

I thought it the most hideous thing I ever saw.

"Gaze at its ruby eyes. Listen to what they are saying to you," she urged softly in that honeyed tone, but whispered the words, "*Iwa* Marie" occasionally.

I looked but didn't hear anything. Didn't feel any anything either.

"You are sleepy. You need to rest."

She watched me with intense curiosity, repeating the phrase.

I was feeling very tired, but after my silent prayer, I found I could gaze at the pendant or look away at will, even as she repeated her soothing words.

After a while, this seemed to irritate her. Suddenly she gasped, dropping the pendant on the table and clutching her heart with a beefy hand.

"You are one of those—those *Christians*!"

She spat out the word as if it were a dirty word and threw a hand to her forehead in a gesture of consternation.

"One of those who can't be charmed…unless…"

She paused. A cunning look came into her eyes.

"Yes, I am a believer in Jesus Christ, the Son of God and my Lord and Savior," I announced firmly.

That statement sent Madame Chevalier into a fit of rage so intense that I thought she might pop a blood vessel. She cursed, moaned and rocked back and forth on the bench, holding her head in her hands.

Wow. Just that simple.

Speaking the Lord's name instantly destroyed whatever hypnotic spell she had been trying to weave. The entire atmosphere in the room changed completely from one of sinister foreboding to a definite calm, an actual peace. Despite Madame's apparent distress, I felt as light as a rainbow and positively joyous.

Standing up, I thought this might be a good time to make my exit.

"So you see, Madame, I'm no good to you at all. I'll just be going now."

I had no idea how or where to go, but I knew Cajun Jack's cabin was not too far away.

The woman snapped to attention.

"You are not going anywhere. I have other methods of dealing with you." She spoke once again with a sudden, calm assurance.

"We will go to the fire ring this night."

I could only guess what that meant and after what I had seen, the thought made me shiver.

The gypsy motioned for me to sit down again. She wasn't going to let me simply walk away.

"I have powers," she began in a confidential tone. "Secret powers that can be shared. You will see this night. Would you like to be my apprentice?"

The question startled me.

She crooned seductively, "You can learn to cast powerful spells. Look into the future. Control others. Make them do your bidding. Think of it. You can gain everything you ever wanted. Fame. Fortune...Love."

Madame glanced at the emerald ring on my finger as she spoke the last word. Probably, she had shrewdly guessed that it was not an engagement ring.

Hers was an offer as old as the Garden of Eden. Forbidden knowledge that would entice a man into believing he could become like God, knowing good and evil. Knowing even the future.

For a fleeting instant she made me see myself winning coveted journalistic honors and awards, writing amazing books predicting the future, gaining the attention of national and international world leaders like many previous prophets and psychics had done—Rasputin, Nostradomus, Edgar Cayce, Jeanne Dixon.

I saw myself the happy bride of an adoring husband. A smiling, handsome man, utterly devoted to me. He looked a lot like Dax Larue.

Those glorious visions made my obscure, and rather uneventful life seem colorless, devoid of recognition and empty of...of love. Then I saw myself growing old, lonely, and dying without ever experiencing any of life's most coveted pleasures.

Who wouldn't want more, given the opportunity?

But what would be required of me?

In answer to my unspoken question, the woman whispered seductively, "You can enjoy the power. All you have to do is...to curse the name of your god." As she whispered the last words, she stared at me with an eager, intense expression.

I shook my head.

"No thanks, Madame Chevalier. You've got it all wrong. I'm not the reincarnation of anybody. And more importantly, I may not have supernatural powers, but I serve the God who is all powerful—both in this world and in the one to come. That's enough for me. I will never curse His name."

A verse from First Corinthians sprang to my mind. No man speaking by the spirit of God calls Jesus accursed, and no man can say that Jesus is the Lord but by the Holy Spirit. I knew then that Madame was truly a witch. Whatever power she had was not from the spirit of God.

The woman's eyes gleamed impossibly red for an instant, as red as the rubies in the obsidian pendant.

"Besides," I asked her the obvious question as I glanced around the small room, "you don't strike me as the sybaritic type. Why would you need me if you already have such great magical powers? Why do you need to find any buried treasure? Can't you just use your hocus pocus and conjure up some coins and jewels?"

A startled look flashed in her eyes, then quickly changed to one of tired resignation. Breathing less rapidly now and speaking in a more controlled tone, she murmured, "I will tell you."

She took another sip from her cup, calming herself further, and then began her story with a tired sigh. "But you won't understand."

I listened as her story unfolded, watching her eyes for hints of insanity.

"Magnolia was a slave in Louisiana, but before she arrived on the slave ship from Haiti, she was a powerful tribal queen. She knew ancient African arts, powerful spells learned from the wisest *mundunugu* of deepest Africa. After Miss Elizabeth taught her how to read and write, she wrote these secrets down in a book."

Madame set her mug on the table and wiped her pouty lips with a paper napkin before continuing.

"Miss Elizabeth was a believer like you. She treated Magnolia kindly and Magnolia became devoted to her, even obeyed her mistress's wishes to forsake her secret arts and worship the Christian God. They made a pact between them, a solemn vow never to reveal the location of the book. They pronounced a curse on anyone who might ever try to open it, and they hid it inside the treasure chest. Then the soldiers came. You already know that they hung Elizabeth."

I nodded, fascinated by this glimpse into the lives of Civil War–era women from such different backgrounds, united by a faith in the Lord.

"Magnolia had to flee for her life, but not before vowing she would avenge her mistress's death. Seeing that Elizabeth's god was not powerful enough to save her, Magnolia went back to her old ways. However, the book of spells could not be opened without an O'Brien present to protect her from the curse."

"What was this curse?" I asked.

I wasn't surprised that she actually believed in the power of curses.

"A blood descendant of both Magnolia and Elizabeth O'Brien, or their reincarnated spirits, must be present together when the book is opened, If not, every curse in the *mundunugu's* book will be unleashed on the one who disturbs it. I have Magnolia's blood in my veins. You have the spirit of Elizabeth O'Brien in you. It must be opened by the two of us!"

She spoke the words with sudden intensity.

I could see a terrible desperation in her eyes, and I knew she would not be persuaded that I was anything but the reincarnation of the long-dead plantation mistress.

"Why didn't Elizabeth and Magnolia just burn the book?"

It was the obvious question.

"Magnolia wouldn't allow that. There is a price to possessing such power. If she burned it, she knew she would die a horrible death. The *mundunugu's* secret arts had to be safely buried."

"So you need this book to add even more power to your own, which is already quite formidable according to yourself?" I asked, still not quite comprehending her insatiable need.

"With this book, you and me, we can do *anything*! Go everywhere. Have everything. *There is no greater magic* than these ancient powers. And I'm offering to share them with you!"

I felt a momentary pity for her, deceived by such a falsehood.

"Look, Madame, I'm sorry, but I'm not the one you are looking for." I tried explaining once more.

"Enough!"

She exploded, bringing a hammy fist down on the table.

"You will come with me tonight. You will see my powers are real. And we will see what you will do to keep your friend among the living rather than the dead."

I didn't like the sound of that.

Madame grabbed my wrist in a vise-like grip, jerked me to my feet and steered me toward the doorway. She shoved me down the rickety steps and into the boat, which was tied up at the cabin.

Bad Leroy was nowhere in sight, and for that I was glad.

Hoisting her hefty frame into the wobbling craft, she quickly loosed the slipknot and started the motor. Daylight was already giving way to deepening darkness underneath the canopy of moss-draped trees.

How long had I been asleep before waking in the gypsy's lair?

Instead of heading the stern toward the lighted channel markers, Madame steered directly into the darkened swamp. She must have had the eyes of a cat, because she sluiced the craft through the black waters at a steady pace. I held my breath, ready for a spill at any moment.

A dim orange glow soon appeared through the cypress trees ahead. Flames of a bonfire came into view under parting curtains of Spanish moss. A few motor crafts and several pirogues were tied to a crude dock made of rough, uneven planks resting on sunken stilts.

Madame quickly tied up her boat to an iron ring on the dock, then jerked me out of the craft and steered me toward a grassy knoll where flames already leaped higher than my head.

Once again I was witness to a voodoo ceremony which had its roots in the heart of Africa. A multifarious group of men and women—black, white, Creole, Cajun, Mulatto—brought scraps of paper wrapped around cinnamon sticks and laid them in a basket. These, I learned later, were written requests to the power of the *Iwa*. Again they danced around the bonfire and chanted unintelligible words. It was an eerily familiar scene since I had previously witnessed it only a short time ago.

The celebrants glanced at Madame Chevalier, but seemed not to notice me at all. She left me standing at the edge of the firelight under the watchful eye of a withered albino crone, her claw-like hand gripping my wrist with surprising strength.

Evidently, I had been brought here for a demonstration of Madame's power. Was I supposed to be impressed by the gyrating forms which grew ever more exaggerated as the fire leaped higher and the drum beat faster? Sweat glistened on bare arms and chests. Eyes rolled back, leaving only the whites to be seen. Lips moaned and parted. Jaws went slack. The dancers looked more beastly than human.

After several minutes of leaping, moaning and gibbering, the lot of them fell silent in an expectant hush. Madame Chevalier stepped into the firelight and lifted her arms to the moon, which had seemed to hide its face in shame behind the clouds until this moment. A single shaft of moonlight bounced off the fabric of her silky robe, creating the appearance of a radiant aura around her. She looked like a fat moon goddess.

From the other side of the flames I could see dim figures approaching, carrying a familiar wooden box.

Oh no! Was she going to kill me and bury me in that box just the way she buried poor Tex?

I tried to calm my fear, telling myself she needed me to open her treasure box. The voodoo priestess remained completely frozen, arms upraised, head thrown back, lips silent.

Dark figures brought the crude coffin around to my side of the fire ring and placed it on the ground. Two men with crowbars began working to remove the lid, which lifted easily enough.

Once again Madame repeated the words, "*Iwa* Marie."

I couldn't see inside the box from my vantage point and I didn't want to. At that moment, the stillness was broken by a collective gasp from the dancers. They appeared to exhibit absolute astonishment or terrified awe.

I shrank from the crone's grip as a shudder racked her body. I could see...

Something moving...

sitting up...

sitting up and...impossibly...climbing out of the crude sarcophagus.

The something, rose to stand on stiff legs, eyes open but unseeing.

Could it be? I blinked and rubbed my eyes.

It was...

the *thing* was Tex.

Disbelief overwhelmed me. Thinking I must have consumed some hallucinogenic powder in the chicory coffee, I could only stare in shocked awe with the rest of the celebrants.

It was Tex alright. He took a jerky step or two and stopped. His features were glazed over by a hideous lifelessness. The pallor of his skin, the blueness of his lips and those blankly staring eyes certainly gave every appearance of death.

Yet there he was, standing upright.

"Zom...bie. Zom...bie. Zombie!" The chanters began repeating the word. They moved around the fire ring once more, slowly at first and then gained momentum. Tex stood transfixed, unseeing and unmoved.

The albino crone trembled, gasped and stepped toward the fire, releasing her claw-like grip on my arm and leaving me behind where the shadows began. So intent was her focus on the Tex-thing that I saw my chance to move without drawing attention. Madame appeared to be in a trance-like state and the dancers were equally oblivious. I started backing slowly away from the murky firelight, finding my footing carefully, afraid of slipping off the grassy knoll into the surrounding mire.

Two steps back.

No one appeared to notice.

The entire group exhibited a state of total awe, entranced by the living-dead man. Judging from their stunned reaction, this was a miracle they did not see every day.

I moved back into the deeper shadows, one careful step at a time. When I felt I must surely be invisible in the blanketing darkness, I turned and ran for the boat dock.

I dared not take Chevalier's motor craft. Even if I could figure out how to start it, the noise of the engine would bring pursuers who would surely overtake me. Instead I chose a pirogue equipped with a pole. My hands trembled as I fumbled to loosen its ties. I was too afraid to look back, afraid I would see them coming after me, or worse yet—Tex, like a creature right out of *Night of the Living Dead*, a horrible zombie pursuing me through haunted Rainy Bay Bayou.

In my haste, I almost overturned the pirogue, but managed to right it and began poling past rusty pine trees, gaudy with fungus, disturbing turtles from their logs and frogs the size of frisbees. They belly flopped into the water, causing me to hold my breath until the muddy firelight faded completely from view.

When I dared to look over my shoulder, all I could see was shadows. No one followed me as yet. But they would. Of that I was certain. The madwoman was not going to let me get away.

Then I realized I had another big problem.

A huge problem.

I had no idea where to go. I'd heard stories about people getting lost in the swamps and never coming out again. Had I escaped from one nightmare only to face another?

I kept poling the boat, more afraid of pursuers than of being lost. Now and again the Spanish moss brushed its fingers across my neck, making me gasp. The thought of snakes and alligators sent shivers through my charged frame.

Tex's story about the skunk ape leaped to my imagination. He must have come from eastern Texas. As a reporter for *Beyond Fantasy*, I knew that hundreds of sightings of the legendary Bigfoot were reported around Jefferson, Texas, during the 1990s alone.

I wasn't sure I believed in Bigfoot.

But then I'd never believed in zombies either. After what I had just witnessed, I wouldn't have been surprised to see an entire Bigfoot family sitting around a campfire enjoying a bowl of jambalaya. In spite of the heavy bayou air, tiny bumps pimpled my skin.

Where was Cajun Jack?

Could I find his cabin again?

Was I anywhere near it?

Pale moonlight penetrated the dense overgrowth only at brief intervals. I could see dimly at best. Maybe I could find those channel markers.

For what seemed like hours, I poled blindly along, hoping against hope that I could find my way to somewhere.

Then hardly believing my luck, I glimpsed lights ahead.

Headlights. Cars moving back and forth on a roadway.

The pirogue bumped against a shelf of solid ground. I leaped out and headed in the direction of those intermittent headlights, stumbling and slogging probably half a mile through grassy turf and shallow bogs, before I hit the roadway. I wanted to kneel down and kiss the solid ground beneath my feet.

Muddy and breathless, I realized I must look frightful in the moonlight. Who would dare to offer me a ride? And though I was desperate, why would I dare accept a ride from a total stranger who might be one of Madame Chevalier's followers?

I began a stumbling walk on the buckling pavement. From its state of neglect, it wasn't a major road. I thought it unlikely that Bayou dwellers would be out this time of night unless they were part of Madame's evil crew, so I decided to dodge into the weeds if headlights appeared. It seemed a rather lonely and abandoned road.

After walking a few miles without passing a single car, I approached a run-down gas station with rusty outdated pumps that might have been there since the 1940s. The place was lighted by a single lantern hanging in the window. Nobody appeared to be stirring about, but I tried the front door anyway. It was locked.

The sound of an approaching vehicle sent me scurrying to find an unlocked door to the rickety old station.

There was a restroom to the side of the building, evidently added on in later years. It was made of concrete blocks rather than clapboard.

The door stood half open on rusty hinges. Inside seemed narrower and blacker than a vampire's coffin, but I felt my way past three stalls and gave a ragged sigh of relief, thinking I could hide there safely until the vehicle passed.

Instead the engine slowed. Gravel crunched under the tires and the engine died. I heard the car door opening. Heavy footfalls coming my way.

Slow, labored footfalls.

I recognized them.

The ponderous, heavy steps of an overly large woman.

Sweat popped out on my forehead and trickled down my armpits. How had she tracked me here? It was too cruel to have come this far, only to be captured once more by the voodoo priestess. Moving as quietly as possible, I stepped inside the third stall, thankful the metal door was already standing open.

Did I dare swing it closed? Would it groan on rusty hinges and give me away? I decided to leave it open.

The obese woman's footsteps neared my hiding place. How could she know? Hinges creaked as she swung open the entry doorway. My breath was labored now, coming in gasps. She would surely hear me!

I tried breathing through my mouth and stepped up on the edge of the toilet seat, hoping to keep Madame from spying my feet. Of course not much was visible in the inky blackness, but the voodoo priestess might have the eyes of a cat for all I knew. She was no natural woman.

There was a sound of fumbling and scratching at the wall. If she switched on the lights, all would be lost. No doubt my muddy tracks would be plainly visible. The room remained totally black. Apparently there was no electricity…a huge blessing for me.

Madame's labored breathing filled the air.

She stepped toward the first stall and fumbled to get the door open. The groaning and creaking sound of the rusty hinges might have been right out of a Dean Koontz thriller.

I felt a sneeze coming on. *Not now. Please not now.*

Pinching my nostrils together, I held my breath.

Footfalls.

Closer than before. The woman was unstoppable.

The second stall doorway creaked open on complaining hinges.

She wouldn't stop there. She was going to find me!

I considered leaping at her and fighting my way out. I knew I could outrun her. But if she had Bad Leroy with her, he could be waiting to grab me.

She gave a snort of disgust. A grunt.

Madame was obviously growing impatient with the hunt.

From outside, a male voice urged, "Hurry up, Winnifred. This place gives me the creeps."

Winnifred bellowed back at him, "I told you to ask for directions, Frank! Now we're lost and this place is a pit. Lights don't work and I don't want to sit on it in the dark. Could be a toilet full of snakes for all I know."

She continued grumbling to herself, the sound of her own voice blocking out any noise of my ragged breathing.

Unable to stifle the sneeze a second longer, I let out a kind of strangled *choo.*

"EEK! One of 'em's hissing at me!" Winnifred shrieked.

Her mad scramble out the door would have made me laugh at any other time. I could hear the sound of heavy footfalls, the creak and slam of the car door.

Relief flooded my body.

Winnifred and Frank!

Lost motorists. Not Madame Chevalier after all.

I thought about running after them and begging for a ride, but by the time I stepped down from the toilet seat and managed to get my shaking knees to hold me up, I could hear the car already moving away.

When the shivering stopped and the weakness in my knees passed, I peered out the door to see only a few dilapidated sheds, a rusty old sedan, and a chicken coop visible in the moonlight. That's when I heard a second car approaching.

This time I chose the sedan for a hiding place, opening the driver's side door on groaning hinges. Once inside I lay down to further hide myself from view. The car passed by at an even speed, not slowing or stopping.

Lying there, hidden from view and relatively safe for the moment, I felt the relief of nervous exhaustion. Badly needed sleep overcame my jangled nerves.

When I next opened my eyes again, sunlight streamed through the dusty windshield and a rooster crowed nearby.

I was startled by a face peering in at me through the passenger window, a freckle-faced youngster, with a missing front tooth and chestnut hair pulled back in tight braids.

"You not be dead," she observed through the broken glass. Her grin broadened.

"No, I'm not dead," I answered, very glad to be able to say that. I sat up.

Returning her smile, I said, "Look, honey, can you tell me where I can find a phone?"

The girl shrugged her shoulders. "You looking for something in there?" She nodded toward the sedan. "I'll tell you what's fun. I like to hang by my heels from the seat. When you're upside down, you can see under the dash. There's all kinds of neat wires to look at. But not in that car. Nutria ate 'em out long time ago." Then she turned and started walking away.

"Wait a minute," I said climbing out of the junker. I must have looked like the creature from the Black Lagoon in my muddied clothes, hair uncombed. I didn't blame her for wanting to get away from me.

"Can you at least tell me the name of this road?"

The girl kept walking. She carried a sack of chicken feed and was headed for the coop. "You don't be knowing where you're at?" she tossed back over her shoulder.

"I know that sounds crazy, but I've had a rough night, and I need to find a telephone. I'll be on my way as soon as I can tell a friend where to pick me up."

The girl turned around and looked me over. "Your earrings made of real gold?"

My earrings? They were actually just small gold-plated hoops. I removed them slowly and held them in one hand, extended toward her. "Tell you what. You can have them. Just tell me where we are and point me to a telephone."

She approached and reached for the earrings. Then her face spread into a delighted gap-toothed grin. "We're on Rainy Bay Bayou Road, just a few miles from the old river road. Paw's got a pay phone inside the station. You can use it if you got a quarter."

A quarter. I didn't have a single penny. But at least I had some idea of my location. Maybe I could talk Paw into letting me use the phone.

I had to ask, "Your paw? Was he home last night?"

She kept walking toward the chicken coop, but nodded over her shoulder.

"All night?" I pressed. There was always a chance he had been one of the followers at the fire ring. I didn't want to risk showing myself to him if so.

The girl nodded again, admiring the earrings in her hand. I headed for the front door, anxious to get back to New Orleans, police or no police. Let them arrest me. At least in jail I'd be out of the madwoman's reach.

Rows of dusty canned goods lined the walls inside the aging clapboard station. A galvanized tub held water and a handmade sign hung over it with the letters "BATE" printed with a red crayon in big block letters. I could only assume the word meant fish bait.

Paw wore a pair of ragged denim overalls and peered at me over smudgy spectacles. His stare reminded me once again of my disheveled appearance.

"Mister, I've been walking for hours. My car's not running, and I really need to use your telephone," I began. It wasn't the complete truth, but I couldn't just say I was running from a voodoo priestess and a zombie.

The thought flashed through my anxious mind that Madame might actually be a zombie herself. After all, she was *supposed* to be a dead woman.

No. That was crazy.

Still, I had seen Tex with my own two eyes, dead as a tombstone, his body laid in a coffin and then raised up out of it again.

What was I to believe?

Could I trust my own senses?

"Cost you a quarter," the man muttered, pointing to a really old-fashioned pay phone inside a dusty booth. I hadn't seen a booth of that style except in some of Mom's old movies.

"Sir, I haven't got a quarter. If you could just let me use the phone, my friend will pay you when he picks me up," I pleaded.

Paw looked me over, spat a chaw of tobacco at the floor, then opened a drawer and pulled out a coin. He tossed the quarter at me across the weathered counter top. He didn't speak a word.

Relieved, I grabbed the coin and headed for the phone. No telephone directory anywhere. That meant I had no choice but to dial Dax's number, the ink on my hand still visible.

Please let Dax still be in New Orleans, I prayed.

Paw might not be so generous as to loan me a second quarter.

Dax picked up on the fourth ring. Almost sobbing with relief, I spewed, "Dax! It's Kaytie."

"Kaytie! Blazes, girl, where have you been? Where are you now?"

His voice was filled with both relief and concern. I might have been flattered any other time. At the moment, all I could think of was getting out of Rainy Bay Bayou.

I babbled out my need for a ride and managed to explain my location somewhere near Old River Road, describing the run-down station as best I could while trying not to insult Paw.

Dax barked, "Stay there. I'll find you. I'm on my way."

"Thank you, sir," I said to Paw, after hanging up. "I'll be waiting for just a little while till my ride gets here if you don't mind."

He didn't answer, just turned his back to me and appeared to busy himself with some paperwork.

For the next very tense couple of hours, a few old beater pickup trucks pulled up one at a time. The drivers paid for sodas and moon pies along with fishing bait. They spoke in a Cajun dialect or guttural snorts and grunts. Most of them ignored me after a brief stare.

I tried to hide my face behind a yellowed newspaper whenever someone entered the run-down place. In truth, I probably drew less attention in my present ragged state than if I had been neatly groomed and wearing my white skirt and jacket.

After several anxious glances through the dusty windows, I gasped with relief to see Dax pulling up in a rented white Ford Expedition. Then I ran and didn't stop running until I was safe in his arms. Strong, warm arms that welcomed me and held me tightly while I began to sob and bit my lower lip, trying to regain control.

"Hold it, girl. Easy now. I'm here," Dax crooned gently, calming me as if I were a spooked horse. I felt more spooked than any horse, and probably looked like whatever it is that spooks horses half to death, but I didn't care.

He held me away from him a moment and looked me over. "Good gravy, girl, you look like you combed your hair with a swamp buggy!"

I ignored the compliment. "Let's get out of here. This place gives me the creeps."

Seeing my tears and trembling lips, Dax lifted me up onto the seat of the Expedition with strong, muscular arms.

A less agitated part of my mind registered, *Finally! Now I get chivalry. It takes a sobbing, half-hysterical, swamp-muddied woman to bring out the gentleman in him.*

He climbed in and stepped on the gas.

"I've been driving up and down these back roads for over an hour. I must have stopped at four shanty gas stations," he said, reaching his right arm around me and drawing me close. I shivered against him, glad for the warmth of his chest. I must have been in shock from the night's events for my body to react this violently, now that my rescuer had finally arrived.

"Do you want to tell me how you managed to get here?" he asked, squeezing my shoulders in a protective hug.

"Yes. I'll tell you everything. But not now. Right now I just want a hot shower and a long nap."

Chapter 6

Marie Laveau

"I'll take you to the Bienville House. I've been staying there since you disappeared on me the second time. And by the way, you'll be glad to know you're no longer a suspect in the murder of Madame Chevalier. The police talked to your chemist pal and he probably cleared you. But they're still looking for you. You're now classified as a possible kidnap victim. It's been all over the news. Makes a good mystery story, coupled with the gypsy woman's murder."

At the time I hardly bothered to associate the two events.

"That's good," I murmured and closed my eyes, simply glad to be leaning my head on his shoulder.

It wasn't a long drive back to New Orleans, but I slept most of the way, slumped against my knight in dusty denim. Dax guided me through the Bienville's courtyard and upstairs to his room where I did not hesitate to enter. Any other time a man's hotel room is strictly off-limits, but this was no ordinary time.

Of course there was that time at his suite in the Lafitte, but that didn't count since I hadn't stayed there.

He offered to go out and bring back something to eat while I scoured my aching body in the shower. The steamy water splashed away all remnants of marsh mud, but it couldn't wash away the memories of the last few nights as easily. I still trembled at the thought of seeing Tex rising up from that coffin.

Maybe Madame *really did have* supernatural powers.

She was a witch in every sense of the word.

I thought back to the book of Exodus and how Pharaoh's sorcerers used "secret arts" to duplicate the miraculous signs performed by Moses to show he was sent by God. The sorcerers turned water to blood. They also turned their staffs into serpents.

Where did their powers come from? Certainly not from God.

Simon the sorcerer astounded the people of Samaria with forbidden arts. He wanted their worship. I had no doubt that demons have deceptive power. The Apostle Paul wrote to the Thessalonians that Satan is going to masquerade as an angel of light and perform all kinds of lying signs and counterfeit wonders *to deceive* even the very elect if possible.

But could an evil spirit actually animate a corpse? Had I seen a *counterfeit* raising of the dead in imitation of Christ's power over death?

The idea seemed too far out, even for demonic spirits with deceptive powers. There had to be another explanation.

When Dax returned with a Styrofoam carton of ham, eggs, grits and hot biscuits, I had wrapped my hair in a towel and was wearing the hotel's luxurious, thick white terry bathrobe belted tightly around my waist. My stomach growled noisily. Dax watched with some amusement as I sat on the bed and devoured the breakfast, gulping down the coffee. Nothing had ever tasted better.

I was licking my fingers when he spoke. "You look like you're recovering nicely. You were so pale, except for the bumps from mosquito bites. Now you have some color in your cheeks and the swelling appears to be going down." He handed me a tube of ointment to dab on the welts.

"You mean I'm a recognizable human being again?" I started rubbing the ointment on my skin.

"A beautiful human being at that. The first time I saw you at the airport, your hair was rain soaked and plastered to your head. Even then you were gorgeous. You were Bananas Foster for the eyes. I had to look away to keep from staring."

"Don't you dare!" I ordered him, suddenly incensed.

His eyes showed surprise. "Don't dare what?"

"Don't tell me I'm beautiful when I'm just out of the shower. Gulping down food like a ravenous hound. Looking like I have measles, and my hair wrapped in a towel."

I suddenly wanted to cry. How dare he tell me I looked beautiful at a time like this. Honesty I could handle. Not flattery.

His expression turned from surprise to amusement. "Okay then, Miss Homely America. Want to tell me what happened?"

"You aren't going to believe me."

"What makes you think that?" he asked as he sat back in the room's only chair and prepared to listen.

"Because it's absolutely too *weird*."

"Kaytie, you're a trained observer. A reporter. You write for a skeptical magazine. Why wouldn't I believe you?"

"Because I hardly believe it myself. It's entirely too far out."

"Try me," he said.

I gave a little sigh of resignation. I had to tell somebody after all. Whether he believed me or not, I needed a sounding board.

"Okay, here goes."

I began with my first kidnapping by the gargantuan fortuneteller calling herself Madame Chevalier—coincidentally and mysteriously of the same name and description as the woman found murdered in my room. Dax listened without interrupting, like a good journalist. He wanted to hear the whole story before asking questions.

I told him about Tex and our slog through the swamp. How Cajun Jack rescued us from the gator and got us safely back to New Orleans. Of course Dax was there when my second kidnapping occurred outside Pat O'Brien's. He also had seen the television report of my disappearance after Detective Broussard woke up on the sidewalk with a lump on the back of his head.

"So it was Madame Chevalier's thug that grabbed you the second time?" he asked, puzzled. "What does she want with you?"

"Dax, the woman thinks I'm the reincarnation of Elizabeth O'Brien, since I have the same name mentioned in the will by the owners of the Lafitte hotel. Madame is a direct descendant of Magnolia, the slave woman who was Elizabeth's loyal maid."

I glanced at his dark eyes. No incredulity. So far so good.

"Her story is that Elizabeth and Magnolia hid a book of spells learned from some African witchdoctor back in the Congo where Magnolia was born. They couldn't burn it because of Magnolia's superstitious fears of a curse, so they buried it with the family fortune and added another curse for protection. If a direct descendant of both Magnolia and Elizabeth—or their reincarnated spirits—are not present, the one who opens the book will suffer a whole series of…really bad stuff."

Dax nodded his head. "Okay. So far this is not so unbelievable. Voodoo practitioners believe strongly in the power of curses. But I do find it highly curious that you have the same name as the woman in the will."

He was right of course. If my name had been more common—say Sally Johnson or Mary Thibodeaux—then the coincidence would have been less weird. There are dozens of those names in the phone books, but how many people have I met with my exact same name over the years? Zip. Zero. Nada. The name Kaytie alone is not so uncommon, but combine it with Flame and it's extremely unique.

"Okay, I'll grant you that one," I said.

Dax nodded. Then he offered an unexpected and surprising bit of information. "The coincidence of Madame Chevalier and the dead gypsy woman's name is not such a puzzle." His eyes had that here-goes look.

"I've discovered there are *two* Madame Chevaliers, although few people in New Orleans are aware of it. They're sisters. Their names are Emerald and Sapphire, identical twins and heiresses to the Lafitte property."

"Twins!"

I might have guessed it. Dax had good investigative reporter skills. He'd obviously uncovered records from the county clerk's office and the county recorder of deeds. Or was it the parish clerk's offices? Anyway that explained why there were two Madame Chevaliers of the same description.

"The twins actually inherited the haunted hotel years ago when they were very young. Someone was hired to run the place for them."

My mind was already running ahead. Twins. That explained the mystery of the two Madames, one dead and the other out chasing me around.

Dax continued, "Later, when they were adults, one of them, Sapphire, died of a sudden illness. I found a copy of her death certificate."

"Wait a minute!"

Just as the mystery seemed solved he was throwing out the explanation.

"What good does it do to know there were twins if one of them had already died before they found the body in my room?"

"I'm convinced that Sapphire actually faked her own death some years ago and was still alive until that shooting."

"Faked her death? But why?"

I was already beginning to guess that the sisters could avoid paying double income taxes on hotel revenue and probably also pocket a nice profit from their fortune-telling income.

Dax had another theory.

"The Chevalier sisters were experts at duping clients who never guessed they were dealing with *two* women instead of one. The pair dressed alike so they could appear to be one and the same woman. This gave them the apparent ability to show up in two places at the same time. It's called astral travel or soul projection. Charles Manson was supposed to be able to do it. The street urchins tell me that Madame Emerald Chevalier is very good at it."

"Go on," I prompted, beginning to see their double scheme had more than one level.

He paused a moment with a knowing look in his eye.

"I believe she was trying to compete with the legendary witch queen of New Orleans, Marie Laveau."

Of course growing up in Louisiana, I'd heard of Marie Laveau.

"A witch queen, huh? Wasn't she just a legend?"

"Oh she was *very* real. She's still quite famous as either a saint or one of the most powerful voodoo priestesses that ever lived, depending on who you ask. Actually, few hard facts are known about her life. According to one story, Marie was born in 1794 in Saint Domingue, Haiti, the beautiful daughter of a wealthy white planter and an African slave woman by the name of Darcantel Maguerite. It's not recorded just how she got to New Orleans, but she married twice and had numerous children. Both her husbands died prematurely."

I could picture the young Mulatto girl growing up on the plantation, becoming a woman determined to make her own future far from slavery.

What might she have done to achieve it?

Sell her soul to the devil?

Dax continued, "When she reached New Orleans, Marie was a free woman of color. She learned to survive quite well, eventually moving into a house at 1020 St. Ann Street between Rampart and Burgundy, not far from Congo Square, a place that became famous for voodoo rituals. It's no longer there today, but at one time it was a real draw."

"How does a free woman of color earn a house on St. Ann Street?" I asked.

"The story goes that a wealthy merchant had a son who was facing certain conviction for a crime. The merchant went to Marie and begged her to help. On the day of the trial, Marie placed three Guinea peppers in her mouth and went to the cathedral where she knelt before the altar for over an hour. After that, she hurried to the Cabildo and somehow slipped the same three peppers underneath the judge's bench. Incredibly and against all odds, her *gris gris* powers worked. All evidence pointed to the young man's guilt, but the judge set him free. His grateful father paid Marie a nice bundle of money and deeded the cottage to her."

"So the trial's outcome was credited to voodoo power and Marie's three Guinea peppers. It's just as possible that somebody bribed the judge. What else did the woman do?" I asked, unimpressed.

"She gained notoriety in New Orleans by her apparent knowledge of upper society's secrets, which I suspect she learned by her work as a hairdresser for fashionable white ladies. This allowed her to enter their homes where she probably overheard conversations and secrets, just like hairdressers do today. Of course, she never hesitated to use inside information to her advantage."

I nodded, imagining how easy that would be. "I see nothing really supernatural about the woman from what you've told me so far."

"Oh, there's more. Although raised as a Catholic, Marie became the voodoo priestess and held rituals on Congo Square, which at that time was outside New Orleans. She also held gatherings on the shores of Lake Ponchartrain where she spent much of her time in a flimsy shanty. One story is that a hurricane passed over New Orleans. Her shanty was ripped off its foundation and hurled into the water with Marie floating on the roof. It's said that when she reached the lake shore and stepped on land, the fury of the storm suddenly abated and the water became smooth as glass."

I muttered, "Good timing. That's all. But I can see how that might have impressed the locals."

"Not only the locals. Marie was said to be beautiful of form. Men from all across the country traveled to New Orleans, just to see her dancing nude on the shores of Lake Ponchartrain. Legend has it that the serpent-god *Dumballah* coiled sinuously around her bare flesh as she writhed and swayed."

My silent question had an answer.

She *had* sold her soul to the devil.

Aloud, I remarked, "Silly men. Diddley squat. They don't have to leave Bourbon Street to see a show like that."

Dax continued, "The well-bred New Orleans ladies of higher society began to call on her. They were willing to pay a pretty price for love potions, hoping to rekindle lost love or to attract a new passion."

"So how does all this figure with our Madame Chevalier?"

I could see a pattern emerging. If Madame Chevalier could attract a following like Marie Laveau, she would have a very lucrative income.

"There is one legendary secret surrounding Marie that Madame would probably be willing to do anything for. The historic voodoo queen supposedly possessed the secret of...eternal youth." He spoke with drama in his voice.

"Eternal youth? Marie's not still alive is she?" I meant it satirically.

"No, she's very much dead. Buried in the St. Louis Cemetery. But legend has it that a notorious Haitian sorcerer by the name of Cagliostro traveled to New Orleans in the 1800s in order to learn Marie's powers, or perhaps even to murder her. Instead they became lovers. It's said that he taught her the secret arts he'd learned from the Darkhold. The secret of his own eternal youth."

Dax's voice took on a more emphatic tone. "Here's the clincher. Marie's followers didn't realize there were actually *two* Marie LaVeaus. They were mother and daughter."

"Ah ha! Now I get it. They did the soul-projection thing."

Dax nodded knowingly. "Yep. And they fostered the myth that Marie had eternal youth. That's how she kept her youthful appearance for years, even as she aged. Her daughter simply assumed the mother's identity. The mother eventually died in 1881, but her convinced followers believed the daughter was actually Marie, the ageless voodoo priestess, somehow eternally youthful."

"They had to know that she died sometime."

"Yes, they know she died, but not until she had lived virtually two lifetimes as a young and beautiful woman. They've made a shrine out of Marie's grave, even though the daughter, who bears the same name, is buried in the same cemetery."

I couldn't help thinking how those who are willing to believe mere illusion are so easily deceived. How many with spiritual gifts have strong desires to become wealthy, famous, drawn in by a web of deceit designed by the master deceiver to ensnare them.

"What about the daughter? How did she die?"

"The second Marie was very much alive in 1895 when a hurricane hit New Orleans. Hurricanes have plagued the Crescent City more often than we realize. Anyway, witnesses claimed that they saw Marie floating downriver on a log, chanting voodoo songs. That's the last report of her I could find."

His theory made sense. I could see the parallel.

Two Marie LaVeaus. Two Madame Chevaliers.

Madame was clever. If she wanted to build a reputation like Marie Laveau, she could certainly do it by using her supposedly dead twin sister as a double.

Dax's next words echoed my thoughts.

"Madame Emerald's followers are convinced that she can actually spy on them in spirit form while they're completely unaware of her presence. They don't dare disobey her slightest orders."

I thought of Pirate Man who seldom spoke a word and seemed completely under Madame's control, ready to do her bidding without question.

Dax continued, "The sisters' soul-travel scam is very impressive and convinces high-paying clientele that Madame has great supernatural powers. I suspect that's just one of many ruses the sisters have practiced over the years."

"So it was Emerald's twin sister who turned up dead in our hotel room at the Lafitte. But who killed her? And why?"

"Think about it, Kaytie. The woman you've been dealing with was probably willing to have her sister bumped off rather than share Magnolia's book of spells. She truly believes in the secret arts recorded there. She knows very well that her own power is limited to trickery and artful con jobs. But with Magnolia's book, she probably thinks she won't have to resort to charlatanism and chicanery anymore."

I nodded emphatically.

"She believes it alright. You should have seen the madness in her eyes. I can imagine the woman would commit murder if she thought her sister was a threat to her. Now all she has to do is show up with a whole new identity and nobody will ever suspect her, since there was supposedly only one Madame Chevalier alive anyway. It's a plot for the perfect crime."

I saw the scenario on the screen of my imagination. Sapphire, already supposed to be dead, had gone to my room that night, thinking she was going to persuade me to come with her to find the buried book. Instead, someone shot her in the back of the head.

"But why commit the murder in my room?" I puzzled aloud. "If I was going to be any good to Madame Chevalier, she wouldn't want me arrested. Or maybe she thought she would get the information she needed and then turn me over to the police? I'd be conveniently out of her way."

Dax looked thoughtful. "My guess is that the hit man messed up. He wasn't supposed to kill her in the hotel room. He followed her there. Something surprised him, and he shot her ahead of the plan."

I visualized Pirate Man with his scarred, tattooed face and Satan-filled eyes hiding in the halls, sneaking through the doorway, stalking the gypsy woman as she entered my room.

"Something startled him," I continued the thought. "He fired before she had time to turn around. No one heard the gun fire because of the thunder. Then he ran down the servants' stairway and out into the alley. Emerald must have been waiting for him in a car. They followed me to Jean Claude's place, jumped Tex, shoved him in the trunk and waited for me in his cab."

Dax nodded. "With her sister out of the way, Madame Chevalier must believe she will be the most powerful sorceress in the world, surpassing even Marie Laveau. If only she can find that buried chest."

I began spilling the rest of my incredible story. "Dax, she tried to hypnotize me. She must have been thinking she could take me back into recalling a past life so I could show her where the chest is buried."

He listened attentively. So far so good.

Did I dare tell him the rest?

Encouraged by his steady confidence, I blabbed on. "She also tried to terrorize me in the swamp. I saw her followers bury poor Tex in a wooden coffin. And then later, he...he came out of it!—looking like a total zombie."

Gulping as I spilled the tale, I watched his eyes for any hint of disbelief.

Of course Dax is an investigative reporter for the *Supernatural Seeker*. If anybody believes in zombies, he should be the one. But not without some kind of evidence. Good reporters document their stories.

I had to ask him, "Do you think I was drugged into seeing things that weren't real?"

"I believe you saw what you described, Kaytie. Is Tex a zombie? Probably. But not in the sense that most people understand the word. I traveled to Haiti just before the U.S. invasion in 1994, to do a story on zombies. The London *Daily Mail* had carried a story claiming that literally battalions of Haitian zombies had been created to stop invaders. My editor sent me down to check it out."

The guy was a walking library of weird information. I listened, eager to know what he had learned.

"Go on."

"Haitian people don't doubt that zombies can be created from a dead body which is not yet decomposed." He paused and sipped coffee from a paper cup.

Eager to hear his tale, I asked, "So? Did you find any real zombies?"

"Of course I didn't find any proof of the dead being raised. Instead I discovered there are certain elixirs. Potions. The ingredients are right out of a witch's brew. Boiled and powdered human bones, lizards, the slime from a puffer fish and the skin from a certain type of toad."

I made a face. "Yuck! What kind of effect does the brew have if it doesn't kill you first?"

"The skin of the puffer fish and the toads actually contain powerful neurotoxins. These can be lethal. In smaller doses the victim shows every appearance of being stone cold dead, but remains brutally conscious, even while he is buried alive."

I shuddered involuntarily. Shakespeare's *Romeo and Juliet* sprang to my mind. Juliet drank such a potion, giving her the appearance of death. I'd always assumed that detail of the famous love story was merely fiction.

Maybe it had some basis in fact.

"The voodoo priest, or *bokor,* secretly administers an antidote and the effects begin to wear off. You described Tex as appearing zombie-like when he rose from the coffin. That's exactly the way a victim would appear until the drug wears off completely. The body can eat, hear, and speak, but appears to have no ability to think or reason, and no memory. Sometimes there is permanent nerve damage. The poor guy acts like a robot and becomes the slave laborer of the *bokor*. Haitians will do anything to avoid becoming a zombie themselves."

By this time I was totally convinced that one of the Chevalier twins had faked her own death. With a potion like Dax was describing, it would have been easy. The woman drank the potion. The other sister staged her funeral. New Orleans conveniently buries their dead above ground, so it would have been easy to escape from the coffin. Someone simply opened it later that night, administered the antidote and Sapphire hopped up, free to go about her life. No taxes and lots of gullible people willing to pay big bucks for a session with a gypsy who could materialize in two different locations simultaneously.

Whew! It felt good to hear an explanation that finally made sense, so I kept on talking.

"Madame tried, but she couldn't hypnotize me, and that's when she accused me of being a Christian. The woman really believes that she can't charm a Christian unless that person first curses God, and of course I refused to do that."

Dax raised his brows at this. "Hmmm. That's interesting. She fears the power of your religion? Your Jesus?"

For a moment, my heart thudded around inside my chest. Was Dax saying he was NOT a Christian? That meant the end of a beautiful dream for me before it had even begun. If Dax did not share my faith, then he was totally unsuitable and off my list as a romantic interest.

Not that I was romantically interested of course. Attracted yes, but I certainly wasn't jumping ahead to a relationship.

Still he was so handsome. How could a girl not notice?

I resolved right then and there to *stop* noticing his impossible good looks.

"What do mean, *my* Jesus? Don't you believe in Him?"

He looked at me with the same tolerant expression I'd seen on the faces of the "intellectually enlightened" when they talk about Jesus.

"I respect your faith, Kaytie. Just as I respect the Moslems, the Hindus, the Buddhists and any other faith."

I groaned inwardly. Forget those flashing eyes. That chiseled mouth. The stubborn chin.

It would not be easy. However, I had no wish to become unequally yoked. As my poor dear friend Dora always said, "It's no laughing matter when the yoke's on you."

Dora had married the man of her dreams. Soon enough he turned into her worst nightmare. She always advised me that God warns Christians not to marry unbelievers for a good reason. After all, who wants the devil for a spiritual father-in-law?

I had to ask, "So you're saying you don't believe in God?"

"I have written for the *Seeker* long enough to know that I live in a world where almost anything is possible. I believe in god. I just don't think there's only one way to worship him. The world is filled with people who serve god in their own ways and traditions. For the Jews it's honoring Jehovah. For you, it's Jesus. For Islam, it's Allah. Then there's Buddha. I don't think god is displeased with any of them. They all follow moral teachings. They practice kindness to their fellow man."

I wanted to tell him how only Jesus' life fulfills hundreds of Old Testament prophecies—specifically and to the letter. How no other god in the entire world has ever claimed to declare the end from the beginning and then *done it.* How every other religion in the world offers a type of counterfeit righteousness—salvation earned by good works—instead of the righteousness that comes only by faith in the Savior. How Mohammed's bones and every other prophet's bones can be found still inside the graves, but the tomb of Jesus is empty, mute testament to the fact that He rose from the dead.

Many ways to God? Not so. Jesus said, "I am the way...No man comes to the Father but by me."

The deception of religious *tolerance* is so prevalent today. Not that I would ever advocate intolerance such as Islam practices. The Koran actually urges Islamics to *kill* infidels who refuse to convert. Islamics stone offenders to death, or cut off their hands and feet, whereas Christians are taught to love their enemies and to pray for those who despitefully use them.

I wanted to tell Dax so much about my Savior. But there is a time to speak and a time to be silent. I sensed in my spirit that this was not the time to speak to Dax Larue. He didn't have ears to hear. Not yet.

Still I couldn't help saying, "I'm sorry for you, Dax."

He seemed not to register my words. Instead he wanted to discuss the strangely accurate prophecy from Maggie, the ancestress of the Chevalier twins.

"I've interviewed enough mediums to know they aren't all fakes. Some of them are quite gifted. I believe Maggie had a definite psychic gift of prophecy. She foresaw your exact name. Therefore, it is possible that you're connected in some way to the spirit of Elizabeth O'Brien."

"Hold on. Wait a minute. There are genuine gifts of prophecy described in the Bible. But, Dax, there are also *counterfeit* gifts that are not from God."

"What do you mean?" he asked.

"Think about it. Evil spirits have access to information from the past. After all, they were *there*. They know all about historical people's lives. The Bible calls them familiar spirits. It would be easy for a familiar spirit to imitate a dead person's mannerisms, speech—to have knowledge that only the dead person and his living relatives would know. That's how lonely people get tricked into thinking they've contacted relatives from the other side. They receive a little accurate information. Then they're willing to pay more money for more contacts. And more."

Dax appeared interested without being skeptical, so I continued. He might as well know where I was coming from. After all, how could I be crazy for believing the Bible?

"Evil spirits apparently have some access to the future. *Limited* access. Or maybe limited *control* is a better term, for they can tempt people into wrong behavior with predictable outcomes. That's one reason the Bible strictly forbids *any* communication with the dead through these familiar spirits. Today they're called mediums, channelers and psychics."

Arching an eyebrow, Dax questioned, "Evil spirits predicting the future? Does that include astrology? Horoscopes and other forms of fortune telling?"

He appeared more curious than outright skeptical.

I nodded. "God absolutely forbids seeking information about the future by *any* means—the stars or secret arts like tarot cards, tea leaves and crystal balls. One of many warnings against these methods is found in Deuteronomy 18:10,11,and 12. I don't deny that some accurate information can result, otherwise it wouldn't be a temptation. But it's never a hundred percent correct."

That caused a look of skepticism.

"Kaytie, I've interviewed talented people with real psychic ability. I know it's real. So how do you know which one has a 'counterfeit gift' as you put it, and which one has a true gift of prophecy from God?"

"How many psychic mediums do you know who are one-hundred percent accurate in their predictions?"

He took his chin in one hand, striking a thoughtful pose. I could tell he wasn't coming up with a name.

"Nostradomus? Jeanne Dixon? Edgar Cayce? None of them predicted with complete accuracy. Right, Dax? God gives us a test to determine which are His prophets and which are not. Any prophet whose words do not come to pass with one-hundred percent accuracy is a false prophet, according to the Bible."

"You're saying God expects His prophets to be correct all the time? Totally correct? That's a tall order."

"Absolutely. He's God, declaring the end from the beginning. What He speaks, He brings to pass. And every prophetic utterance recorded in His word has been fulfilled completely, or is being fulfilled. It's in the news everyday. Just look at what's happening in Israel."

His expression was thoughtful. "But aren't these prophecies rather cryptic? I mean, anyone can read Nostradomus and interpret his predictions in a variety of ways."

"God's prophets are very specific. Did you know that seven hundred years before Christ was crucified, King David predicted the exact words which Jesus spoke on the cross and also described the exact manner His death?"

"I didn't know that. You're saying a true prophet is a hundred percent accurate? And one whose gift is not from God is not completely accurate?"

The concept appeared difficult for him to grasp. "Let me say it again. If a word comes from God's Spirit to a prophet, it *always* agrees with the Bible and it always comes to pass, and that's how you can tell a false prophet. He gets messages from another spirit, the wrong spirit, and these messages are often not accurate. And there's one other surefire way to tell a false prophet."

"What's that?"

"By what they believe about Jesus. That test is also in the first letter of John, chapter four. Don't believe every spirit, but test the spirits whether they are of God, because many false prophets have gone out into the world. Every spirit that confesses not that Jesus Christ is Lord come in the flesh is not from God. I may not have quoted that word for word in King James English, but you can look it up."

He looked puzzled. "I know a few psychics who would agree that Jesus came in the flesh."

"Sure, but it means a little more than that. Would they agree that Jesus is Lord and Savior? That's the difference. Most mediums do believe in a god or some higher power. But they will tell you Jesus is just a man on a higher spiritual plane, or some such nonsense. They'll even talk about Him as a wondrous prophet or a teacher to be honored. But they *never* proclaim Him as the living, only true Lord and savior."

His brow furrowed. "Hmmm. Do you think mediums and psychics are being deceived?"

"Perhaps they are deceived. I know they deceive others. God asked the Israelites why they would look for answers from the dead when they should be going to Him for guidance. He wasn't happy about this. He actually commanded the Israelites to stone false prophets to death."

"The death penalty for a false prophet? That's pretty serious. Why would God do that? It seems to me that many people have found great comfort in the belief that there is an afterlife."

"Think about it, Dax. False prophets can deceive the people into thinking there is a pleasant afterlife apart from Christ, and this can lead to their ultimate destruction. God wants us to live by faith in His word. We shouldn't base our faith on the word of spirits who tell us everything is peaceful on the other side of death without Christ. It's dangerous to think we can rely on answers from the paranormal realm." I looked at Dax with hope that my words were penetrating his armor of skepticism.

"Dax, I know you believe that there are psychic gifts, and it's true. If these were just harmless parlor games, God would not strictly forbid them as He does in Isaiah 8: 19-20. He specifically said don't listen to mediums; what they say can't keep trouble away. The fallacy of believing in everything—horoscopes, cards, consorting with the dead for answers—is that you end up without a standard for truth and will ultimately believe in anything."

He inclined his head and I could see the beginnings of agreement in his eyes, so I kept talking. "Let's put it this way. Suppose you are the child of a loving father and he has given you some guidelines for living successfully, but instead of following his words, you run to other sources with opposite standards. You choose to respect these other sources while ignoring your true father's words. Don't you think he would be hurt?"

He merely shrugged noncommittally. I could see the question coming before he asked, "What are these people with psychic gifts supposed to do with them? Like that television medium, Ann LaBouinne, for instance. She's been seeing visions of dead people since childhood. I mean, sometimes she can help police locate missing persons. That sort of thing."

"Dax, I only know that if I had dreams or visions, I would pray and ask God to confirm to me that they come from Him, or else take them away. I want to trust in Him alone to show me how to help others. And there's also this warning in Thessalonians. Satan can appear as an angel of light, performing signs and lying wonders to deceive even the very elect if possible. Ann may very well believe in a creator, but if she is not a true Christian, then I seriously doubt her psychic gifts are from God."

Getting to the heart of the matter, Dax asked, "So you think the prophecy regarding your name came from an evil spirit?"

"That's exactly what I'm saying. Maggie was channeling a demon, and the thing used my name. This is not a prophecy from the Holy Spirit. Look at what it's led to already. A murder. A woman seeking ultimate power through forbidden sources. She's clearly under the control of demonic spirits. Who knows what harm her followers may be doing?"

A half smile crossed his face. "Demons able to counterfeit spiritual gifts? For the purpose of keeping believers from going to God for guidance, you say."

He had this irritating habit of asking me to repeat myself. Intent on the conversation, I didn't mind.

"Look at it this way. Satan was created as an angel of light, a beautiful, and musical being. That made him proud. So proud he wanted to ascend to a throne even higher than God's. Just imagine that. The thing that was *created* wanted the worship of his Creator. He even asked Jesus to bow down and worship him. That's his nature. And he's never stopped trying to get the worship that belongs to God."

"How does he expect to be worshiped? There's not a large number of actual Satan worshippers in the world."

"He goes after it by tricking people into seeking alternative sources for their answers. Sources like Madame Chevalier. When people turn to forbidden methods, they're really opening themselves up to Satan's influence. After all, he's called the prince of this world, father of lies and the great deceiver. Just look at what happened to King Saul when he went to seek advice from the witch of Endor, an Old Testament medium."

Dax cleared his throat. "I haven't read about King Saul, or the witch of Endor, but that's an interesting theory. And you really believe these evil spirits—demons—exist?"

Oh boy. He was so uninformed about biblical truth. How can you have faith in God's word if you don't even know what He says?

I had to try to explain. "Guess I never really thought about evil spirits much until I read the Bible for myself. Jesus had to deal with demons. Scholars say that up to a third of His ministry involved demons. Anyway, if Jesus acknowledged them, I can't deny their existence. Just look at all the evil in the world. People who hear 'voices' telling to them kill. To commit suicide and do other outrageous things."

An expression of doubt crossed his face, but I kept talking. "Look at the Son of Sam. He heard voices telling him to murder couples in New York City. The Night Stalker, Richard Ramirez, strangled multiple women. He was a self-confessed Satanist. Then there's self-proclaimed Messiahs like David Koresh and leaders like the Heaven's Gate cult leader. What did they find but death? It's obvious these men were hearing the wrong voices."

The *Supernatural Seeker's* star reporter considered a moment, then shook his head. "I believe the only good and evil in the world comes from the heart of man himself. But if you *are* right, and there are demons, then there must be angels too. Maybe you should pray to yours for protection."

Now it was my turn to shake my head. "No, Dax. We're not supposed to pray to angels. There's not one prayer to an angel recorded in the Bible. True, they are spirit beings sent to help believers, but it's God who does the sending, and it's Him alone we should pray to."

He gave me a half smile. "This is all very interesting, but I have a plane to catch. Now that you're safe and relatively sound, I need to get back to Chicago. My editor is jumping up and down to get my follow-up story on the haunted hotel. He wants it in the next edition of the *Seeker*."

I could have told him a thing or two about the ghost lady—an image projected on powdered mist, but he was already grabbing a suitcase.

"Look, *Mrs.* La Rue," he used the title with a hint of teasing mischief in his voice, "stay here in this room as long as you need to. It's paid up through the weekend. I left you some cash for necessities. When you get back to Chicago, we'll continue this conversation. That is, if your fiancé doesn't mind. Ashton Wilson, Wilkerson? He does live in Chicago doesn't he?"

"It's Wilkins. And yes, he lives in Chicago."

I scrambled in my memory, hoping I had given him the right name for my fictitious boyfriend. Oh well. If he didn't remember it either, I was in the clear.

He leaned over and planted a quick kiss on my forehead. Then he was out the door.

* * *

I tried calling my editor several times that afternoon. The line was maddeningly busy. Finally giving up, I ordered room service and fell asleep, planning to call Ed early the next morning at a time when I knew he would be at the office. He'd be anxious to hear from me. I was just as anxious to get back to Chicago. That, I could not do until he wired me some money for a plane ticket.

It seemed my head had barely hit the pillow when the phone rang.

"You can't escape."

The voice slithered through the telephone wire and crawled into my ear, squeezing the drowsiness out of my tired frame.

"You can't escape your destiny, lady, you aren't who you think you are," the caller hissed.

He had a kind of wet, choking sound in his voice, as if a rope were being tightened around his throat and slowly strangling the life out of him.

But dying men don't usually bother making threatening phone calls do they? After what I'd seen in the bayou, I wouldn't have been surprised if a dead man walked into my hotel room and asked to borrow my hair dryer.

Exhausted as I was, I felt incensed that this jerk was disturbing my sleep. It was time for the whole mistaken identity thing to end.

"Get this, wacko, I'm not who you're looking for!" I informed him angrily, then slammed the phone down.

Obviously, I don't hit on all eight cylinders when my sleep is disturbed by a choking voice in the night. Who was this creature? The word *creature* seemed more adequate to describe the ghastly tones I'd heard. Unwanted thoughts of zombies sprang to mind.

With a chill, it dawned on me that Madame Chevalier was lurking out there somewhere. She obviously had a link to the hotel industry. The witch woman knew my room number.

Knew my phone number.

Knew where I was.

Chapter 7

Morris

What if she sent her thug to get me? What if Pirate Man was on his way right now? Creeping up the stairs to my room?

I pulled the covers off my head and sat up in the dark. This was no time for inactivity. Leaping out of bed, still wearing the Bienville House bathrobe, I groped for a light switch; the room sprang starkly into view. Thankfully the drapes were drawn. The digital clock showed 2:15 a.m.

Where were my clothes?

Oh, yeah, I recalled, I had no clothes but the swamp-muddied sundress I'd been wearing since the second time I was kidnapped. I'd rinsed it out with the hotel shampoo. It was hanging in the shower, still dripping wet.

I had to get out of this room. *Okay, maybe I'll have to wear it,* I thought as I opened the closet on the slim chance that someone's wearables might still be hanging there. Someone's were. Dax's red pullover and a pair of his blue jeans. I pulled on the jeans, tied them round my waist with a strap from the sundress and wiggled into the roomy pullover, which smelled of after-shave cologne, the expensive kind.

No need to pack my bags or grab my purse. They were gone, probably forever.

Wearing a pair of hotel slippers, I padded into the dimly lit hallway and peered down the back stairwell.

No sinister kidnapper lurked there.

No gypsy woman or zombie.

Not even the lost Winnifred and Frank finding their way to a room after being lost in the wetlands. Everything was as still as an abandoned tomb when I scurried down the stairs and out into the courtyard.

On the street I faced another dilemma. Dax had left me a hundred-dollar bill for necessities, but where was I going to be safe?

Madame obviously had a direct link to the New Orleans hotel managers and concierges. I couldn't go to another one.

While I stood there debating what to do, a yellow cab pulled up. This time I looked before I leaped, making sure no zombie, voodoo witch or scar-faced pirate was at the wheel. Relieved I climbed in and asked the lady driver to take me to the only place I could think of, Bruce and Jacqueline Boudreau's residence out past the Old Vegetable Market.

Edgy. Nervous. I kept looking over my shoulder, unable to shake the feeling that someone was following me.

As usual, traffic moved through the French Quarter, even at this pre-dawn hour. New Orleans has a 24-hour-open-door policy if the manager so desires. Pedestrians also may carry alcoholic beverages in plastic containers or cups and drink as they walk. But I was not interested in watching for tipsy tourists along the sidewalks.

I was far more concerned that a voodoo queen, a pirate man or even a zombie lurked about in the shadows.

When we arrived at the Boudreau house, I asked the driver to wait until I roused the occupants just in case they weren't home. I didn't want to be left standing on their front porch without access.

The doorbell refused to chime, so I pounded loudly on the wooden door. After a long moment, a porch light switched on and Bruce peered through a tiny crack demanding, "Who is it?"

I didn't blame him. Who would want to open the door for an unknown caller at this hour?

"Mister Boudreau, it's me, Kaytie O'Reilly. I'm a friend of Jack's, remember?"

He peered cautiously at me through a chain on the inside lock. Then he opened the door and I practically leaped inside.

"I'm so sorry to disturb you at this hour," I babbled gratefully. "But I had nowhere else to go."

As I tried to explain, Jacqueline entered the room, wiping sleep from her eyes and tying a cotton wrapper around her slender waist.

"I saw it on the news," she said. "You were kidnapped. The police have been looking for you again. Are you okay?"

"For the moment," I answered, glancing nervously at the darkened street-side windows, seeing only our reflections mirrored there. Jacqueline moved to draw the drapes.

"Is someone following you?" Bruce asked.

I nodded. "It's possible. But I don't think so."

I desperately hoped I was right. It would be unthinkable to expose Jacqueline and Bruce to any harm.

What had I been thinking by coming here?

I berated myself for not going straight to the police department. After all, Jean Claude should have cleared me as a suspect.

That's when it happened. The front door exploded wide open as Pirate Man burst into the room followed by a second man who looked like an escapee from a circus freak-show. Hundreds of finger-like nodules, tumors and bumps covered his neck and ears. His face had an even bumpier texture than cottage cheese and was the color of a leprous gourd. His wide mouth stretched under a pendulous nose like the mouth of a frog. His eyes, glittering through tiny slits, had almost disappeared among the protruding growths.

A third figure entered the room.

A zombie.

I gaped at Tex, who looked as ghastly as an animated corpse, moving and breathing somehow.

Stunned into momentary silence, I reeled at the sight of this gruesome trio.

Surely I was trapped in the throes of a hideous nightmare and would wake up any moment, safe in my hotel bed. I collapsed on a sofa, which felt solid enough beneath my shivering frame and did nothing to reassure me.

This was no dream.

Gourd Face aimed a gun in the general direction of Bruce and Jacqueline. "Nobody move. We want the woman."

That unmistakable wet, strangled voice was the same one I'd heard on the telephone.

He turned his yellowish eyes toward me, and then repeated the words, "You can't escape your destiny."

I almost rolled my eyes in disgust at this repeated assault on my identity, but the shock of the moment was overwhelming.

"What do you want with her?" Bruce demanded in a voice devoid of fear. He looked husky enough to handle all three miscreants—if they had been unarmed.

"She won't get hurt." Gourd Face nodded toward me while moving toward the couple. "You two just keep your mouths shut and everything will be okay," he rasped, herding them into the small bedroom. "But if you go to the police, you won't see her alive again."

He shut the door and looped some kind of locking device around the knob, rattling it to make sure it held securely. Grunting with satisfaction, Gourd Face turned his attention to me, sitting stupidly on the sofa. I looked to Tex, hoping for a hint of recognition in his eyes. He didn't appear to know me, however I noted he moved less woodenly, not yet fluidly, but not quite as robotic as he'd appeared at the fire ring. The drug's paralytic potency must have been wearing off. I hoped so.

How had he survived his fall from that third-story ledge?

If indeed he *had* survived. I wasn't completely convinced Tex was truly still among the living.

"Come with us," the freak ordered, nodding his head, the cluster of appendages jiggling obscenely.

Without a moment's hesitation, I decided this would be a good time to faint and did so, sliding down from the sofa to the floor. If they wanted me, they were going to have to carry me out of the house, and that might attract attention.

That was my desperate hope.

Undaunted, Pirate Man grabbed my wrists. Tex grabbed my ankles. They carried my limp body between them as if I were a dead deer, out the door, down the steps and straight to a waiting van where they tossed me through the side panel onto a bench seat.

If I screamed would anybody hear me?

I sat up trying to reach the door handle as the van started moving.

"Keep your head down," the strangled voice ordered.

He hit the gas pedal and the vehicle leaped forward almost tossing me to the floor.

"What do you want with me?" I demanded. "Is Madame Chevalier paying you enough money to risk a federal kidnapping charge?"

Gourd Face didn't bother to answer.

* * *

Dawn colored the sky in pink hues before the van finally pulled to a stop somewhere outside the Crescent City.

Tex woodenly lifted me out of the vehicle, his eyes staring blankly ahead.

Could I pinch him, slap him out of his stupor?

Probably not.

Where were we now? The gleaming white columns of a colonial plantation manor towered over us, and fields of lush farmland stretched on either side of the manicured lawn. We weren't headed toward the elegant structure with its graceful porches. Instead we were traveling toward a tall hedgerow, a path winding and twisting beneath fragrant arches of flowering vines.

With Tex guiding me through the maze we eventually reached what appeared to be a gardener's cottage. Gourd Face tapped at the door. Half expecting yet another grisly creature to open it, I was pleasantly surprised to see an affable old fellow with graying hair and twinkling blue eyes. He blinked in the morning light.

"I'm Morris. Morris St. James," the disfigured man whispered.

"Oh, yes, Mr. St. James. I wasn't expecting you this early." He squinted and greeted his unlikely visitors with a cheerful tone.

"Come in. Come in. Dear me. I must get my eyeglasses and put the coffee on. Why what would Sylvia say?"

"Never mind the coffee," Gourd Face whispered in that strangely soggy voice. "Have you got the chest?"

"The chest? Oh dear me. The chest! Why, certainly. You've come about the chest. Have you brought the key?"

"Let me see it!"

"Well, yes, of course, sir. Of course. I must say I know we agreed that you would see the chest. It's just that since we talked, I've wondered if I've done the right thing. How do I know it truly belongs to you? You assured me you would bring the key."

"You uncovered it on the grounds of the old Lafitte sugar plantation didn't you?" Morris stated, adding, "That's where I last knew of its whereabouts. Of course it belonged to my aunt."

"Well now that's true enough. It was probably fifteen years ago. I was working as chief gardener at the Lafitte Hotel. I'd just removed the stump of an ancient live oak tree which had been struck by lightning, and there it was grown over by roots, so entangled I had to cut it free. I took it to old Mr. St. James, the proprietor at the time. He thought his daughters would be interested in the chest—something about a family legend. The poor fellow was struck down by illness before he could contact them."

The gardener rubbed his squinting eyes and continued. "Mr. St. James was on his death bed when he made me promise to keep the chest until the sisters showed up. I tried to find them without success, so I brought it home to Sylvia. She kept it all these years, thinking they would show up one day and claim it."

He looked straight ahead at nothing in particular and continued his story.

"Never could open it, you know. It takes a special set of keys. The locksmith couldn't help. It's got several locks with terribly intricate mechanisms inside. He said it had been designed in England or Ireland, probably over two hundred years ago. Once I tried to hacksaw into the battered material that covers the metal lining, but Sylvia stopped me. She feared it might hold something wicked. Said she sensed it was kind of a Pandora's Box, and we'd best leave it be."

He took out a handkerchief and dabbed at the corner of his eyes. "That little woman had amazing intuition, bless her soul. I learned to listen to her over the years. Yes indeed. I learned to listen. I always regretted it when I didn't. But that's a lesson we husbands learn over the years. If the little wife is not happy, nobody is happy. And that's another thing I tell young husbands. Let the wife be right. Would you rather be right or happy? My Sylvia had a genuine gift of intuition though. She just knew things, bless God. She knew things and I learned to listen."

The two creeps shifted from one foot to the other, obviously impatient. Tex remained impossibly still.

Still as a dead man, and of course he looked the part too.

"We forgot all about the old chest eventually. Then after Sylvia passed on, I ran across it again in the attic and ran the ad in the newspaper to alert members of the St. James family. I didn't figure any of them would come looking for it, but then you called."

Here, the old fellow shifted his gaze and appeared to take note of the sinister-looking threesome he had admitted into his cozy home. His squinty eyes widened slightly.

"You are a descendant of Mr. St. James, correct? Do you have a driver's license? Dear me, you do have the key don't you?"

"Just bring me the chest!" The tumors and nodules on Morris's face jiggled as he choked out the words, struggling to add volume to his whispery voice.

I had visions of his vocal cords covered with the same kind of growths that appeared to cover his head.

"Oh yes, the chest. But I mustn't forget my manners. Please be seated and rest yourselves while I go to retrieve it. I should have invited you to sit down at once. Why, what would Sylvia say?"

He turned and shuffled out of the room, leaving us standing in the tiny parlor, me leaning against Tex, who held my arms behind my back in a steely grip.

Gourd Face looked at Pirate Man, silent as usual. He walked to the chintz-covered sofa and sat down with a nervous shrug, apparently deciding to wait as patiently as possible for the old gardener to return. What choice did he have?

A grandfather clock chimed, filling the room with momentary sound and reminding me that I faced yet another day as a captive.

I was getting very tired of the role. Time to end this, I thought, glancing around me, wondering if I could enlist the help of the old man.

Tex's grip on my wrists remained vise like.

From my vantage, I could see through a window, which overlooked the back lawn of the cottage. I tried not to register any surprise when I saw the old gardener scurrying toward an outbuilding under a stand of oak trees.

Was he going to retrieve the chest, or was he making his getaway?

Evidently, his eyesight was worse than I thought, because he trustingly re-appeared moments later, transporting a well-worn chest in a wheelbarrow. It looked ancient and mysterious, even menacing.

I understood at once why Sylvia had not wished to have it opened.

"Here it is, gentlemen," the old fellow announced breathlessly upon re-entering the parlor. "You did bring the key of course?"

Gourd Face stood up and reached for the chest. "*She's* the key," he rasped, nodding toward me. He grabbed the box and started dragging it out the door.

"Wait—" The old fellow's voice was cut off by a sharp blow to his chin. Pirate Man knocked him to the floor before grabbing a handle on the opposite side of the box.

I screamed as Tex dragged me out the door and hoisted me into the van.

The scurrilous pair hauled their coveted prize between them, straight for the vehicle's sliding side-panel door and quickly loaded it, unaware that Tex climbed into the driver's seat.

Before they realized it, Tex had started the engine and hit the gas pedal, nearly ejecting me through the still-open door.

"Hang on, Kaytie!" he yelled.

"Tex!" I gasped, clinging to the seat, my legs flailing through the opening.

We careened up the driveway, clipping several hedges.

Above the gravel-crunching sound of churning tires, Tex yelled again, "Kaytie! You still with me?"

"I'm here. Tex! Is it really you?" Struggling to right myself, I managed to climb into the passenger's seat beside him, grinning from ear to ear.

"It's me, alright. Hold on, girl. We're gettin' outta here!"

"Yes!" I whooped, glancing behind us to see the outraged goons leaping, shouting, and growing smaller as we quickly outdistanced them.

"Omigosh! Tex, I'm so glad to see you—I mean, to see you back among the living again," I babbled while I located the automatic button to close the side-panel door and keep the chest from sliding out.

"I'm sure enough back!" Tex exclaimed, opening and closing his left fist as if testing his muscle control.

He picked up even more speed once we hit pavement, careening down the road like a fox with its tail on fire. We zipped down a two-lane highway, screeched around vehicles and dodged oncoming traffic. Seeing a tour bus coming at us head-on, I yelped and ducked my head. Tex jerked the wheel and we wobbled back and forth, leaning crazily on two wheels until the vehicle righted itself.

The next instant I was thrown to the floorboard as the van screeched around a sharp curve.

"What are you doing down there?" Tex exclaimed, spying me crunched underneath the dashboard.

"Oh, I just decided to check out what's under the dash," I muttered, trying to steady myself. "I've heard there's all kinds of interesting wires to look at down here."

The van passed a vegetable truck, clearing the driver's side by a paper-thin margin, and rocking from side to side.

"Lord have mercy!" Tex muttered.

Yes indeed, I silently agreed, climbing back into the passenger seat and buckling my seatbelt.

"Check behind us. See if anyone's following. If those creeps find a car on the grounds, they won't hesitate to steal it," Tex ordered, echoing my own thoughts.

All I could see were angry drivers waving fists, their mouths forming words which I doubted were compliments on our driving skills.

Tex whipped around a slow-moving old beater and jerked the van even farther onto the shoulder of the oncoming lane, facing a terrified semi driver leaning on his horn. We barreled down the outer limits of the wrong lane, passing three more startled motorists.

Then we saw the bridge ahead.

I gripped the edge of my seat, expecting to veer across the path of traffic and straight into a deadly collision, or crash through the guardrail of the bridge and into the water. Neither option appealed to me.

That's when Tex did the darndest thing.

He hit the brakes, jerked the wheel and steered off the road into a thick stand of trees. We bounced through the undergrowth, slowing to a stop as curtains of Spanish moss closed behind us.

"What are you doing?" I demanded. "We have to get away from here!"

"Look at the gas gauge. We're not going anywhere very far."

I groaned in consternation at what I saw. We were down to less than an eighth of a tank.

"Diddley squat!" I hit the dashboard with a closed fist.

"I know, I know," Tex agreed. "Let's just sit tight for a moment or two. If they're already on the road, they can't see us in here, and they'll pass us by."

"You're sure about that?"

"No, ma'am, but I shore do hope so."

I *shore* did hope so too.

We waited out some tense moments. No vehicle showed up with freaky people inside demanding us to accompany them. No zombies stumbled upon us. I started to breathe a little slower.

Then unable to wait a moment longer, I started asking questions.

"Tex, how did you survive that terrible fall out the window? I thought you were a goner for sure."

"The tree. I snagged my shirt on a branch of that overhanging tree and it slowed my fall. Then I landed on a slanted roof over a porch on the lower floor and slid right off it to the ground. Didn't hurt me none, but before I could run, someone grabbed me. Next thing I knew I was inside a wooden coffin. Couldn't speak. Couldn't move. I thought I was going to die in that box...buried alive."

He shuddered at the thought.

So did I.

"Do you remember being raised up out of that coffin?"

Tex nodded. "They injected me with some kind of drug. I could move then, but I still couldn't speak. Musta been some kind of hallucinogenic concoction, because what I saw next was right out of a horror movie."

"I know. I was there. Madame evidently wanted me to think she could raise the dead, and let me assure you, Tex, you looked very dead. If I ever believed in zombies, it would have to be after seeing you in that condition."

Tex nodded. "That was her plan. She wants you to think she has great power and that you can save me—or even yourself—from being a zombie. But that's only if you cooperate with her. She's convinced you'll lead her to a book of secret spells. I overhead the whole conversation before the drug wore off."

"But how did she identify me as the woman she'd been waiting for? I didn't even use my name on the register at the Lafitte."

"The woman has paid informants all over the French Quarter. Every September thirteenth they watch for you. She had a woman working in the hotel who recognized you from that old photo, the one she showed us of Elizabeth O'Brien. You gotta admit, you're a dead ringer."

I nodded. "Yes, but I don't necessarily like your adjective after what we've been through."

"Adjective? Oh, you mean *dead*? Sorry. Okay, let's say you could be Elizabeth's twin. Speaking of twins, you probably already know that Madame Chevrolay has a twin—*had* a twin. I figure the informant notified both sisters as soon as you went upstairs to the Pirate Suite. And I'm guessing the twin was the woman who got bumped off in your room. She was there, going through your things to verify your name."

"Bad Leroy killed her?"

"That's my guess. I heard him say they found your reporter's badge with the name they were looking for—Kaytie F. O'Reilly—and that's how they knew they'd hit pay dirt. Then the other woman, Madame Emerald, decided she wanted you all to herself. She wasn't going to share the spell book with her sister. There was bad blood between the two women anyway. From what I gathered, it started years ago when they both fell in love with the same man."

I could well imagine there existed small affection between the two women, each consumed by greed and hunger for power.

"Anyway, Pirate Man Leroy is fiercely loyal to the sister who nabbed you and me. She's made promises about what she will do for him once she gets her hands on that witchdoctor's book. He intends to see that she gets it."

Stifling a sneeze, I asked, "Did he intend to shoot Sapphire?"

"I don't know. I figure Leroy heard someone coming in and fired the gun. The maid started screaming. Then she ran out the door."

I nodded, thinking how so many people will do anything for power, or even the mere illusion of power. And for what? Every timeworn statue of great heroes, kings, and conquerors stands as mute testament to the fleeting moment of fame compared to the vastness of eternity. Once again, I was glad I wrote for a journal dedicated to exposing deceitful and dangerous ideologies. *Idiot*-ologies, my editor calls them.

"How did they find me at the Bienville House? I didn't register there either."

"No, but your journalist friend did. Madame's thugs figured you might run to him since you were with him at Pat O'Brien's. With their hotel spies, they had no trouble gettin' his room number. Morris—if that's the gourd face guy's real name—called Larue's room just hoping you'd answer the phone. And you did. They were coming after you when they saw you catch the taxi. I was just a zombie along for the ride, still under the power of that witch's brew at the time. We followed you to the Boudreau place."

"If only I had run to the police instead. I never meant to put them in danger."

It was too late for regrets. My thoughts turned back to Tex.

"How long before the antidote started wearing off? Were you yourself again before we left the gardener's house?"

"The numbness started wearing off this morning. I kept a hold on you though, 'cause I didn't want those thugs to know it yet."

"Is Leroy drugged the same way?"

"Don't know. But I do know this. Madame Voodoo Queen has a couple of misfits—including that side-show freak with the tumors growing all over his face—who believe she's going to cure them of their diseases once she gets hold of her book of spells. That's why they're willing to risk anything to get you, girl. You're the key. They know she won't open it without you there."

"So that's her power over them. The promise of a cure."

I felt sorry for the poor misguided souls. If only they knew the answer was not in the darkness of African spells but rather in the Light of the world.

"Tex, what are we going to do now? We've got the chest. They won't stop at anything to get it back."

I considered the possibility of turning over the box to Madame Chevalier and letting her open it in my presence. However, once she got her precious book of spells, would she just go away and leave me alone?

Not likely. The risk of exposure would be too great. She would practice her evil spells on me. Poison me and leave me in a zombie state. Bury Tex and me both alive somewhere in the swamp. The very thought sent shivers through my frame.

Tex spoke my thoughts aloud. "They won't let us be. Even if we give them the chest, I figure they'd have to do away with us."

"Maybe we should go to the police. That's our best hope. What if we turn the chest over to the authorities and get as far out of New Orleans as possible?"

Tex nodded slowly. "Maybe that's the thing to do. But first, we gotta get outta here. Go for gasoline. Or catch a ride."

"Going for gas is not a good option," I reasoned. "One of us would have to walk—no telling how far. Those two men are bound to be prowling the roads. They know we didn't get far if they bothered to check the gas gauge at all this morning."

'"Maybe they did and maybe they didn't."

"We can't risk it, Tex."

Tex considered for a moment.

"Okay then, we leave the van here, but first we bury the chest. That's our insurance in case they find us again. Then we try to find a ride."

I couldn't think of a better plan, so I climbed out and helped Tex lug the chest farther into the woods. The ground was soft as mud in places.

Tex wondered aloud, "Should we risk sinking it in the mire or just cover it up with brush?"

"I think maybe that's the better plan. But we have to wipe out all our tracks in case they find the van."

I remembered how the trunk had been buried among the roots of the old tree in order to keep it from sinking into the watery soil. We located several natural thickets, piles of brush, dead foliage and fallen trees along the bayou banks, finally choosing a place between the exposed roots of a taller tree where a growth of palmettos further obscured the box.

"The less we disturb the brush, the better," Tex commented as he stood back to survey our hiding place. I stared at the tree with its jagged scar down the trunk, branding the scene into my memory.

Then we each made a broom of sorts with leafy branches and began wiping out our tracks. The usual afternoon rain shower would do the rest. Unless the thugs had tracking dogs, they would be hard pressed to locate the hidden chest without one of us.

Trudging back to the van we debated whether to drive it as far as the remaining fuel would allow in hopes of finding a gas station.

"What's that sound?" I jumped, my nerves crackling with tension left over from our harrowing ride.

Tex cocked his head to one side, listening. The sound of music (no movie-title pun intended) followed by a vitamin commercial came clearly through the trees. Funny how you can't get away from advertising. Here we were on the edge of the bayou, entangled in a matter of life and death, and a voice was telling us why women need more calcium.

Tex grabbed my hand and guided me through the trees to the water's edge where we spied a large swamp buggy tied to a tree, the radio blaring.

"Ahoy, there!" Tex hollered.

No answer. He climbed aboard the bobbing craft, calling, "Anybody around here?"

Still no answer.

Turning and reaching a hand to assist me, Tex waited for me to climb aboard.

I hesitated.

"We can't just take someone's craft. We should wait for the owner and offer to pay for a ride,"

"I know, but what if the owner doesn't show up for hours? We have to get to the police station and file a report. The sooner the better."

I shrugged. Desperate times call for desperate measures, but stealing? I remained on the shore.

"Now look here, Kaytie. I waded through the swamp with you on my back and nearly got eaten by a 'gator. I climbed out of a third-story window at your insistence and almost fell to my death. And I ended up in a coffin and became a sure-enough zombie. It's time you did something for me."

He had a point. I took a step toward the craft.

"Hold it right there, you two!"

A woman's voice spoke from behind me. I turned to see an attractive, middle-aged woman dressed in khaki shorts and shirt, wearing an official-looking badge on her shirt pocket, sunglasses and a straw hat.

She held a handgun, the barrel lowered to the ground. "I overheard your entire conversation, so I know you aren't regular thieves. You're in some kind of trouble."

"Beggin' your pardon, ma'am," Tex stammered. "We're in serious trouble and we'd be mighty grateful if you could help us out."

The woman walked toward us, holstering the gun. "I'm Fish and Wildlife Agent Ogle. Beth Ogle. Want to tell me who you are and what kind of trouble you're in?"

"You wouldn't believe it," I answered, expelling a sigh of relief. Finally, someone had appeared to help instead of harm us.

"We've been kidnapped by a madwoman, a voodoo priestess and her thugs," Tex started explaining. "We escaped in their van this morning, but we ran out of gas. They'll be looking for us. If we could just get back to the New Orleans Police Department..."

Beth eyed us with a quizzical expression, as if seeing an oddity of nature like maybe a two-headed frog. I wouldn't have blamed her for hauling us straight to the funny farm.

"Okay, you were kidnapped," she stated, slowly digesting the wild tale. "And your names are...?"

"I'm a New Orleans taxi driver, Chuck Owens, but she calls me Tex," he nodded toward me. Only then did it occur to me, I'd never bothered to learn his given name.

"I'm Kaytie O'Reilly, investigative reporter for *Beyond Fantasy* magazine based in Chicago." I extended a shaky hand. "We're pleased to meet you Miss Ogle. *Very* pleased."

Beth hesitated, then grasped my hand in a brief shake.

"I suppose I can get you back to N'awlins. You can tell me more on the way."

She climbed up to the roomy buckboard-style seat mounted in front of what appeared to be a giant fan.

"Well don't just stand there. I haven't got all day." Beth indicated that I should join her and Tex on the seat. I didn't hesitate this time.

Chapter 8

Sofronia

Beneath the jangled layers of my over-stretched nerves, I had time to be impressed by the ingenuity of the swamp buggy's design. It zipped along powered by the whirling fan blades, skimming the surface, able to navigate the shallowest of waters. A canopy of branches dripped moss overhead.

Beth guided the craft and we filled in the gaps of our story, both of us talking at once until she barked, "Hold on. I may have two ears, but I can only hear one of you at a time."

I let Tex do most of the talking, painfully aware that our story sounded like one of those bizarre episodes from a tabloid, the kind with screaming headlines such as "Vampires Sank the Titanic!"

Beth listened quietly, nodding her head from time to time. When our story ended, she remained quiet. I didn't know what to expect from her. I wanted her to say something.

Anything.

Finally unnerved by the woman's silence, I blurted, "Beth, can you tell us where we are?"

"We're on the Marngouin Bayou. It runs into Lake Veret. It's a little out of the way, but I've got a motorboat there. Another bayou connects Veret to the Mississippi Riv*ah*, and that'll take us straight into New Orleans. Of course, we intersect Routes One and 405 along the way. I could drop you there and let you thumb a ride." She raised her eyebrows at us with a slight grin.

We both shook our heads.

The water route was safer. Things had turned in our favor at last. The thugs wouldn't find us now.

That's when the wind whipped up, churning the water to a white froth around us and causing the swamp buggy to dip erratically.

"That squall line wasn't supposed to hit until later this afternoon," Beth noted, a crease appearing between her eyebrows. "We're going to have to pull over and ride out the weather."

She turned the buggy into shallow swamp water. Trees swayed back and forth, alternately bowing and lifting their branches in a dance of obeisance to the wind gusts.

Thunder rumbled and a jagged flash of lightning speared the belly of a low thunderhead. Because of the overhanging foliage, we hadn't noticed the rapidly approaching storm until it was upon us.

"We're gonna get soaked," Beth muttered, pulling a couple of yellow rain slickers from a backpack while steering toward an outcrop of dry and.

"Here, you two can share," she handed one to Tex, then unfolded a wrinkled map and studied it for a moment. "There's an abandoned ranger station near here. It's pretty run down but it can give us shelter."

We climbed out of the swamp buggy, now bucking and leaping on the wind-whipped water, and tied it fast to the trunk of a sturdy tree. Large drops had already started pummeling the leaves overhead.

"This way," Beth directed, brandishing a flashlight.

We followed, huddling under the slicker, holding it tightly to prevent the wind from jerking it out of our hands. Sure enough, a small building made of concrete blocks appeared in the gloom, its door hanging open on rusted hinges. We ran for it as the swollen clouds spilled on the marsh.

Inside, Beth found a candle and lit it. The place had little to offer but dust and a roof. Wind-driven rain whipped through a broken window, but we found a dry corner.

I couldn't wait any longer to ask, "Beth, do you think we're crazy?"

She eyed me a moment. Then she cleared a space in the dust and sat down on her slicker, motioning for us to do the same.

"I believe your story. Since I've had this job, I've seen plenty of evidence of voodoo cults in the bayous, and I know they do some pretty weird things. Heard of a woman a few years back, working in the fields of a sugar plantation. People said she was a zombie so I visited the place. She certainly acted like one."

Puzzlement furrowed Beth's brow. "Here's the weird part. I knew this woman before her supposed death. Knew she had an unusual scar on her right arm. I looked for it and it was sure enough there. She was the same woman alright. So I decided she couldn't have really died. There must have been a mistake. Later I checked the records and found her death certificate, all official and authentic. The whole thing gave me the creeps."

As I listened to her story, the wind moaned and howled around the building like an angry, wounded thing. Sitting there in the flickering candlelight, once again in the middle of a swamp, I thought it the spookiest story I'd run across in my entire year of reporting for the *Beyond Fantasy*—not counting what had happened to Tex and me.

I knew we weren't out of our own difficulties yet. That unwelcome thought and the fury of the storm unnerved me.

Tex described how his own zombie experience involved the use of a paralyzing drug and an antidote to revive him later.

"Makes sense," Beth agreed, appearing relieved to find a natural explanation to the mystery.

The woman inspired confidence by her calm, decisive attitude. We couldn't have asked for a better rescuer, I thought. She knew her way through the swamps and could see that we got safely back to the city. She could also be very helpful when we talked to the authorities. We needed someone who could assure them that we weren't a couple of loonies.

The scream that burst forth from my throat was totally involuntary. In the flash of lightning, I saw a gap-toothed witch through the broken window.

Unexpected.

Unwanted.

Totally unlovely.

Beth patted my hand as if to calm me while looking toward the window and saying in a calm voice, "Come on inside, Sofronia."

Sofronia appeared at the doorway and hesitatingly entered.

"I be out fishing," she said by way of explanation. Wet and bedraggled as she was, her gap-toothed grin did not add any charm to her features. She wore baggy trousers and a man's work shirt over her withered frame. Gnarled hands had been callused by years of hard work. I couldn't help thinking of the wicked witch from *The Wizard of Oz*; however the word *wicked* did not seem to apply to the woman, now that I saw her more clearly.

"You get caught in the storm too?" She nodded toward Tex and me. Then peering at us more intently, she stated, "You be them that the voodoo witch is lookin' for." It was an observation rather than a question.

"How did you know that?" I asked, astounded.

"Word travels in the bayous. Sofronia knows things." She pushed a wet strand of yellow-gray hair back from her forehead. "You gonna get away from her sure enough."

"What do you mean?"

"She fears your power." The old crone gave me a knowing look.

"My power?"

"You have a greater power in you. She don't be working her spells on you without real harm to herself. She's afraid. But she keep trying cuz she want dat book. She wants the secret to living forever young."

Amazed at her apparent knowledge, I thought of the moment in Madame's enchanted shack when I spoke the name of my Lord. How the atmosphere of the room had changed completely and how Madame's fit of rage followed.

Suddenly consumed by a desire to know what Sofronia believed, I asked, "What faith do you follow?"

She made herself comfortable, seating her rickety frame on a corner of Beth's slicker before beginning her story.

"I be here in the bayous since born. I be knowin' all about the voodoo, the hoodoo and the black magic. There is power in these." She spoke with a solemn conviction in her voice, the voice of experience.

I was vaguely aware of the wind and thunder. Rain pelted our shelter, but inside with Beth's calming presence and now Sofronia's too, I felt safe, almost cozy.

Beth interjected, "I've known Sofronia for years. She's a lady who doesn't speak unless she has something to say. And when she does, it's worth listening to."

Tex and I turned our eyes to the old woman, who looked less like a witch and more like a wise old grandmother now that I could see the light in her eyes.

"My grandma, she took me to the meeting house when I be small. I heard the preacher. He be yellin' and shoutin'. The people, they be yellin' and shoutin.' Me, I just be scared. So I don't go back when I growed." A regretful expression clouded her face.

"I go to the fire rings. I see what they do. I know they make things happen. I want to be where there is *power*. So I stay with them for long times."

"What kind of things can they do?" Tex asked, his eyebrows raised inquisitively.

"They can affect the weather. Sometimes cure the sick. More times they make sickness come for revenge. Make *zombies*. Tell the future."

I glanced at Tex, wondering if he knew the ruse worked by the Chevalier twins.

He exclaimed with a tremor in his voice, "There's two things I don't want to be in this world and both of 'em's a zombie!"

Sofronia's voice took on a dramatic and slightly fearful tone. "I see many times the *houngan*—the priestess—at the fire ring when her spirit leaves her body and a demon takes over. For years I thought it was her *loa*, her ancestors. We believed they would protect us. I found out it was not a kind spirit but an evil one. It give her power. She do supernatural things."

"Where does this power come from?" I asked.

Sofronia's eyes bored into mine. They were clear and blue, lit from within by a steadfast spirit.

"Not from the Lord. *Houdun* believe they get powers for good and for evil. Years I watch. I learned. Then one day I be sick. Bad sick. I send for the *houngun*. She want money to heal me. I couldn't pay. She left me on my bed. I laid there, knowin' I be dyin'. I remember the words from the meetin' house where Grandma made me go when I be a child. *Whoever calls on the name of the Lord will be saved.* I called out to Jesus, the God of the Bible. He heard, and He healed me. I didn't have to pay. That's when I went back to the meetin' house to learn about Him. I found out His power is real. There is no greater power."

The look on her face was one of peace and joy as she continued, "I always wanted something real, a real God that can change things for good, not bad. I found Him in the Bible's words. His power not be for sale. The power of love. It cannot be bought. Cannot be used. Is free to all who come to Him."

Her expression changed to one of knowing. "From reading His book, I found out that everything God asks His people to do, the devils ask their people to do. That's why the voduns make blood sacrifices. The spirits ask for blood."

I smiled at Sofronia, gladdened by her story, happy to hear she was a true believer. "Sofronia, how do we deal with this witch woman?" I asked, already trusting her wisdom.

"You give her what she want. Give her dat book. But first you pray. Ask the Lord to bind it. Make it useless to anyone. Ask the Lord for His protection over you. And nothing shall by any means harm you." Her words were filled with simple faith.

I nodded slowly, thinking over what Sofronia said. Maybe that was the wisest thing to do.

Why hadn't I thought of it myself?

So simple. Just pray and believe.

But did I really want to put myself within Madame's grasp again? Did I really want to turn over the book of spells which could be used to deceive trusting people such as Sofronia had once been?

Even if the book was only superstitious junk, wouldn't there be others who could be fooled into a wrong or harmful way of living, thinking Madame could use it to help them?

What it all came down to was one simple thing.

Did I really believe in the power of prayer? I wanted to say a resounding YES! I also had doubts screaming in my ears.

Tex looked at me with a huge grin. "Kaytie girl, I think this lady has the right idea."

"Just a couple of hours ago, when we were back there hiding that chest under the trees, you didn't think so. May I remind you, Tex, you said Madame would have to do away with us for her own safety?"

Tex remained silent, pondering my words.

Beth had listened quietly to the entire conversation. Now she spoke up. "Look here, you two. I think Sofronia is right. The woman takes the power of faith seriously. Just as the power of voodoo is taken seriously by people of different faiths."

I glanced at her with a question in my eyes.

Beth saw the question and elaborated. "You remember when that Florida state senator, Alberto Gutman, tried to say his opponent had used voodoo against him to win the election? That was in 1998. The National Labor Relations Board even got into an investigation of claims that employees were using voodoo to organize a union at a Florida nursing home."

I hadn't known of these instances, but I listened, hoping Beth was right.

She suggested, "Here's a plan. We can all go together. She can't risk killing all of us. We can tell her that we left a letter with the authorities, explaining where we are. Let her know that if anything happens to any of us the law will come looking for her."

Tex slapped his knee. "Butter my biscuits. That's a plan if ever there was a lasso on a steer's neck."

I looked from one to the other. "Would you really be willing to go with me, Tex? Beth?"

Tex hesitated briefly before nodding his head yes. I could tell the idea did not appeal to him, but he also wanted to be free of voodoo threats.

Sofronia added, "I go with you. Madame knows me. She knows her power can't harm me since I am a Christian now. The curse without a cause cannot come. She be fearing me, like she fears you."

Turning to the woman, I asked, "Sofronia, I don't know how to find her. Will you take us to Madame Chevalier?"

She nodded her head. "She works the crowds in Jackson Square some days. But that's no good for you. Her followers may be waiting to grab you. This meeting has to be on your terms. You must meet her before the next full moon, two weeks from now. She will be in the bayou to meditate and call on her *loa,* her most powerful spirit guide to help her deal with you. That be the time when she is weakest, and she will fear your faith most."

Two weeks.

I could let the police know I was still alive, call my boss, have him wire me some money and catch a plane back to Chicago. Then I'd book my next flight back to Louisiana.

I would return, wouldn't I?

We began making plans at once, exchanging phone numbers, meeting places, and calendar dates. Tex seemed a little apprehensive.

"I don't know if I want to drive a taxi around N'awlins for two weeks with that woman and her thugs looking for me."

"Tex, you can drive a cab anywhere. Go to Baton Rouge or Lake Charles. Go back to Texas for a couple of weeks. They can't find you there."

Sofronia raised her hand. "They can find him anywhere. You too." She turned her knowing eyes toward me.

We looked at her, stunned.

"She won't let you go. There is nowhere to run. You be meetin' her again. Either on her terms or yours. I will tell her you come. She wait. She has to wait. Just like you have to come back and face her. Or you never be free. She will harm all the people closest to you, the ones you love most, if you try to escape her."

"Can she really do that?" I asked, chilled by the possibility.

"She is not without power. She can cast spells that will hurt even those who don't believe in her power. Make them sick with fevers. Cause fires to burn their houses down. I've seen it happen. If her spells don't work, she sends her slaves to do the harm."

I couldn't take that kind of risk. Sofronia was right. I had no choice. I had to return to Rainy Bay Bayou. I didn't want to live in fear of being wakened by that choked and whispery voice in the middle of the night. More importantly, I didn't want anyone I knew to suffer harm from the witch woman.

"How do I send her the word that I'm coming?"

"I send her the word. She will know it is true."

Tex and I both breathed a sigh of relief. I was even more gladdened that we had run into Beth first and then Sofronia. Both were unexpected sources of help. Heaven sent.

Rain pelted our shelter, but now it pounded a rhythm of hope. At last we had a plan. Possibly a dangerous plan, but a plan nevertheless.

Would each of us be willing to carry it out? I knew I couldn't do it alone. I needed these people, Beth, Tex, and Sofronia.

I needed the power of faith like never before.

* * *

"Kaytie Flame O'Reilly, don't you ever put us through this kind of anxiety again!" my boss exclaimed when I walked back into our small Chicago office on Friday morning.

Ed gave me an uncharacteristic hug and sat me down with a cup of coffee to "debrief" me. He'd been very alarmed when he heard the news of my disappearance and possible kidnapping, and he'd waited anxiously for some word of my whereabouts. I never heard a happier voice than his when I called him from the New Orleans Police Department. He wired the money for a plane ticket immediately.

Taking a chair next to mine, he listened intently, nodding from time to time but remaining speechless throughout the entire story. At the end of it, he jumped up, almost knocking the chair over. "You've got a scoop here, young lady! Zombies. A voodoo priestess. The homicide. What a story!"

I grinned, pleased that he was pleased. Then he looked at me directly. "You're not going back?" He spoke with a question in his voice, and that told me he already knew the answer.

"Ed, I have to go back. The Fish and Game agent and Tex will go with me to visit Madame Chevalier. And Sofronia too. I'll be safe. The police have heard the entire story. They're looking into it. They're also getting court permission to open the burial crypt and find out if the body of Madame Chevalier's sister, Sapphire, really is inside that coffin where she was supposed to be buried years ago. If not, Madame has lots of explaining to do. Detective Broussard is already looking for Bad Leroy. If he can find Leroy with the murder weapon, he won't have any trouble proving who shot the woman in the Pirate Suite."

"Then why not let them handle it? You don't have to go back. Madame and her thugs may get locked up for a long time. Too long a time to care whether they ever get their hands on that old treasure chest."

That was exactly what I was hoping for. However, I had to remind myself, "They may also be wily and clever enough to escape the law. What have the police actually got on Madame anyway besides attempted kidnapping? Possibly tax evasion. She may not be directly responsible for the murder. Even if she's convicted, she could get out in a few years, and then what? She's determined as a hound after a bone. She would come after me again. Now that she knows who I am and where I'm from, there's no way she wouldn't find me. The woman is hell-bent on finding that book." I didn't tell him what Sofronia had said. That Madame would harm my loved ones.

Ed sighed. "I don't like it. We'll talk more about this later." Then he turned to pick up a notepad lying on the desk. "Oh by the way, in addition to your usual callers, you've been getting several messages from Dax Larue. He's been as anxious to know where you were as we've been. I had to promise we'd let him know you were okay as soon I heard from you. He's asked you please to call him at this number." He handed me the slip of paper.

I smiled at his editorial "we."

Ed was like a father to me, and I was touched by his concern, gladdened by his warm welcome. Larue, on the other hand, could wait.

* * *

Once again at my desk in comfortable, familiar surroundings, I started to work on my story for *Beyond Fantasy*, briefly wondering how Dax had written his story on the staircase apparition. Would he be embarrassed when I exposed the hoax?

Not ten minutes passed till my desk phone rang. It was him.

"Well, well, well, Miss Kaytie Flame O'Reilly, also known as *Mrs.* Larue. I'm so relieved to hear you're back in Chicago safe and sound, and before you say a word, you're having dinner with me tonight."

"Dax, I think not. I have a lot of work to do in the next few days," I began, but he cut me off.

"Come on, Kaytie. You stood me up on that first night at the Lafitte. And don't forget, you owe me a hundred bucks, which I'll gladly forgive if you let me pick you up at six. Shall I call for you at your office? We'll go someplace nice."

I did owe him the money. And I suppose I had stood him up in New Orleans. Being kidnapped by a witch was no excuse to break a dinner date. I might as well get this over with.

"Okay. Six it is. I'll meet you downstairs in the building's foyer."

Telling myself that this would be my first and last dinner date with Dax, I turned my attention back to my story. The words quickly flowed from my fingertips to the computer screen, and I felt some amazement at what I had actually been through.

Ed looked in on me shortly after five and gave me the go-home signal. I nodded. I'd worn a black pinstripe jacket and matching slacks, a crisp white blouse and black pumps. The look was Nancy-Grace professional, not dinner-date elegant. It would do nicely for Mr. Larue, I thought as I checked my compact mirror.

Just a little lip gloss. A touch of liner. No mascara or glamour makeup. I was ready for the evening.

He pulled up outside our office at 4:45 p.m. in a classy, silver BMW, probably a company car, I thought. The *Seeker,* sponsored by its parent corporate television network, maintained a large staff and had tons of money. It wouldn't do to let their star reporter drive just any old car.

Grinning from ear to ear, Dax greeted me with a bear hug and then escorted me to the passenger door. "You're looking absolutely gorgeous," he said. "No swamp water in your hair. No mosquito bites."

"And this time I'm not dripping wet from being left in the rain while someone else grabbed the last taxi," I quipped as I climbed inside.

"Kaytie, that isn't fair. I was blinded by the rain. I didn't even know you were there until you told me to move over. Do you think I would have left you standing there if I'd known?"

I only raised an eyebrow at him, thinking he certainly might have. After all, he had barged ahead of me to check in at the hotel.

Dax had made reservations at the top of the John Hancock Building on North Michigan Avenue where the view of Chicago is breathtaking on a clear evening. It was a place for shoulder straps, dangling earrings and glitzy heels, and indeed there were plenty of those in the place. Glamorous women and elegant men, as well as smoothly tailored professionals were stopping by after hours for cocktails. Waiters in crisp white shirts and neatly pressed trousers moved quietly between the sumptuously laden tables. City lights stretched below us in a dazzling display like multicolored sequins embroidered on a black velvet landscape.

I maintained a professional attitude, confident in my pinstripe suit. Dax wanted to hear all about my escape and seemed genuinely interested in what happened after he'd left me at the Bienville House.

Telling him my swamp adventure over a table draped with a formal white cloth and softly glowing candlelight made Rainy Bay Bayou seem remote and very surreal.

"If I'd known you were in any real danger, I would never have left you!" he exclaimed after hearing the entire tale.

Then he stated flatly, "You're not going back."

Seeing me nod my head in way that clearly meant *yes I am*, he added. "I'm sure your fiancé—that Wilkerson? Wilson guy—wouldn't want you to go back. You did say he lives here in Chicago, right?"

I sighed. Time to be honest.

"You might as well know, he doesn't live anywhere except in my imagination. I made him up. I didn't want you to think I was chasing after you when I invited myself into your hotel room."

I knew it was a lame excuse for lying. Actually there is *no* excuse for lying.

Dax grinned broadly. "I thought so. With your middle name, it seemed a little too coincidental, even though strange coincidences do seem to find you. You didn't use the exact same fictional name for your imaginary fiancé, but of course Ashton and Flame are right out of the famous Civil War novel. Which one of your parents chose your name? Let me guess. Your mother."

I nodded. "She's a movie freak. Loves the old classic movies. Clark Gable is her all-time favorite actor. I can't count how many times I've sat through that movie, watching Ashton put up with that selfish Flame woman. I don't know how he could stand her for *four* whole hours. Mom always said the movie was a good history lesson. I never knew if the lesson was supposed to be on the Civil War or the war between the sexes."

Dax chuckled. "I'm glad to know you aren't an imitation of the Flame in the movie. She's one woman I wouldn't put up with, even for half an hour." His amused look turned to one of puzzlement. "You got your name in a natural enough manner. But I'm still intrigued by the gypsy woman coming up with it in her will. You have to admit there *is* something supernatural going on here."

I nodded, thinking we had already discussed what I thought was going on. The gypsy's conjuring up my name may have the thumb print of the supernatural on it, but it definitely was not God's thumb print.

He interrupted my thoughts. "I suppose you don't believe in reincarnation."

"Nope."

"You don't think it's even a remote possibility?"

"Nope."

"Wanna tell me why not?"

"Because I believe what God said about it."

"And what is that?"

"It's appointed unto a man *once* to die and after that the judgment. God never said we had to be born over and over and go through a progression of lives, each time striving to be better than before. Or that we must suffer in other lives for the times when we weren't better."

"I thought Christians believed in being born again."

I had to restrain myself from rolling my eyes. "*Born again* is a term for the birth of a new spirit in man. Not a new body. It happens when someone asks Jesus to come into his heart. Until then the human spirit is separated from God."

He looked slightly amused. "Then after this spiritual birth, you're perfect? You don't have to go through a progression of lives in order to burn away the dross from the silver and become a paragon of virtue?"

I looked at him with some amazement. "Do you know of anyone who has attained perfection on this planet? Besides, if we could develop righteousness by living out numerous lives, Jesus wouldn't have had to come and die for our sins."

"I see. Jesus did it all. We don't have to do it?"

"I know that sounds simplistic. Think of it this way. A guilty man is under a sentence of death and can't possibly reverse the court's judgment against him just by changing his ways. The law demands a penalty. No matter how hard the convicted man tries, he can't undo his death sentence with good behavior alone. Then, suppose someone steps in and pays the penalty for him, by dying in his place. Justice is satisfied. The debt is canceled and the convicted man is set free. Now all he owes is a debt of gratitude to his benefactor."

I didn't say it aloud, but I was thinking, *Actually he owes more than gratitude. He owes Jesus his life.*

"Okay, okay. I get the picture. Now let's talk about you." Dax reached across the table and took my hand in his. "I don't like it that you're mixed up in this. If I can't persuade you not to go back to the bayou, then I'm going with you."

I was disappointed that he had not apparently listened to my analogy. I also was surprised by his declaration that he would go with me.

Next, it occurred to me, and I said it while removing my hand from his.

"You just don't want to miss the scoop on what happens when the voodoo priestess finally opens her precious book of spells."

"Kaytie!" He looked genuinely disappointed. "Do you really think I'd stoop so low? That story is yours and yours alone unless you give me permission to write my version. You have my word on it. Trust me."

His midnight eyes pleaded.

I truly wanted to believe him. Evidently he could see that.

"Now it's settled." He grinned. "I'm going with you."

I started to protest once more, but he raised a hand. "End of discussion."

We ordered chocolate mousse for dessert, and when it arrived I wondered if I was adding a few more pounds of trouble than I wanted to deal with. I promised myself to stay out of Larue's close proximity on the next trip, no matter what emergency might arise.

When the waiter left the guest check, I promptly took it and paid for the meal, which came to eighty-seven dollars. "Including the tip, I have paid back the hundred I owed you," I announced. He protested, but I remained firm, relieved to settle the debt.

He drove me to my apartment building, parked on the street and wanted to see me up the stairs.

"No thanks. If I can find my way around the Louisiana swamps, I can surely find my way up to my own apartment."

Turning toward me and taking my hand in his, Dax said, "I don't doubt you are completely capable of finding your way to anywhere you wanna go. It's your charming company that I don't want to give up so soon."

For a moment, I was dazzled, knowing I would enjoy spending more time with him as well. Warning bells went off in my head. He did not share my faith. He was not suitable as a romantic interest. It was definitely time to go. "I'm sure you have plenty of charming company available at your beck and call."

"Oh yeah," he rolled his eyes. "The *Seeker* hires bodyguards regularly to protect me from hordes of desperate women chasing after me." He teased with mock exaggeration. Then he changed his tone. "Come on, Kaytie. You don't see any wild female fans following me around, do you?"

I glanced at the immediate area. "Not at the moment. Not unless it's that one disguised as a bag lady over there on the other side of the street."

He glanced at the stooped woman lumbering beneath a large plastic bag slung over her shoulder. "Hmmm, I'll definitely have to check *her* out," he said with mock interest. Then turning his eyes toward me again, he added, "Look, I know you're not exactly one of my biggest fans, but we're really not on such opposite sides of the professional fence. You already know that. Just because I write for your magazine's competitor doesn't mean we can't be friends."

"We're on opposite sides of the theological and philosophical fences, Dax. That means we can't really be anything but friends as far as I'm concerned." I said it firmly, hoping to divert any unwanted advances in the future.

Dax looked perplexed. "Oh, you mean the religious thing. I'm not up to your spiritual standards?"

"Just so you know. If you want to be friends, that's fine with me. But let's keep things strictly professional."

He smiled and extended a hand. "Friends it is."

I was glad I had laid out the ground rules. Glad he accepted the terms. Because in that moment I saw a goodnight kiss in his eyes. A kiss that I very much wanted.

And wanted even more to avoid.

Chapter 9

Who Has Seen the Wind?

Forget that kiss, I kept reminding myself during the next two weeks. My mother called daily from Baton Rouge and spent hours on the phone making sure I truly was okay. She'd had her entire church congregation praying for my safe return from New Orleans. I thanked God for those prayers, wondering where I would be without them. Now it looked like I would be needing them even more.

Larue maintained a respectful distance, calling only once to tell me that we were booked on the same plane back to the Crescent City.

I didn't know how to stop him from coming with me.

It's a free country.

At Chicago O'Hare Airport on the day of the flight, I boarded alone, not seeing Larue at the gate. I buckled my seatbelt and opened my briefcase to proof the final copy of my story one last time. It was sensational enough to have made the highly popular *Supernatural Seeker*, but still factual enough to be respectable material for the *Beyond Fantasy.*

That pleased me greatly. My article was the headliner, written entirely in first person. First person articles don't happen too often for a novice journalist. My boss also was pleased. Pleased as pie—peach pie, I thought, smiling. He always treated me like a peach and I loved him for it. I could never write for another editor. Ed was just the best.

The stewardess began a demonstration of how to use the seat cushion for a flotation device, and I was thinking Dax must have changed his mind, when he hustled down the aisle looking for his seat.

"Kaytie, there you are! I got held up in traffic, but I made it," he exclaimed breathlessly as he stored his carry-on bag in the overhead storage compartment.

He looked like a male model for *GQ*, as desirable as ever in snug-fitting blue jeans and a white sweater stretched over broad shoulders. Taking the seat beside me, he buckled up just as the captain announced our departure. I had to remind myself again to forget that almost-kiss in his eyes, so real I could almost taste its sweetness.

We were on our way back to Rainy Bay Bayou and the infamous Madame Chevalier with her evil crew. Only this time it was by my own choice. I experienced a momentary shiver down my spine.

What might be waiting for me there?

"I read your story in the *Fantasy*," Dax eyed the rapidly approaching clouds as we climbed toward them, leaving Chicago a miniature city below.

"The one about the woman who claimed to have visions before the World Trade Towers disaster. You make a good case for your prophetic-gift theory. Did you actually know this woman?"

"For two years," I nodded. "Vidya was in a Bible study group with me. She described two very tall 'pillars' surrounded by clouds of smoke in her vision and didn't know why the image filled her with such dread. This happened at least a month before the attack. If you read the entire article, you already know that Vidya used the word *pillars* instead of *towers* because she's from India, and English is her second language. She just didn't have the word *towers* in her vocabulary before nine-eleven. Our group didn't have the slightest idea how to interpret her vision. Not until we saw the news on the screen and the twin towers burning and surrounded with black smoke, exactly as she had described."

I didn't tell Dax how Vidya had also described an evil visage appearing in the smoke. How an image on a CNN camera later captured what appeared to be a wicked, leering face in the clouds over the burning towers. The photog had even drawn a circle around the face. I keep a copy of it in my nine-eleven reference folder.

Dax raised a brow. "Why would God give this obscure little eastern Indian woman a vision of such a hugely impacting event?"

I had to admit I didn't know. "That's a question that's led me to study prophetic visions in the Bible. Most of the time, the prophet saw things coming which he couldn't change, warnings of coming judgment. It's God's mercy to allow people time to repent. Prophecies also serve to confirm that God is God, knowing the end from the beginning."

"Oh yes. We've talked about this before. But how do we know that over the course of thousands of years and translation after translation, the Bible's books are even the same today as when they were first written?"

Dax's question was the same old ploy first used by Satan in the Garden when he put doubt into Eve by questioning what God really said. Just get someone to question God's word, and he's got them where he wants them, because then they don't have a standard for truth.

A stewardess was making her way down the aisle with coffee and soft drinks. I ordered a glass of orange juice and Dax ordered coffee. Then I turned to him.

"One way we know is because we have the Dead Sea Scrolls found in a cave by a Bedouin explorer. One of the scrolls was a three-thousand-year-old manuscript, the book of the prophet Isaiah. The cross of every *t*, the dot of every *I*, and every word is exactly the same as in the Bible today. It's a small thing for God to watch over His word and keep it accurate in the hands of copiers and translators."

I was thinking once more how there is no greater proof of God's divinity than the very existence of the Bible. For centuries, skeptics have not been able to dismiss it or to prove one single line is untrue. In fact, actual science and archeology have only served to confirm it time and time again.

As fascinated as I was by the subject, I could tell Dax was not interested. He tried to appear so, but he kept fidgeting with his briefcase. "Do you believe God gave this former Hindu woman a vision merely to convince your Bible group that God's word is true?"

"No, everyone in the group was already a believer. It caused us to respect her when she spoke of dreams or visions. We *know* that she hears from God."

"Ummm," he murmured. "Has she predicted other things of significance to America?"

"Not that I'm aware of. You have to realize Vidya doesn't just decide to dream up a vision. She's a woman of prayer and she waits on God. Visions don't happen because she wants them to. In fact, she'd rather not know what's ahead. It's just too awesome and terrifying."

"I don't understand. Why wouldn't God give this vision to the president? Someone in authority who could do something to stop it?"

"Perhaps He did and that person didn't recognize it or act on it. Or maybe it was something that could not be stopped. We are creatures of free will, you know. If God steps in and stops every act of evil or violence, He would be circumventing man's free will."

I could hear in mind what Dax was thinking. The mystery of evil is another of Satan's ploys. If he gets us to blame God for the bad things that happen to people, that makes God the bad guy.

Without waiting for him to ask, I said, "I know it's hard to understand why God allows evil in the world. But actually He didn't create anything that wasn't good. Evil entered the world when Adam sinned."

Dax's expression remained noncommittal.

I wasn't getting through that barrier of intellectual reasoning.

"I don't attempt to explain God. If I could do that, He wouldn't be God. All I know is that He's a God of love and I have faith in His loving kindness, no matter what evil men do."

Dax looked thoughtful. "Faith. I have difficulty with that concept. We're created with minds that reason. We want to explore. We want proof of what we believe about the universe. Why should our creator give us these attributes if we're expected to have faith in something we can't see?"

I took a sip of juice and silently asked for wisdom to answer his questions.

"Proof? You experience proof of the unseen every day. You can't see the wind, but you can plainly see where it's been as it moves the trees or whips the waves to foam. You watch it fill the billowing sails of a boat. You saw its power in the devastation of Katrina."

Dax looked out the window at the cottony cloud formations above and below us. He nodded slowly. "Who has seen the wind? Neither you nor I. That's the first line of an old poem I learned in grade school. You should have seen my sixth-grade teacher. She was a real looker. Everything a guy could want...including a nice beard."

He made me laugh in spite of the seriousness of our conversation. I could see Dax as a sixth-grade boy—a cute one. Girls chasing after him.

Somehow, every time I thought of him, girls were part of the picture. I wouldn't let myself ask if he had a steady girlfriend. In fact, I told myself, it would be a good thing for me if he did.

So much for the spiritual conversation. He wanted to talk about Madame Chevalier and what we were going to do. I didn't have the plan all worked out from A to Z, but I had a peace in my spirit.

It didn't keep fearful thoughts away entirely.

I had to choose not to let fear become my focus.

* * *

This time we checked into the Lafitte Hotel asking for separate rooms. I wondered briefly if the concierge was puzzled by our sudden "divorce." She appeared to be delighted and could hardly stop fluttering her eyelashes at Dax. Unlike our first arrival, Dax made certain that I was ahead of him at the desk. I wondered suspiciously where his gentlemanly manners had suddenly come from.

As soon as I unpacked, I called Tex's cell phone and found him driving a fare through the French Quarter to the Toulouse St. Wharf. We agreed to meet for dinner to discuss our next move. Sofronia and Beth would be there too, he assured me.

There was nothing to do for the moment, so I decided to walk, do a little sightseeing on my own. Being from nearby Baton Rouge, naturally I had visited New Orleans several times with my parents as a child and a few times thereafter.

Charmed by the sights and sounds, I decided early on that there was no other place like New Orleans in the world. I was delighted to find it had lost none of its eclectic charms even after the devastation of Katrina.

I've always enjoyed the city's racial diversity, its population having grown up on the backs of French Acadians, the Cajun generation of the immigrant French. And there were the Creoles named for the first generation of immigrants from France, Spain, Haiti and Africa. The descendants of the first arriving slaves were largely from the African Zulu tribe.

Most of the language on the streets was typical southern Louisiana with lots of "y'all" and "where y'at" phrasing. Of course visitors from every state and nation spoke with varied accents, but I also caught a few words from the beautiful Creole language, a language influenced by French, African, English and even a few Indian words. It was a language born of African slaves owned by French masters—slaves who had proudly determined to maintain their own identity and so had created their own language.

The French Quarter remained largely untouched by Katrina, retaining both its old world charm and decadence. Some of its buildings were under repair for roof damage, and others had boarded-up windows.

Bourbon Street's peculiar smell of rotting vegetables had not been washed away by the flood, so I walked on Royal to St. Peter, a block from the old

Cabildo where the Louisiana Purchase had been signed in 1803 after Napoleon abandoned his hopes of establishing a new empire in America.

I was glad to see the historic building with its cannon still guarding the entrance. My sense of history and the impact of the past would have been wounded had these structures suffered irreparable damage.

The Cabildo adjoins St. Louis Cathedral, the oldest structure of its kind in the country, now a museum. I joined other visitors slipping inside for a peek at marble tombs, intricate stained-glass windows and various sculptures.

Across Chartres Street from the Cabildo is Jackson Square where old Andrew himself rides a war horse with both hooves raised in the air. The park is usually surrounded by street vendors, the aromas of delicious red-beans-and-rice in a paper cup or gator on a stick, artists, street musicians and entertainers.

I could hear happy music from what sounded like a giant calliope on the "rivah" excursion boat. A talented youngster performed a tap dance to the delight of spectators, drawing attention away from the mimes in colorful blue and yellow costumes

I hadn't walked far when I saw her. Madame Chevalier sitting before a fascinated tourist, both of them peering intently at the palm of the man's hand.

Stopping short, I stepped back, not wishing to be seen, but curious. There was something different about the voodoo priestess. Her red and blue gypsy costume and dangling baubles and bracelets were the same, but she appeared shrunken, thinner by several pounds. Instead of triple chins, she had only two.

I wanted to observe her more closely from an obscure vantage point, but pedestrians were thinning at the moment. Fortuitously, a wedding party had just entered the area, the white-gowned bride and tuxedoed groom dancing in the lead, followed by bridesmaids in pink satin, tuxedoed groomsmen in pink ties and matching cummerbunds. Family members and well-wishers were followed by jazz musicians playing a lively version of "Basin Street." I joined the procession to keep myself hidden from the woman's eyes.

Watching Madame from the corner of my eye, I marched around the square with the revelers, enjoying the merriment when a voice at my ear sent chills through my frame.

"Come with me."

It was the unmistakable choking voice of Morris, the gourd-faced whisperer. I whirled to face him. He wore a low hat and large sunglasses, neither of which adequately concealed the cottage-cheese texture of his mushroom-colored skin. The pocket of his jacket bulged as if he held a gun aimed directly at me.

This could not be happening.

What had I been thinking to come here?

Wasn't this exactly what Sofronia had warned me about?

How stupid could I be?

"Come with me," he whispered once more.

"What if I don't?" I challenged, glancing at the wedding party moving on down the street. Several walking-tour groups were arriving in the square. "You aren't going to shoot me."

His voice was thick with anger. "We have other ways of dealing with you. Ways that are far less pleasant than a bullet."

The implication of his words was chilling. I thought of the zombie potion, remembering how the neurotoxins can leave the victim in a permanently brain-damaged state. Tex had been one of the lucky ones to revive unharmed. It would be easy for Gourd Face to jab me with a needle. But we were far away from Rainy Bay Bayou at the moment. Surrounded by the sightseers, I took courage.

"Look around. You don't want to start something out here in front of all these people," I argued. "Besides, I know where the chest is, and I'm willing to turn it over to Madame."

His demeanor registered surprise, then exuded sudden hope.

"You will bring us the chest?"

I nodded.

"Take me to it. Now!"

Before I could move, he grabbed my arm in a viselike grip and started shoving me through the crowd.

"Hold it right there."

Another familiar voice spoke with steely authority. Detective Broussard. He flashed a badge in one hand while holding a gun in the other and leveling it directly at Morris, who released me with a ragged, tired sigh.

My own sigh was one of great relief as Broussard clapped the handcuffs on Morris's wrists.

"You're under arrest for attempted kidnapping. You have the right to remain silent," Broussard began Mirandizing Morris while reaching into the man's pocket to remove a small-caliber, chrome handgun.

"Miss O'Reilly, will you accompany us to the station? I'd like to get your statement."

I felt like throwing my arms around his neck and hugging the detective out of sheer gratefulness. Instead I followed him, shaking from both the rush of adrenalin and great relief.

* * *

Broussard turned Morris over to be booked and processed into jail, then seated me in his office and we talked once more of the Chevalier sisters.

"We received the court's permission to exhume the twin's body," he began with a serious face.

"And?"

"And guess what. The corpse was there. Hadn't cooked enough yet and was still recognizable as Sapphire Chevalier, the twin, right where she was supposed to be."

I was stunned. I'd been so certain the twin had faked her own death. It seemed the only logical explanation.

"Then who was the body in my room at the Lafitte?" My mind flooded with questions which I had previously answered by the wrong theory.

"We're waiting for the autopsy report. Certainly the corpse in the hotel room fits the description of Madame Emerald Chevalier."

"What about the one in the grave? Could she have been an impostor? Some poor woman who died and was deliberately dressed as one of the twins?"

Broussard nodded slowly, his brow wrinkling.

"That's possible. But why would she want to impersonate the gypsy woman?"

"Who knows? Now we've got three Madame Chevaliers! Two of them already dead and a third one determined to kidnap me. What's going on?" I threw up my hands in a gesture of consternation.

"We'll have more answers when we get the coroner's report," Broussard noted. "Until then, you have to be more careful. I can't spend all my time following you around New Orleans waiting for the next thug to grab you off the street."

"I'm sorry," I muttered, thinking how foolish my actions had been.

"I know you plan to turn over the chest to Madame soon. She's already aware that we're on to her. We've had our suspicions about her from time to time, but never could prove she'd done anything illegal. Now here's what I want you to do. Arrange to have her meet you somewhere in public where we can be watching to be sure you aren't harmed. If Bad Leroy is with her, we can pick him up at the same time."

I thought it a great plan, the more public the better as far as I was concerned. But I also knew that Madame would not open her precious book of spells without me at her side, and she would not be likely to open it in a public place. We talked over possibilities.

"Sofronia insisted it be opened at the woman's swamp lair in Rainy Bay Bayou," I explained. "She said it should be around two weeks before the full moon when Madame's powers are weakest."

Broussard shook his head. "I don't like it. The gypsy knows the area too well, and my men could get lost."

"Wait a minute," the thought hit me. "I have a friend who's lived near Chevalier's cabin for years. Cajun Jack. He can find his way around the bayou blindfolded. I know he could direct your men to her place and also keep them out of her sight."

Broussard looked thoughtful. "That might work. How do we contact him?"

"His daughter, Jacqueline, can call him. He keeps a cell phone in his power boat."

The detective agreed to contact Jacqueline before he drove me back to the Lafitte. By then it was late afternoon, and I was anxious to shower and dress for dinner.

Anxious to see Tex and Beth.

I might as well admit it.

I was looking forward to seeing Dax as well.

* * *

The phone in my room rang just as I stepped out of the shower. I grabbed a towel, picked it up and heard a whispery voice.

"You can't escape your destiny!"

"Come on, Dax! You aren't going to scare me that easy."

Dax chuckled. "Where have you been?"

"You don't want to know."

I didn't want to tell him either, knowing the scolding I'd get for my audacious sightseeing excursion.

"Meet me in the lobby. I'm dying to see you."

Hastily dressed in casual clothes, I hurried downstairs to the lobby where Dax met me with a dazzled grin. His eyes sweeping me from head to toe.

"Kaytie, you look amazing."

I glanced at him with a slightly skeptical expression in my eyes.

"Honestly, Dax, I think the word 'amazing' has been hugely overly worked and shows a lack of imagination. I expected something more from a skillful writer who knows how to avoid trite language."

His grin widened. "Let me try again. You are a stunning vixen, an exotic example of female pulchritude. Your esoteric essence festoons the moments I spend in your company, desalinates the hours I spend waiting to see you again. Shall I go on?"

"Yes, please," I nodded imperiously, amused at his outburst of flattery.

"Shall I compare you to summer's day?"

I frowned slightly. "That line has been done before. Try again."

His eyes twinkled with mischief.

"Your lips are as enticing as the coral of a rainbow over a sunrise pool and I'm thinking of drowning myself if you don't turn them up in a smile at me immediately."

I smiled.

"Ah, the rainbow has turned upside down, and now I'm tortured by the promise of those lovely, luscious lips."

"Passable descriptives, for a writer who is good at exaggerating the truth," I couldn't help jibing. "I'm sure you'll do even better with practice."

Dax laughed heartily. "Exaggerate the truth? Never!"

Before he could begin another outpouring of such nonsense, I informed him, "We're meeting Tex, Beth and Sofronia for dinner at a little place he knows. Actually, Tex will be picking us up here any minute." I glanced at my watch. "We should be watching for his cab."

Dax nodded, took my elbow and guided me to the entrance where we could see a few taxis already waiting at the end of the green canvas canopy. "That's him," I nodded toward the last cab pulling up, and we headed out.

"Miss Kaytie, I shore am glad to see you again," Tex greeted me with a warm handshake. "You too, Mr. Larue."

"And I'm relieved to see you've made it safely through these past two weeks."

I couldn't help glancing around the interior, remembering the last time I'd climbed inside this very vehicle. No voodoo priestess, Pirate Man, or zombie this time. Not even an Avon lady with a bag of lipstick samples.

"Not as relieved as I am," Tex exclaimed. "I've been as nervous as a chicken wandering into a KFC by mistake."

He talked while he drove, seemingly on automatic pilot, explaining how cautious he had been about picking up fares.

"Nobody that even comes close to looking like a gypsy or a pirate gets inside my cab!"

A few blocks away, we arrived at a quiet little seafood and oyster bar where the waitress greeted Tex with a smile.

"Your usual table, honey?"

"Put us in the back room, Ethel. We have business to talk about. Oh, and we're expecting two more ladies."

Ethel nodded and showed us to a private room. The place reminded me of a spaghetti house with its checkered tablecloths, plastic bottles of mustard, the mandatory bottles of Louisiana hot sauce and a variety of Cajun spices. Before we could finish the shrimp appetizers, Ethel escorted Beth to our table, still wearing her Fish and Game ranger's uniform.

After greetings and handshakes, Beth sat down across the table from me.

"Beth, what's wrong?" I blurted, noting the look at her eyes.

"It's Sofronia. She's in the hospital. Had an attack of some kind. I've been to see her but she was out of it. Doc says she might not make it. Anyway, here's the other bad news. I doubt if Sofronia was able to contact Madame Chevalier before she had the attack."

We sat there blinking stupidly.

Sofronia ill? Unable to contact Madame with our plan?

Of course that explained why Morris had tried to grab me at Jackson Square. He hadn't known we were planning to turn over the chest to the boss lady.

Tex broke the silence. "You mean that we don't know if Madame is expecting us to bring her the danged treasure chest?"

His eyes darted toward me. I knew what he was thinking.

"I'd have contacted the woman myself if I'd known before today," Beth explained. "I just found out about Sofronia this afternoon. She's been hospitalized for the last thirteen days, so it's not likely she got word to Madame."

"Call me a biscuit and slap me with molasses! I've been driving around this city for two weeks, and Bad Leroy and that gourd-faced freak could have grabbed me at any time!"

Tex pulled a handkerchief from a shirt pocket and wiped his brow.

"Dang! They could have shot me with that zombie potion and I'd be a robot again."

I could see more white than color showing in his eyes.

Dax spoke up. "This doesn't change anything. We have a good plan. I say we stick to it. We can find the woman in Jackson Square, right?"

I nodded, still unwilling to admit my near-disastrous encounter with Leroy earlier that day.

"So we just tell her that we'll bring the chest to her, to wherever, and let her know that the police will be waiting for our safe return."

He reached for my hand under the table and squeezed it reassuringly.

The concern in Beth's eyes changed to a slightly puzzled look. "I think that's what we have to do. She won't try anything if she gets what she wants. But it's too late to send word to her."

Before I could ask her what she meant by that, she remarked, "I don't like it that Sofronia is—"

"Is what?" I asked, sensing there was more to the story.

Beth took a deep breath. "I've seen cases where people believe they've been hexed by spells. They moan and talk out of their heads. That's what Sofronia is doing."

"Are you saying that Madame put a spell of some kind on her? But how could she even know that we had any contact with Sofronia?"

I was thinking there wouldn't have been time for that, since the old woman had come down with the fever right after I flew out of New Orleans.

"I don't know. Maybe it is only swamp fever. I just don't like it. Didn't Sofronia say the witch would harm the people around you?"

"She did say Madame could harm people close to me. People I care about."

I glanced at my friends seated at the table with me. They were the only people I knew in New Orleans, other than Jean Claude, Detective Broussard and Cajun Jack's family. I thought of my mother in Baton Rouge. My editor in Chicago. Of course I had friends in both Louisiana and Illinois. I wouldn't want harm to come to any of them.

I had only met Sofronia one time. Now she was lying in a hospital bed, out of her mind with fever. Maybe the witch had nothing to do with it, but how did I know? Sofronia had definitely believed Madame possessed certain powers.

She didn't fear those powers from the pit of Hell, I thought, suddenly angry. *Neither should I.* After all, I had already faced up to Madame's sorcery once before and had overcome it by speaking the name of Jesus. She was the one who had wilted. I wasn't about to give in to the fear of witchcraft now.

Steeling myself for their disapproval, I confessed my afternoon visit to Jackson Square and my frightening brush with Gourd Face Morris.

"At least that's one goon we don't have to deal with anymore, now that he's in jail," I finished lamely. Their expressions ranged from angst to relief.

Dax flashed a look at me that reminded me of my dad after I'd once used one of his new golf clubs for a ball bat. His eyes were threatening, however, he did not let go of my hand.

Beth nodded. "The moon will be full two weeks from *tonight*. We must get the chest to Madame before tomorrow. Sofronia told me that this is the night when the priestess is more vulnerable, and timing is everything to a practitioner of spells. That means you have to recover the chest and reach Madame in the bayou before morning. She doesn't know you're coming. That could work to our advantage. She'll be alone. She won't have time to round up her thugs. With four of us and only one of her, we should be safe enough."

I had expected to have at least another day to prepare myself for the venture. The sudden time constraint threw me a little off balance. "It has to be tonight? I thought any time this week was good."

"It's got to be tonight. Madame will be at her bayou shack to call on her spirit guide. You'll get the chest, and I'll contact Detective Broussard."

Would another day really make any difference? I reasoned that once the priestess got her precious book we should be able to leave Rainy Bay Bayou safely enough. Especially if she knew the police were aware and watching her. Still I was only half convinced. Would Broussard be able to get his officers out to Cajun Jack's place in time?

Would it matter?

Even if he didn't arrive, surely there were too many of us for Madame to contend with alone.

Besides, what did she have to gain by harming us? The kidnapping charges?

I was beginning to suspect that Madame had little fear of the law in New Orleans. She was a con artist. No doubt she could con, bribe or conjure her way out of legal scrapes.

I turned to Tex. "Do you think you can find the way back to her shanty?"

"I know I can. I can find my way back to anywhere if I've been there once before. My folks always said I have a nose like a bloodhound. I know where the wharf is and how far we have to go to reach those lanterns marking the channels. We'll get there, alright."

* * *

Less than an hour later, Dax, Tex and I headed out Highway 10 toward the old plantation manors. It would have been an enjoyable drive any other time. We passed the Houmas House, built in 1840. That's the place most often featured in Hollywood movies about the South because of its magnificent spiral staircase. Next, the Belle Helene, an 1841 structure with southern-style square columns inviting visitors into the past. We drove by Mount Hope, a nineteenth-century farmhouse, charming as well, even in the dark.

Tex knew exactly where to turn in order to locate the road we'd followed after escaping from the gardener's cottage.

Traffic thinned when we approached the bridge over Bayou Marngouin, the place where we'd first run into Beth.

I kept glancing nervously back over my shoulder.

There were headlights behind us.

"Tex, don't stop yet. Slow down and let that car go around," I urged.

Two more cars and a rickety vegetable truck passed before the road behind us became completely dark. Tex pulled over and backed up slowly. He drove the cab off the roadway and under the trees.

The familiar sounds of the bayou filled our ears. Crickets chirruped, frogs alternately sang or belched like tubas, and night birds called. The smell of damp vegetation grew strong. Like a blanket of black lamb's wool, darkness wrapped us with heavy, humid air.

We began our search for the hidden chest, equipped with small flashlights. I'd taken extra care to memorize the location in my mind, but with only the thin wands of yellow light, the woodsy area looked very different. It had a haunted, surreal quality, ground mist swirling and mossy drapes floating like ghosts in the branches.

I half expected to see a vampire's coffin rise up through the marsh grass. Of course I don't believe in vampires or zombies or ghosts. Not in the daytime. At night in this spooky setting, my imagination, fired by recent and chilling experiences, I wouldn't have been surprised if Bigfoot had appeared and started practicing a cha cha for an episode of *Dancing with the Stars*.

After several minutes of stumbling beneath moss-draped branches through the undergrowth, I recognized the tall live oak scarred by a charred streak running down the gnarled trunk, probably a lightning strike from when Katrina barreled through.

"Over there." I pointed.

Tex and Dax moved ahead of me. They quickly shoved aside the palmetto leaves and brush piles from the ancient chest. With a sense of foreboding, I stared at the rotted leather barely covering the rusted metal box.

What kind of evil did it actually hold?

Could the legend of Magnolia's book have been merely that? A legend without substance. Would Madame open it to find it empty? Or were the lost secrets of an African sorcerer about to be unleashed on the world?

An evil more dreadful than anyone could imagine.

Questions without answers filled my mind. I prayed silently that turning it over was the right thing to do.

I couldn't shake the feeling that we were being followed while we lugged the thing back to the cab. It was the same sensation that haunted me after leaving Count Ribaldo's unholy gathering. Once, I felt certain I glimpsed malevolent eyes peering through the trees. With a gasp, I whirled the flashlight's beam toward it.

Nothing was there.

Nothing I could see.

* * *

Beth didn't meet us at the boat dock. After an hour, we decided we couldn't wait for her any longer. It was already well past midnight.

Tex amazed me with his ability to find the way. He didn't miss a turn. As we floated our rented power boat underneath the softly glowing channel markers, I considered that Madame Chevalier might be sleeping inside her cabin. What if she were not even there? Moments later, we rounded a turn and saw candlelight flickering in the windows. There was something sinister in that light, rather than warm and welcoming.

She must have heard the approaching sound of the boat's engines, because the door opened and Madame's bulky frame appeared, limned in shadowy silhouette, strangely menacing against the candle glow.

"You have come," she stated simply.

No surprise registered in her glittering eyes as I stepped out of the craft and began climbing toward her.

"The tarot cards predicted it."

A slight chill prickled my skin at her words. Maybe we didn't have the element of surprise after all.

Still, with Dax and Tex behind, me carrying the chest, I felt in control of the situation.

"Yes, Madame, I have come. We have some business to settle, you and I."

Her eyes fell on the chest and she gasped involuntarily. The two men hoisted it into her cabin, panting and puffing. Then they turned to watch her, warily.

"You brought to me the chest!"

She breathed the words with surprise and something akin to mad glee. Her eyes glowed as fiery as the ruby eyes in the pendant which hung around her neck.

"The police are fully informed of your activities, Madame," Dax explained, "and even now they're here in Rainy Bay Bayou. If we don't return safely to New Orleans, they will come for you."

I hoped he was right and Beth had been able to contact Broussard.

I added, "Just so you know, we don't intend to press kidnapping charges. We're only here so you can open this thing, and then we're out of your life for good. Understand?"

She waved a beefy hand as if what I said were of no consequence to her. Wearing the flowing white caftan which swirled around heavy ankles, the woman turned toward a shelf. Numerous fine braids moved around her shoulders, making me think of Medusa with serpents growing from her head instead of hair. Again, I was aware that Madame had diminished in size. Somehow, it seemed she had also diminished in strength.

Maybe Sofronia had been right. This was the hour of her vulnerability. She turned back again holding a curious key in her hand.

"My father gave me this before he died. He said it had been kept in the family since Magnolia's time. Now at last the time has come to use it!"

Madame's eyes blazed and sweat popped out on her forehead. She knelt down beside her prize, then suddenly glanced up at Tex and Dax. The two of them were waiting silently, intensely curious as to what was about to happen.

"You be not afraid of what this might do to you?" she asked, slipping from perfect English to a Cajun accent.

Tex raised his eyebrows questioningly, looking at Dax first and then at me. Apparently he felt somewhat reassured.

"I reckon not," he said with a slight shrug.

Dax had assumed his cool, winning-hand expression.

Madame turned back to her work with a *whatever* shrug and inserted the key into the first lock.

"Hold on there," Tex interrupted, raising a hand. "What might happen if we *are* here? I mean, nothing can go wrong since Kaytie's here too, right?"

The voodoo priestess did not remove her hand from the key, but she paused.

"Don't know. She is here. That is *all I* need."

No one spoke for a long moment, until Dax interjected, "Go on. Open it."

Chapter 10

The Chest

Hesitating no longer, the woman began unlocking a series of intricate mechanisms. I could see why the old gardener's locksmith had been unable to open the chest. It had been cleverly designed by an old-world expert who well knew that his clients would be keeping their most valuable possessions inside.

One by one, Madame turned the interior locks which had not suffered rust as had the outside metal. Each lock turned easily. After several moments, the final lock sprung open with a slight click. By this time we were all holding our breath.

Slowly, Madame raised the lid. A third metal lining nesting inside the second had kept out moisture successfully. That was evident from the condition of the velvet fabric covering a strand of pearls. Underneath the pearls were other pieces of jewelry, an exquisite diamond pendant set in finely crafted gold, sapphire earrings, an enormous ruby ring, and several delicate gold chains.

One by one the woman removed pieces of jewelry. These might have adorned the slender throat of Elizabeth on those occasions when she entertained, dancing in the grand ballroom underneath the chandelier that now hung in the Lafitte's hall.

Gazing at the past, I glimpsed a hint of the graceful and elegant life once lived by plantation owners, a life forever gone with the winds of Civil War, the bloody and epic struggle to re-unite our fledgling nation.

Madame opened a yellowed parchment packet containing paper money, Confederate money, now without value except to a museum curator or a collector.

At the very bottom of the chest lay a leather-bound volume, appearing to be in good condition. Madame gasped when she saw it and eagerly grabbed the book. With trembling hands, she opened it carefully, as if fearing she might damage the thin, yellowing pages. They remained intact.

I could see large block print letters, as if a child had written them in faded ink on the first open page, "Magnolia."

I glanced at Tex and Dax. We were still breathing regularly. No Pandora or evil genie rushed forth. No vile spirit materialized to leer at us. We stood there, perfectly unharmed at the moment.

With a sense of relief, I broke the silence.

"You have your precious book now, Madame Chevalier. We'll be leaving. But first let me give you this bit of warning. My church has prayed that if you ever attempt to practice any spells in this book, all the curses written there will come upon you. After all, Elizabeth was a Christian woman and it was her wish that these spells remain buried forever. That wish and her prayers are still effective today, and my church wishes to honor them."

I had no idea of the reaction my words would cause. Madame reached up with both hands, grabbing fistfuls of her Medusa braids, shrieking at me.

"What have you done!"

Tex and Dax stood gaping at her, ready to restrain her if she threw herself at me in her fit of rage.

Sofronia was right.

The woman feared my faith.

* * *

Morning sunshine brought shopkeepers out to sweep and wash down the walkways in the French Quarter. Over coffee and the famous beignets at Café du Monde, Dax, Tex and I spoke of our last night's adventure with a sense of great relief. It seemed kind of anti-climactic that the chest was finally in the witch woman's possession, opened and seemingly useless to her now, by our observations.

How simple the entire episode had been, after the dreadful moments I'd gone through trying to avoid it.

"I thought she was going to pop a blood vessel," said Tex with a chuckle. "She looked like a Texas tornado was about to blow her away when you said your church had been praying. She shorely *does* fear those Christian prayers."

I glanced at Dax, pleased to see him nod in agreement.

"Why don't you call Beth and find out why she didn't show up?" Dax suggested.

I fished my cell phone out of my purse and dialed, relieved when Beth answered.

"I'm sorry I couldn't be there," she began. "I had to go to the hospital. Sofronia took a turn for the worse and I couldn't leave her. She doesn't have any living relatives. I'm glad I was there to hold her hand, because she died this morning. She was smiling when she went, like she could see Heaven opening up and the angels welcoming her home," Beth explained.

"I'm sure that's exactly what she saw," I whispered, wiping a brief tear from my eye. It was hard not to weep, even though Sofronia was in a far better place. I knew I should try to smile instead and be glad for her glorious homecoming.

"We're still not sure of Madame Chevalier's true identity," I said, changing the subject. "The police found her twin in the grave, right where she was supposed to be. Now they're working on the identity of the woman who was shot in my hotel room."

"Let the police figure it out," said Beth. "They have both corpses. They'll find out what's going on."

Somewhere in the back of my mind swirled the unwelcome thought of voodoo and zombies. I shoved it underneath a layer of reason.

"You're rid of the chest and safely back in New Orleans. The woman has no further use for you now," Beth assured. "The trouble is mostly behind you. I suppose you will be going back to Chicago."

"Yes, I'm flying out this afternoon. What do you mean, *mostly* behind me?"

"That Larue has his eyes on you, girl," she warned. "He looks like he could be trouble. Don't you let him sweet talk you into anything without a license. Tell him you ain't no used car. Let him know you have to see some real commitment first."

Because Dax was sitting right next to me, I could only murmur, "Uh, huh," before saying my farewells and ending the call.

I explained to Tex and Dax about Sofronia's death.

"Did the doc say it was swamp fever?" Tex wanted to know.

I could see the question behind his query.

Had Madame somehow caused the old woman's death?

Unfortunately, there was no way to be certain. The slight chill I felt did not disappear as quickly as the thought of zombies.

* * *

Tex and I shook hands inside his cab when we arrived back at the Lafitte. "Next time you're in N'awlins, look me up." He grinned. "But not if you're planning on getting us kidnapped again. I've had enough scrapes to last me till the cows start wearing Beef Burger ads draped all over their hides."

That's when Dax took my arm possessively and said, "The next time Kaytie is anywhere near the slightest hint of danger, I plan to be there to keep her safe."

He didn't know it, but he was the danger, already near me.

* * *

I called the airport to catch an earlier flight back to Chicago and was planning to leave that afternoon, so I excused myself to pack. Dax had to visit Mike's Crescent City bookstore on Chartres St. He was looking for a book on the famed witch queen of New Orleans, Marie Laveau, hoping to find further parallels between her life and the Chevalier sisters, who were apparently both dead.

I saw that he wasn't going to just "let the police figure out" the third Madame's identity. He was a reporter onto a story.

Let him have that one, I thought. I only wanted to go home.

I'd just changed into a comfortable pair of traveling slacks and a green silk blouse when Dax rang my room. "Kaytie, can you meet me outside the hotel. I have something important to show you."

"Sure, I'll be right there."

Without giving his request a second thought, I sprinted down the stairway, through the lobby and out the double doors, glancing right and left for Dax.

This time the thug did not use chloroform.

"You will come with me," said Bad Leroy, "if you want to see your boyfriend alive again."

I stood there, paralyzed by this unexpected threat, my mind in momentary shock.

Leroy grabbed my arm and escorted me to a van waiting at the curb.

The van was sinister, its darkened windows hiding the interior from view. Pirate Leroy allowed me to sit in the front passenger's seat. He didn't bother restraining me in any way.

The back seat was unoccupied. I had half expected to see Dax.

Where was he?

Darn!

Had I allowed myself to walk into a trap without substance? Was Dax even now sitting safely in the hotel lounge sipping a mint julep? Had I stupidly climbed aboard for yet another encounter with madness?

"What the devil is going on?" I demanded as Pirate Leroy climbed behind the wheel. "Madame has her precious book! You don't need me anymore."

He remained impassive, starting the motor and pulling away from the hotel.

"What have you done with Dax?" I continued, my heart pounding with anger and tension.

Leroy didn't bother to answer. He drove in silence, quickly winding the van through the busy French Quarter, then following lesser-traveled streets and heading out of the city. I expected to be taken back into the swamps, but it soon became evident that we were on Airport Road heading toward Reserve, Louisiana. We arrived at St. John Aviation LLC, an FBO landing strip. I could see the hangar and a few small planes.

A Blue Star charter King Air Turbo Prop sat on the runway. The pounding of my heart slowed and my hands no longer trembled.

Were we meeting somebody on the plane? My mind whirled with possibilities. None of them made sense.

Leroy pulled onto the tarmac, parked the van and exited, shoving me toward the plane. He pushed me up the steps and through the entry portal where I was greeted by Madame Chevalier herself.

A very stricken-looking Dax was seated in the small cabin which could accommodate up to six people, however the other seats were empty. I was surprised to see Leroy climb into the pilot's seat and don a pair of headphones. Madame took the copilot's seat after shoving me down beside Dax and ordering us to buckle up.

Moments later we were airborne. I turned to Dax.

"Do you have any idea what's going on? Where we're going?"

He shook his head. "I was walking back from the bookstore when he grabbed me. Before I could stop him, he injected me with something and ordered me to call you to get you out of the hotel. Some other goon drove me here and shoved me aboard."

Injected him! I turned toward him in horror.

Were they making a zombie of him too with their evil concoction? His face was unchanged. No glassiness in the eyes. No apparent stiffness or immobility of features.

That's when Madame turned toward us.

"He's healthy enough...for the time being," she announced. "But he's not going to stay healthy if you don't cooperate"

"What do you mean?" I asked. "What did you do to him?"

"Merely a little poison, the same one my dear departed Emerald used on me before her untimely death. Probably the same thing Emerald used on Sapphire years ago. Poor Sapphire never knew what made her sick. She died thinking she had swamp fever."

Madame's honeyed voice again interrupted my whirling thoughts.

"You see, ma petite, I have injected your Mr. Larue with a slow-acting, but very deadly poison."

She saw the look of horror on our faces and rushed to assure us. "Don't worry. I have learned the ingredients for the antidote. They be written down in Magnolia's book which you turned over to me in time. You see, my friends, my dear sister Emerald also injected me! Yes, on the very night you arrived at the Lafitte. That little betrayal cost Emerald her life. Now we must go to Haiti for the antidote, or both of us will die."

She hesitated a moment, then announced in the imperious voice she used for heightened drama, "You will reverse the curse of your church so we can safely take the elixir!"

For once, I didn't feel like smarting off with a frankly-Madame comment. Dax and I sat there in stupefied silence for a moment, each trying to absorb what we had just heard. Finally Dax spoke.

"What if we don't find all the ingredients for the antidote? How long do we have? I mean before the poison kills us?

"Two days. Maybe three."

Calculating from the date of my first arrival in New Orleans, I noted that Madame had already used up nearly three weeks of life since her supposedly fatal injection. If the same stuff had been administered to Dax, why wouldn't he have at least that long to live? Maybe she had given him a stronger dose of the poison.

No wonder the forbidden book had become so desperately important to the voodoo priestess. It was not just ancient secrets she wanted. It had become a matter of life and death.

Her life.

And now Dax's too unless they could find the antidote.

I came back to the maddening question of her identity. Sapphire was long dead and buried, evidently poisoned by her twin sister, Emerald Chevalier. Now we were hearing that Emerald was also dead, shot to death in my hotel room.

If both sisters were already dead, then who was *this* Madame Chevalier we had been dealing with all along?

"Dax, did the parish birth and death records show there was ever a *third* Chevalier sister?" I whispered.

"No. But then I wasn't looking for another member of the family. Who the heck is this woman?"

His words echoed my thoughts.

"I have no idea, but whoever she is, she believes she needs my prayers to make certain she lives."

"Yeah. Well, while you're making certain, I hope you can keep me breathing awhile longer too," Dax gave me a weak grin.

Reversing the curse by prayer? Could I do that? Would it stop the toxins from their deadly work?

I was no expert on Haitian poisons. Still from what I knew about Haiti, we were headed for the right place. Those people should be experts at poison-damage control.

I groaned, thinking the flight to Port-au-Prince might take several hours in this small plane.

"You've been to Haiti. Tell me something about it," I said, hoping to take Dax's mind off the poison slowly working in his veins.

"Any other time, I'd love taking a trip to the Caribbean with a beautiful woman like you. But I probably wouldn't choose the island of Hispaniola." His features expressed regret. "Sadly, *La Perle Des Antilles*, is no longer the sparkling jewel that it was in old Chris' Columbo's day."

I already knew that, but I wanted to keep him talking.

"It had to be a beautiful island to be named Pearl of the Caribbean. That sounds so lovely."

He nodded. "Must have been. It's a mountainous island and probably sparkled like an emerald, green in the sun, a beckoning oasis to sailors with land-starved eyes. No more. Not today. The mountains have been denuded of greenery, and the island's people are steeped in extreme poverty."

"Why is that?"

"The Indian tribe known as the Taino originally lived on the island, but today's population of some 8.3 million are predominantly African, their ancestors brought over on slave ships—slaves who created a Creole society with *Vodou* as their predominant religion.

He knew his history alright. I listened with pretended interest, thinking that as long as his mind was on history, he wasn't thinking of the poison in his veins, but I couldn't help thinking of it, while he talked.

How much damage had it done already? How could we be sure Madame was telling the truth? Even if we did find the antidote, how could we know she would allow him to use it? Once again I was at her mercy. Without me she believed she couldn't have opened the chest. Now, without my prayers to reverse the second curse, she believed she would not be able to practice the shaman's sorceries.

"You probably know that Haiti went through many a bloody battle during the slave revolution against their French colonial masters until it became the first black republic of the world in 1804."

Keep it up Dax, I coaxed silently, then asked, "They won their freedom. Then what?"

"The people haven't done much to advance their nation. It's become the third poorest country in the western hemisphere. In other words, it's not big on the list of islands to visit for a luxury vacation."

I agreed. I'd much rather go to the North Pole than visit Haiti at the moment.

Thinking that hours of precious time would be used up for the flight, I glanced at Dax again for any signs of deterioration.

What would be the first symptom?

Without thinking, I blurted to Madame, "What does this poison do to you?"

She turned to look back at me, sending her snaky braids flying.

"Weight loss. Thirst. Then fever. Sometimes seizures and hallucinations. The final symptoms can last for days…or mere hours. Your boyfriend won't be so pretty when his skin yellows and his eyes pop out."

I saw the determined glint in her eyes. She wanted me to know the grisly details. Wanted to make sure I would undo the binding on the book as a result of my prayers.

What a way to take Dax's mind off the poison in his system. *Right on, Kaytie, get a list of terrible symptoms. That should make him feel a whole lot better.*

Madame removed a kerchief from a bag on her expansive lap and wiped perspiration from her brow. The plane's small, pressurized cabin was air-conditioned and very cool. Dax did not appear to be perspiring. Madame, however, continued to wipe her brow repeatedly.

"What kind of ingredients are we looking for?" I wanted to know.

She answered in a single word. "Frogs."

"Frogs? Aren't there plenty of frogs in the bayou?" Dax asked, eyebrows rising inquisitively.

Madame answered rather patiently. "The marine toads be already mature in the bayous. We need a young frog. Or even its eggs."

She grunted and turned her back on us once more. With a wave of her hand and the word, "Enough," she dismissed further conversation.

Dax turned to me, his tone quieted, "She probably needs a hyla tree frog, a *Bufo marinus*. They're native to the Caribbean and only breed from April to September. It takes forty-five to fifty days for their eggs to metamorphose from tads to frogs. I doubt we'll have trouble finding one. They're noisy. An adult male makes a sound like a tractor's engine. And they're big. Full grown, they can measure from six to nine inches."

Impressed, I remarked, "You didn't learn all that in high school biology."

"No, I learned it from a member of the Bizango Society in Haiti. They're a branch of the Maroons, a sect dating back to the 1640s. In order to escape French socialization, they formed secret bands to keep their ancient African roots alive and followed the tradition of controlling their members by using certain poisons and potions. If anyone has the antidote to this poison in my blood, the Bizangos will."

He seemed confident enough, but I was not so reassured. Here I was, a kidnapped victim once more, going on a frog hunt on the island of Haiti.

How difficult was that going to be?

Here, froggie, froggie. A big frog might be easy enough to find, but how about its eggs?

Then again, maybe we'd just visit the local voodoo market and ask for a nice supply. I pictured us presenting our shopping list: *an ounce or two of powdered human bones and a few dozen hyla frog eggs please.*

The shopkeeper's reply: *Coming right up. Would you like the eggs scrambled or poached?*

* * *

When we landed in Port-au-Prince, I'd been sleeping for what seemed hours, my head lolled against Dax's shoulder. He must have been sleeping too, because he yawned and stretched as we prepared to exit the plane.

"Aren't you nervous?"

I couldn't help thinking I would be jumping out of my skin if I were the one injected with a fatal toxin.

"Look at it this way. We're getting a free trip to Haiti. We might as well relax and enjoy it." He grinned charmingly, but I could see tension lines around his eyes.

We climbed out on the tarmac in extreme heat. There were colorful sun-bleached umbrellas everywhere, straw hats, beaded braids and battered old vehicles heaped with people standing shoulder to shoulder in the truck beds. The aging French colonial buildings were still attractive, but run down. Other structures were covered with graffiti. The smell of an open-air fish market filled my nostrils, along with unpleasant cooking odors.

Women carried huge bundles on their backs or atop their heads and men led donkeys heaped with bundles. Children passed by, their tiny faces pinched, expressions serious. Ninety percent of Haitians speak French and Creole, so I wasn't surprised at the mix of languages I heard from the throngs.

No white sandy beaches lined the shores, but palm trees waved graceful fronds in the occasional breeze. From every vantage point, I could see mountains, their peaks covered by rain clouds. Most had been denuded of greenery due to the deforestation of the hills, but there were a few green peaks remaining.

Madame made quick inquiries of the natives. With the right amount of cash, one fellow told her of a very feared and powerful Bizango sorceress living on the side of a mountain. I heard the words, *"Montagne Terrible."*

We soon hired a produce-truck driver to take us toward the mountain on a poorly paved road. Dax and I climbed into the truck bed and sat among the vegetables, while Madame and Leroy took seats in the cab. We bumped along, passing hovels with clotheslines strung over mud holes and naked babies running about.

Buckled pavement quickly gave way to chug-holes and rutted dirt lanes. The island appeared to be covered only by desert scrub, but in the swampy areas where mangroves grew, I glimpsed flamingos and caiman.

We passed coffee and cacao trees and then began climbing. Higher up on the mountain was what appeared to be a forest of pine trees above us. I spotted a wooden cross through the undergrowth, a chilling sight because on top of the horizontal beam sat a human skull.

Dax nodded toward it and explained.

"Even though the Creole religion is *Vodou,* or voodoo as we say, they have incorporated some aspects of Catholicism. The skull represents their ancestors. Snakes represent wisdom."

I thought back to the snake used in the voodoo ceremony I'd witnessed at the fire ring.

Wisdom?

How did such a repulsive creature come to represent wisdom?

Then making a connection, I recalled the serpent in Eden promising knowledge of good and evil. The same ancient symbol still represented wisdom for the voodoo followers.

I didn't speak of it. This was not the time to get into a Bible discussion with Dax.

Instead I asked, "What's the voodoo religion all about? I mean besides controlling people with poisons and spells?"

I had always considered it a superstitious set of beliefs, but I wanted to keep Dax talking.

"It's rooted in ancient traditions. I interviewed a New Orleans gal once, Sallie Ann Glassman. She was initiated here on the island as a voodoo priestess in 1995 before she went to New Orleans. Sallie believes that voodoo helps you escape self-imposed boundaries into a world of infinite possibilities."

He made a gesture with his hands that indicated all inclusiveness. "Members communicate with spirits of their dead ancestors. That's why they accept the Catholic faith is so easily. Prayer to the dead saints, as they see it, is something they've always practiced."

Dax turned to me with a slightly bemused expression. "I know what you're thinking. Your Bible tells you that communication with spirits is wrong."

I nodded, frowning. He'd brought it up. I hadn't intended to.

"There is only *one* Spirit for believers to communicate with, but many spiritual gifts for believers. Think about that for minute, Dax. Why would you want information from any other source than the ultimate Truth?"

I wanted to add besides that, there's no place in the Bible that says the spirits of the dead are allowed any contact with the living. In fact just the opposite.

It's forbidden. Yes, angels can bring messages from God to believers. But it's the Holy Spirit—not ancestral spirits—who is to indwell believers, to lead us and teach us. All other sources are labeled as deceiving spirits. However, I sensed Dax wouldn't listen.

He said nothing in response to my argument about hearing from the source of all truth, so I asked, "Do *Vodou* followers believe in a god?"

"They do. They call him *Bon Dieu.* But he's not really a personality. They see him more like a vast, abstract energy, so far beyond humankind that he's unapproachable. Voodoo followers have hundreds of intermediary ancestral spirits called the *Iwa*--the ghosts of the dead. They call on the *Iwa* for guidance."

"I've always wondered, just because someone dies, why does that make him Mister Superior Advisor? Why would he know anything more than when he was alive? Does death suddenly increase his IQ points?"

Dax looked out at the rain clouds hanging above the lush green peak ahead. "Ancestral spirits are supposed to offer greater guidance because they've already passed through the veil, so to speak. They're on the other side of life."

The other side of life. Even the most ancient civilizations were aware that there is an "other side." I thought of how the pyramids of Egypt stand as monuments to that insight. The essence of our being does not end with the death of the body.

People are created with an awareness that there is more to existence than just what we can observe through our senses.

That awareness must be God calling us to Himself.

Thinking of the extreme poverty I'd seen on the island, I remarked, "From the looks of these peoples' lives, it doesn't appear that their *Iwa* give very good advice. I think it wouldn't take me long to find another religion. Especially if I had to carry eighty-pound jars around on my head, followed by a dozen hungry youngsters, while my man was sitting somewhere sticking pins in dolls." I muttered this thought half to myself.

Dax chuckled.

"Do these people actually stick pins in dolls?"

He shrugged. "People in New Orleans do. At least that's what Sallie said."

I thought back to that macabre scene at the fire ring in the bayou. A couple of the celebrants had looked to me like they were having seizures.

"Did this Sallie woman say the worshippers could become possessed by their ancestral spirit guides?"

He nodded. "She did say that those who work with spirits may open themselves up to possession. She didn't think of this as a bad thing."

I wrinkled my nose. "Who wants to be possessed by his grandpa? Who needs advice from an ancestor who's never even heard of the stock market, or the Internet, or pantyhose?"

Dax steadied himself as the old truck dipped and lurched.

"Sallie told me there's a spirit called Erzulie Freda. She makes you see a world of beauty. Then there's the *Oggun*. He's a warrior and if you get possessed by him, you see the world as a battlefield."

"That's easy enough without being possessed. Just watch the nightly news. You'll see the world as a battlefield alright. On the other hand, it's plain to see that anyone living in these depressing hovels would want to zone out with a spirit who shows you a beautiful world. Of course Americans use drugs to find that world. Do you know of any good things Sallie has done for her followers?"

"I'm sure they can point to examples. She held a voodoo ritual to change the path of the killer storm when Katrina came barreling over the land."

"Didn't work, did it?" I harrumphed.

"Well actually it did veer slightly from the path it was on, so I'm told."

The truck shifted down and came to a groaning halt. Now what? Everyone climbed out. The trunk of a rotting tree had been dragged across the ruts. It was obvious that the road ahead had become impassable. The two lanes merged into a single footpath, a trail that wound upwards into the pine trees.

Madame began the climb, huffing and puffing, sweating profusely, followed by Dax, then me, and Leroy bringing up the rear. He carried a backpack with several bottles of water and doled it out to us every ten minutes or so. I soon realized the wisdom of that after the exertion of hiking in the tropical heat.

Eventually we stopped to rest in a shaded area, and I looked back to see that we'd actually climbed higher than I thought. The island was spread out below us in a patchwork of earthy colors, surrounded by the wrinkled sea.

It was beautiful from above the filth and squalor, but I didn't feel like singing about climbing every mountain. Nobody bothered to speak. We needed every breath.

Pirate Man Leroy broke out the water bottles and allowed us a few sips. Madame guzzled her entire bottle. She looked ghastly, her skin mottled instead of the *café-au-lait* color. I noticed a peculiar shadow on her lower jaws and the whites of her eyes had turned a sickly yellow.

Wondering if the poison was working in her body past the point of no return, I stole a quick glance at Dax. He looked healthy enough for someone who had just spent most of the night on a plane and then hiked up a mountain in the Haitian sun with poison working through his body. If Madame's calculations were right, they each had only a few days to live. Maybe hours.

That thought sent a momentary flow of ice water through my veins, in spite of the heat. The sensation left as quickly as it came, and again the heat on my skin made me feel as if I were immersed in a skillet of grease hot enough to blacken fish filets. I wondered how Madame and Dax could stand it. However, the temperature was becoming less humid as we climbed higher, providing some relief.

"We go now," said the big woman, who seemed to dwindle in size before my eyes. She was definitely three sizes smaller today. If only her poison could be marketed as a diet formula, she would make millions. Oprah Winfrey, or Kirstie Allie could market it as the end-all diet.

Of course, without the antidote, you really would be ending it all. That little problem might make it somewhat difficult to get approval from the FDA.

Maybe. Maybe not. There's big money in the weight-loss industry, and people have been known to risk their lives to lose pounds.

We hiked again, even higher. I was amazed at Madame's stamina, breathing heavily but plodding relentlessly for three hours more, moving up the path which grew ever steeper and rockier. The area did not seem right somehow for enticing passionate frogs to produce little tadpoles. Yes, there were tumbling streams from time to time, but no lily pads. Still, I supposed Madame knew where to go. After all, her life was on the line.

When the setting sun blazed crimson across the waters beneath us, turning the ocean to scarlet flames, Madame called another halt. "We rest."

I dropped gratefully to the ground, my knees quivering.

Dax plopped beside me. Pirate Leroy and the witch merely leaned against a tree. Moments later the sun dipped into the crimson tide and the land became dark, almost instantaneously. I sensed a spiritual darkness over the island, deeper than the natural shades of night.

Could Dax feel it too? I glanced at him. His eyes were closed.

"Are you feeling okay?" I asked, noticing a pinched look around his eyes and mouth.

His half-grin was born of bravery rather than mirth. He gulped the remaining water from the bottle, unaware that I had given him my portion too.

Madame grunted. "Not far now. We go."

Leroy pulled a high-powered flashlight from his back pack and pushed ahead on the narrow trail.

I groaned, but managed to haul myself up and concentrate on lifting one foot at a time. Every muscle in my body screamed for relief.

Dax followed more slowly. At times, Madame had to shove him along ahead of her. The woman's stamina was impressive. How long could she keep this up?

We hiked perhaps another hour in the dark when a light appeared in the trees ahead of us and soon we approached a small cabin built of loosely piled stones and wooden logs. Hanging in a tree nearby was a human skull. Voodoo symbols served as warnings to passersby. This was no place to stop for a friendly cup of coffee.

Before we arrived at the low-set wooden door, it opened and a slender woman stood watching us, backlit by lamp light from within. She did not offer a greeting, just lifted her hand in a gesture that meant *halt.*

We stopped and stood there staring at her while she sized us up. After a few moments of total silence, she spoke.

"You are here for potions." The tone of her voice was a statement of fact rather than a question.

Madame nodded. "I have the ingredients written here." She produced a folded piece of paper handed to her from Bad Leroy.

The woman did not bother to look at it, but she lowered her hand.

"I am Darcantel Cagliostro. You risk dealing with me?"

The question implied a threat.

Where had I heard that name before? Darcantel was…was the name of the slave woman who'd birthed the infamous Marie Laveau. And Cagliostro was the name of Marie's legendary lover.

Had this woman assumed those names because of their notoriety, or was she an actual descendant of one of them?

Nobody spoke. Madame Chevalier moved a hand to her throat where the obsidian pendant's ruby eyes gleamed in the night. Darcantel glanced at the medallion. Perhaps she recognized it as a symbol of status, identifying the voodoo woman standing before her, because she stepped back. She peered at the lot of us.

"Enter." She stated the word in a tone of command rather than hospitality.

Nothing about her countenance was welcoming, or the least hospitable. Instead her carriage was like that of a perturbed queen condescending to lowly subjects.

We filed through the narrow doorway into the shack.

I didn't expect the same exotic colors and enchanting appeal of Madame's bayou cabin, and I wasn't surprised. The place was anything but charming. Candles of black wax and lanterns provided the only light in the room, revealing rough plank flooring, a low bench table and a straw pallet. From pegs on the walls hung various plants and even small animal carcasses. The ceiling also was filled with drying herbs and roots suspended from strings tied over the rafters. Pungent odors filled the air.

In cages and glass jars on the floor were small creatures, frogs, a snake, rabbits, field mice and birds. Stacked on a crude shelf along the length of one wall were jars filled with various substances, sinister liquids in hues of toad green, bird's egg blue and blood red, as well as powders and grains.

The woman had a veritable pharmacopoeia of herbal remedies—or poisons—stockpiled in the cabin.

"Sit," she commanded.

Madame chose the bench seat at the table. Dax and I plopped gratefully down on the rough floor. Pirate Leroy leaned against the cabin wall.

For a moment, all I could do was stare at the exotic woman before me. Her dark beauty was both sensuous and sinister. Her eyes, blacker than the deepest cave, glittered with forbidden knowledge. Finely braided ropes of dark hair fell in a thick curtain to her narrow waist. She wore a flowing gown of some rough fabric, dyed canary yellow, draped over one shoulder and tied at the waist with a rope of orange beads.

Yellow and orange beads had been woven into the braids. Gold bands circled her upper arms. Multiple bracelets jangled around her left wrist and a bright orange fabric had been tied around the right hand. She might be a queen of black arts, but the woman obviously liked bright colors.

I could see little evidence of African or mulatto ancestry. Her finely sculpted exotic features might have been Egyptian, or even Western Indian. She did not bother to look at me or Dax. Locking eyes with Madame, she appeared to be sizing her up.

"You not be female," she declared suddenly.

"That is correct!" Madame exclaimed in a pleased voice. "I am no female. You be as skillful as they say."

That declaration drew my full attention.

Madame, not a female?

A man?

Here was a completely unexpected turn. How long had he passed himself off as a woman? Did his followers suspect his true identity? Questions swirled in my mind. Stealing a quick glance at Leroy, I saw no hint of surprise registered on his stony face. He *knew* his boss was a man. Apparently he'd known it all along.

It was then I recognized the shadow on the lower half of Chevalier's face for what it was. A beard! He had not been able to shave since we'd left New Orleans.

"Comment vous appellez-vous?" Darcantel resorted to French to ask our captor's name.

The man known to me as Madame Chevalier replied, "*Je m'appelle* Onyx Chevalier, the only living descendant of Magnolia from the New Orleans O'Brien plantation."

Some place in my startled mind guessed that Chevalier must be the *brother* of the deceased Chevalier twins.

Darcantel spoke disdainfully. "I don't know of your ancestress, dis Magnolia."

"Ah, but you know of Marie Laveau." He spoke the name in a velvet tone, implying that he knew she would be impressed.

"Marie Laveau!" Darcantel's voice whispered with a kind of awe. She peered more intently into the she-male's eyes.

He'd definitely struck a chord.

"Magnolia was Marie's apprentice," Chevalier began calmly. "Magnolia came to Haiti on the slave ship. Then later she be sold to the owner of a sugar plantation in New Orleans. She went to Marie Laveau's gatherings in Congo Square and became her secret apprentice. She learned from Marie, powerful spells, so she could be set free."

Darcantel listened passively. Her eyes glittered but her expression remained unchanged.

With a tilt of his chin toward the ceiling, Chevalier repeated, "I am Magnolia's only living descendant."

The Bizango woman's eyes blazed with the fire of excitement.

"What is that to me?" she said coolly and inclined her head upward, giving her the appearance of looking down her patrician nose at a servant.

Chevalier paused, then declared in a most dramatic voice, "Marie Laveau is my *Iwa.*"

Darcantel remained passive, appearing unimpressed, however something in her posture shifted. She studied the she-male in silence for a moment before assuming a posture of fierce defiance.

"The *Iwa* be no slave in Haiti. We be free!" She spat out the words with determination.

Slowly her expression changed to one of intense curiosity.

"Your *loa* is Marie. She is your spirit guide? You channel her messages?"

Chevalier nodded slowly, a gleam of triumph in his eyes.

"*Oui!* I channel her messages. I know her arts. Her secrets!"

These last declarations were uttered with a kind of jubilance, a secretive glee filled with a seductive promise. It was plain to see he had something of value to the sorceress of Terrible Mountain.

Glancing at the list in her hand, the dark beauty's eyes narrowed, then widened.

"You have poison in your blood." It was a statement, rather than a question. Evidently she recognized the ingredients as the antidote.

Chevalier nodded, swiping one hand across his perspiring brow. The time had come for striking the bargain.

"What will you give me?" she asked, her face an unreadable mask, both beautiful and terrible.

Ah yes, the fee. Like most physicians, the witch wanted payment up front. I doubted that she would honor a medical insurance card.

Chevalier motioned to Leroy who produced a drawstring purse. Darcantel reached for it and emptied it out on the plank table. Gold coins dropped into a heap.

I wasn't surprised. I half imagined they were pirate's gold from Leroy's evil treasures. She did not bother counting them.

"Unnh." It was a snort of disgust followed by a question. "I have no need of that. You have more?"

At first I thought she wanted more coins. She peered intently at Chevalier once again. Then stepping forward with an in-your-face manner, she repeated in a conclusive tone, "You have more."

That's when I realized she wanted something other than the valuable golden coins.

Chevalier looked at her with resignation.

"I have Magnolia's book. The secret spells from the most powerful *mundunugu* of Africa be written there."

"Dis I have already," Darcantel announced impatiently. "What else?"

She was driving a hard bargain. The she-male paused and again, a knowing look glittered in his eyes. Then he whispered seductively, "I have the secret of eternal youth!"

So that was it.

I realized it wasn't merely riches or more powerful black arts. The three Chevalier siblings had actually believed they could find immortality in the ancient *mundunugu's* volume. Emerald Chevalier had been willing to kill her siblings for it. Now the brother must share this ancient knowledge with the Bizango sorceress in order to get the antidote, or he would also die.

What would sharing the secret mean to him? Would the distance between Darcantel and him be great enough to diffuse their competition for secret power?

It had not been enough for Cagliostro. He had traveled from Haiti to New Orleans to kill Laveau rather than compete with a priestess whose powers exceeded his own. Instead, he'd become her lover and shared his dark sorcery with her.

The power of seduction had been greater than witchcraft.

Or had it been a combination of both that had diffused Cagliotro's dark ambition?

Now once again a powerful priest and a priestess of an ancient and dark religion were facing each other. While Darcantel was at least as beautiful as Marie had been, it was doubtful that she would find Chevalier's obese form the least bit attractive. This time history would not repeat itself.

I watched in fascination as a flame of desire lit up Darcantel's eyes. "I will see dis book."

Chapter 11

Darcantel

Pirate Leroy was already drawing the leather-bound volume out of his backpack. He glanced at Chevalier, then handed it over to the dark-eyed sorceress.

She nodded and held it against her breast, closed her eyes and breathed in slowly. We waited, watching her for a reaction.

Maybe witches don't need to read? Maybe they just absorb the information through their skin and nostrils, I theorized, my imagination fired by the powerful presence of the two *vouduns.*

There was an overwhelming sense of the presence of dark spirits swirling in the confines of the cabin. I could almost hear the triumphant shrieking of demonic forces somewhere inside my head. Very real fingers of fear clutched around my heart. For a moment, I couldn't catch my breath. It was a repeat of the same terror I had experienced at Count Ribaldo's ceremony.

A still, small voice rose up from deep within my spirit, "Greater is He that is in you than he that is in the world."

The words calmed me, relieving the overwhelming fear which I recognized as more than natural anxiety. It had been an assault on my soul, and I had no way to combat it except by the sword of the Spirit, which is the word of God. Thankfully, I had taken the time to put those words in my heart so they could return to me at this critical hour.

After a long moment, Darcantel opened her eyes once more with a look of exasperation.

"The spirit of dis book be bound," she stated simply.

I recognized her ability to perceive beyond the immediate physical evidence. I once had this same ability myself before I asked Jesus to be Lord of my life. I'd always been able to pick up information from an aura surrounding others. My paranormal perceptions had once been very real, but I never saw anything good in a person's life.

It was only after my baptism that I realized the gift for what it was, a counterfeit of the spiritual gift of discernment.

How glad I was to be free of it.

No one knows the horror of seeing only darkness ahead in another's life. As a believer, I'd learned the joy of knowing that, through prayer to the Father, evil is overcome by good.

"Dis book be bound," the witch repeated accusatively.

That's when Madame-Monsieur Chevalier turned and pointed his stubby finger directly at me.

Everyone's eyes turned toward me. It was obvious they expected me to do something. I didn't know what to say. My silent prayers went up for help.

Darcantel glided across the room, her movement fluid, sinuous. The thought of a serpent crossed my mind. She peered into my eyes with a penetrating look that might have stripped away my remaining confidence, but the verse, "Greater is He that is within you," rose up even stronger from within my spirit.

A moment later, slightly puzzled, Darcantel glanced away and turned toward Dax, peering at his face closely and uttering some unintelligible words, ending with the observation, "Him be dying too."

Then suddenly looking back at me, she asked, "What will you do to save him?"

She perceived at once that I was the key.

Here it was. The moment of decision. They expected me to pray aloud that God would not bring any curses on the one who chose to practice the spells in the book. Chevalier must hear that prayer before he dared to take the antidote written there.

Should I really ask God to unbind the curse from it? It was either that or let Dax die a horrible, agonizing death.

I could pray, but would God hear? How could I ask Him to unleash forbidden knowledge, a most evil sorcery, into the world and then expect His blessings?

Help me, Lord, I prayed again silently. *I don't know what to do.*

He who confesses not that Jesus is Lord come in the flesh is under a curse already.

I heard these words in my spirit.

What a sudden revelation!

I didn't have to fear what would happen.

The voodoo priest and priestess had already cursed themselves by their own choice to worship false gods, regardless of what spells they practiced in order to control and manipulate their world. The evil they might do was already in the world—had been in the world since the most ancient time. And it too was already defeated.

Relief flooded my soul, followed by confidence, a spiritual boldness.

"Alright, everyone. Bow your heads and I will pray to the Lord to remove the curse."

Leroy and Dax slowly bowed their heads. Onyx Chevalier did not. Darcantel stood with chin held high.

"Darcantel bows to no one," she stated haughtily.

"You *will* bow your head or leave the room," I answered her, my voice filled with sudden authority.

She blinked, then moved slowly across the room, pausing at the doorway. I sensed that it galled her to give in even this much to my demand. The man known to me as Madame Chevalier followed her, muttering to Leroy, "See that she reverses the curse on the book."

They would not bow their heads to my Lord, but they would bow their knees one final day, of that I was certain.

When they were out the door, I looked at Leroy and saw him for what he was, a pathetic man with false hope. Perhaps he thought that he was going to be cured of some unknown illness. Maybe he believed in voodoo power, but more likely he believed in Chevalier's promise to furnish him with the power of wealth. Likely he would not deny the reality of God, but that had little impact on his life. Like so many believers, Leroy was far more passionate about serving himself than serving his Creator.

I knew that Dax was not yet a Christian, but he also did not doubt the existence of a Supreme Being. The two people left in the cabin with me were hardly what I would call prayer warriors. Still, they weren't completely doubtful.

Dax, "Will you believe with me?"

I needed the support of agreement in prayer. This was a dark battle I faced, and the Dark Side was far more real than any *Star Wars* fan could possibly imagine. Once again I sensed the presence of evil, less potent than before but still swirling like storm-tossed clouds, dark shadows in the room.

Maybe he didn't know what I was asking, but Dax nodded his head. His future uncertain, he might have been willing to do whatever it took to save his life, but I hoped he had also heard some of my words during our talk of spiritual matters. Those words were seeds filled with the power to take root in the good soil of his heart.

Okay, I thought. *This is it. Jesus, I need you. Send your angels.*

I began to pray.

"Father, in the name of Jesus and by the power of His righteous blood, I come to You. I ask You to look upon that atoning blood and not my own unworthiness. In that name above all names, let the harm in the spell book be sent into outer darkness. Let the curses without cause be reversed and rendered harmless. I pray that blinders be removed from the eyes of those who are spiritually deceived and that they shall come to know the Truth that sets them free."

I waited a moment, and hearing no words rising up from within my spirit, I added simply, "Let the lies be bound and the Truth be loosed. Amen."

It was a prayer based on what I believed God could honor. Not exactly a freeing of the curse on evil. Not a prayer for granting voodoo practitioners complete liberty without consequences, but Bad Leroy heard what he wanted to hear. The word *reversed.* Evidently he was satisfied because he nodded his head.

Instant relief? Light overcoming the darkness? Not immediately.

I had to believe without seeing. The flooding of peace and joy was not the same as when I had spoken the Lord's name during Chevalier's attempt to hypnotize me. The room did not instantly fill with spiritual light. But there was a definite shift in the atmosphere.

The darkness lifted slightly, yet I remained aware of its hovering presence. I silently offered thanks to God that Light would overcome the darkness. Slowly, peace beyond understanding began to fill my spirit, driving out all remaining fear.

Leroy went to the door to retrieve the beautiful witch and odious wizard with a brief nod, indicating their purpose had been accomplished.

Darcantel re-entered the mountain cabin with the grace of a panther, her proud head held high. She strode to the book and clutched it once again to her breast, eyes closed, breathing slowly, seeming to inhale its very essence. The she-male, Onyx Chevalier, followed her inside, intently watching her every move.

When she exhaled at last, her eyes flew open in an expression of glee. Then she opened the volume and rifled through its yellowed pages. A look of satisfaction settled on her exotic features.

Lifting Chevalier's notepad with the list of ingredients written on it, she nodded. "I will make the elixir to stop the poison."

It appeared a bargain had been struck, although the pair did not discuss any further terms of agreement. She paused, glancing first at Dax and then at Chevalier.

Pointing to Onyx, she spoke, "You will each take small amount. A second draught must be followed in two days. Not before."

Dax looked dumbfounded. Darcantel turned to him, repeating her instructions.

"The second dose will not be effective for forty-eight hours." She walked toward him, peering into his eyes with the air of a diagnostician. After a moment, she said simply, "That be almost time enough."

"Almost?"

Dax obviously did not like the sound of that. Neither did I.

Darcantel smiled for the first time, revealing a set of impossibly pointed, small white teeth, filed to vampirish points, giving her the look of a feline predator, savagely beautiful and dangerous.

"Will be very close, but with the first draught, you might survive."

Dax raised his eyebrows and sighed.

What option did he have? A hospital? It was unlikely that any doctor, even a Haitian doctor, could undo the damage in time.

The Bizango woman quickly pulled some herbs and roots from the walls. Next she turned to the animal cages where an unfortunate toad met a sudden end at the point of a wicked dagger.

While she mixed, pounded and stirred, she began a sing-song chant in a language unknown to me. Onyx Chevalier watched her hungrily, wiping sweat from his feverish brow.

Lifting a glass jar of liquid, she eyed the contents. "The ingredients must age. Color must turn scarlet red or will not work," she noted.

Pouring an amber liquid into the mixture, she watched with satisfaction as a slight chemical reaction caused a bubbling, fizzy effect much like baking soda might produce. Fumes escaped the brew.

I had never seen anything more like a witch's cauldron of double toil and trouble.

She placed the receptacle over a flaming candle and stirred as it heated, her face alight with an eager anticipation. The mixture bubbled and a peculiar scent filled the room.

Taking a wooden goblet from a shelf, she poured most of the steaming liquid into it and carefully set it down on the plank table in front of Chevalier.

"Drink," she ordered. "You will sleep." Darcantel indicated the straw mat on the floor.

Onyx eagerly lifted the brew and gulped its contents, gasped, clutched his throat and staggered toward the mat where he collapsed with a moan.

I shivered, wondering if he would ever rise up again. The look in Dax's eyes echoed my own doubts. There was little we could do if Darcantel wished to finish him off. Or the rest of us for that matter. We were completely at her mercy.

She poured the remainder of the brew into a second wooden goblet and turned to Dax. "Now you. Drink this first draught."

Dax reached for the goblet and eyed it skeptically. I knew he was thinking of the unknown ingredients. How did he know she was telling the truth? This could be a fatal concoction.

"Die if I do, or die if I don't?" He shrugged, weighing his options. "Okay, down the hatch."

Darcantel watched him swallow it to the last drop. She grunted with approval. I too watched him with intense anxiety, expecting him to react as Chevalier had. There did not appear to be any change in his demeanor.

"I will mix again." Darcantel spoke, then turned to her work and began mixing, stirring and chanting, soon pouring a second brew into a pair of small glass vials.

Addressing Dax, she stressed once more, "You must wait until the antidote is ready. It has to ferment in order to stop all the poison."

She emphasized the word *must.*

"How long will that take? I don't exactly have all the time in the world," Dax muttered, forgetting that she had already mentioned forty-eight hours.

"The first preparation has bought you some time. Maybe enough time. The second must ferment for two days."

"So I have to wait for two days before I can drink it?" Dax took the vial and studied the mustard yellow contents.

"You wait until the color turns ruby red. If you drink before the color is red as the blood of a goat..."

"Yes?" Dax waited for her to complete instructions. "What will happen?"

"You will die."

"Oh, is that all?" he muttered flippantly. "A slightly unpleasant side effect."

He placed the glass tube carefully inside a zippered pocket on his khaki shirt. Leroy placed the slightly larger vial containing Chevalier's repeat-dose inside his backpack.

By this time, Onyx Chevalier had slipped into a regular breathing pattern of sound sleep that soon became a heavy snore. I knew then he would recover.

Darcantel motioned for us to sit on the bench at the table with her.

"Dis book, he want to keep it. When he wakes he will take it with him. You copy down for me."

I glanced at what I had previously assumed was an ornamental wrap on the woman's wrist. It was actually a colorful bandage, stained by a small spot of blood, and I supposed the wound had rendered her unable to write legibly.

She handed over a quill and a bottle of ink. The last time I had used one of these things had been eons ago at Cajun Jack's fishing cabin. This time I wrote on paper instead of my hand, copying the words so laboriously printed long ago by the slave girl, Magnolia, in large, kindergarten letters. Many had originated in the *mundunugu's* dark mind and unknown language and were unrecognizable, but I copied the letters.

There were strange chants, spells for gaining favor, for controlling the weather and for attracting lovers. There were incantations for calling on the ancestral dead. I copied lists of ingredients for *gris gris* bags and prayers to *Dumballah* and *Oggun* for protection from evil. Chants for communing with the *loa* and for capturing the *ti bon ange,* that part of the soul that connects to the body, in order to leave it and fly away in spirit form. Poisons used to induce paralysis—to create a zombie. Rites for initiating priests and priestesses into the voodoo religion.

There were many other things too vile to speak of, including a sacrificial rite for allowing one to enjoy perpetual youth—the hope of Marie Laveau's followers. Her infamous name appeared in the pages from time to time along with notations of forbidden knowledge gleaned from the voodoo queen. At one point, the slave woman had written that Marie knew how to cure yellow fever with herbal remedies and had helped hundreds to recover from the disease, but the ingredients were not listed.

There was also an entry dated May 20, 1862, describing how Magnolia had passed out copies of the hated Yankee Major-General George Butler's portrait to New Orleans ladies of ill repute. These women had promptly placed his likeness inside the bottom of their tinkle pots. Magnolia indicated that "Butler the Beast" took umbrage at the insult and issued an order. She copied the edict word for word: "If any female by word, gesture, movement, or insult should show contempt for any officer or soldier of the United States, she shall be regarded and held liable to be treated as a woman of the town, plying her vocations."

Beside the name of Butler was an incantation in the African language, doubtless a curse upon the man. It was plain from Magnolia's notes that Butler was not a popular man in the occupied city.

I promised myself to look up the history of that period when I got back to Chicago, a city that now seemed very far from this remote and wicked place on *Montagne Terrible.*

Before morning, my eyes ached and my hand cramped. My soul felt polluted, contaminated by evil.

Priestly authority included wantonly erotic liberties. Little wonder that the AIDS epidemic had exploded throughout Haiti. Sexual promiscuity was promoted as part of their worship.

What a religion of fear, of controlling others to do your bidding through curse or threat. Of imposing your will on unsuspecting people instead of allowing them the freedom of choice. What good is love gained by deception, commanded, even demanded instead of earned?

Darcantel watched me, reading some of the pages from time to time and grunting with satisfaction. She appeared to have no need of sleep, unlike Dax, now quietly slumped over against the wall next to Leroy, who was loudly snoring, using his backpack as a pillow. When I reached the final page, I laid my head down on the table and closed my eyes.

* * *

The crow of a rooster wakened me. Light streamed through the chinks in the walls. The cabin apparently had no windows. Dax was seated at the table, sweating profusely. His eyes had taken on the same sickly yellowish cast I had seen in Chevalier's eyes only the day before.

Fear for his life flooded my being. Madame had said he would die within a few days of the injection. The complete antidote would not be ready for at least a day, a night and most of another day. Would the initial dose keep him alive long enough for the second preparation to become effective?

"There is water at the spring. Fill your bottles and go," Darcantel spoke to Leroy. He gathered his back pack and left the hovel.

Turning toward Dax, she examined his eyes.

"You will make it down the mountain," she predicted.

I hoped that didn't mean she expected him to die before he could take the second draught.

"Remember to wait until the mixture burns red as fire before you drink. Should turn in two days, maybe three."

* * *

Our hike down the mountain was much easier than climbing it had been. By midday we were over halfway down.

Dax looked positively ill, but he kept up a good pace. Onyx Chevalier fared much better. The yellowish cast to his eyes had turned almost completely white again. Heavy as he was, he managed to outpace even Leroy.

We stopped under the scant shade of scraggly pine trees to catch our breath.

"I don't want to guess what's in this vial." Dax shuddered, removing it from his zippered pocket to study its contents. It had turned from mustard yellow to muddy brown. He placed it carefully back inside and zipped the pocket. The next instant he was on the ground in the midst of a slight seizure.

"Dax!" I yelled, running to shove a stick between his teeth to prevent him from biting his tongue.

What if the witch had lied to us? What if she hadn't really mixed the antidote at all and Dax was dying? I had no way of knowing.

Chevalier watched him with eyes unblinking. The seizure passed quickly, Dax groaned and sat up.

The she-male spoke. "You will make it down the mountain. We go now."

I helped Dax up from the dirt, anxious to see that he had water. The tropical air grew more humid by the moment, and he would probably require even more fluid than normal because of the chemicals in his blood.

We started down again, following Chevalier and Leroy.

"Kaytie, my beauty, if I get out of this alive, I may just visit that church of yours," Dax said in a weak voice. "Say a little prayer for me?"

I nodded and prayed silently that he would do both. Some part of my tired mind registered great delight at his request.

* * *

By nightfall, we had caught a ride to Port-au-Prince. Leroy had re-fueled the plane and filed a flight plan with airport officials. They advised us to wait out a series of squalls before takeoff, so we sat on the runway.

Chevalier seemed disinterested in food, as did Dax, but I was famished. They had guzzled all the bottled water from the spring on the hike down and now were breaking out the supply left on board.

"Got any pretzels or peanuts?" I asked, my stomach growling.

Madame didn't bother to respond. Dax groaned.

Concerned, I asked him, "You okay?"

"I'm just thirsty. The thought of food makes me nauseous."

He had another night and day left before he could safely take the antidote. Chevalier had the same hours to wait, but he appeared to be faring better than Dax. My guess was that Dax's poison had been a far more concentrated dose.

"We go now," Chevalier muttered with a nod that sent his long braided ponytail swinging. "I have clients that cannot be kept waiting."

"We aren't cleared for takeoff," Leroy answered.

"We go now," the big man insisted.

I glanced nervously at the frequent lightning illuminating the low-hanging clouds.

"Hey look, if it's the New Orleans police you're worried about, we can just call them and tell them we're fine," I volunteered, remembering how we had warned Chevalier that we must arrive safely back at our hotel soon, or they'd come after her-him. I still had trouble thinking of Onyx as a male.

"We're not really in that big of a hurry," I offered lamely, thinking perhaps the threat was what motivated him to get into the air.

"We go NOW!" the big man ordered sternly. "There is no wind yet. We can get into the air safe enough. Besides, I have plans for you."

He glanced back at me with a look of pure malevolence.

I gulped, wishing I hadn't made my law-enforcement threat sound so serious on that night at his cabin in Rainy Bay Bayou. I had talked of police investigating Chevalier's clientele and reporting him to the IRS for tax evasion as well as other charges, remembering with a chill that now he had also confessed to murdering his sister, Emerald.

How could he ignore that one? He had plans for us alright. I didn't care to imagine what he might have in mind.

Dutifully, Leroy took the controls and eased the plane slowly forward. We could hear an urgent voice from the control tower speaking French and doubtless forbidding him to proceed.

I peered through the cabin's small windows. The runway looked empty. All other pilots were following orders to remain on the ground. Leroy flipped a switch on the control panel and the voices ceased abruptly. He continued to taxi the small plane toward a runway, already wet with rain.

I rolled my eyes at Dax. "Aren't we supposed to be waiting for the squall line to move out?"

He nodded. Beads of sweat glistened on his forehead.

Leroy prepared for takeoff. An airport vehicle with flashing red lights approached us rapidly from behind, but the plane continued to pick up speed.

I buckled my seatbelt and held on for a white-knuckle flight.

Liftoff was smooth enough. The plane climbed toward dark and dangerous skies thick with roiling clouds.

I didn't like the feel of it. Alarm sirens sounded in my head.

Lightning ripped through the clouds accompanied by gusts of wind.

We hit turbulence and the plane bucked and rolled sickeningly. Leroy donned his headphones and began trying to contact someone—Miami maybe? Or a weather report.

Dax looked too ill to be concerned, his face deathly pale in the brief flashes silvering the small interior.

Hold on, Dax, I silently urged. We had a long flight and hours ahead before he could safely take the antidote.

Leroy continued to climb higher, looking for a smoother ride.

We didn't find it.

Instead, there were stomach-churning dips, ear-popping dives and dizzying climbs, air pockets and downdrafts that would make a roller-coaster ride seem as gentle as a baby's rocking chair by comparison. The engine whined and strained. The entire fuselage shuddered.

When we finally hit smoother air, relief in the cabin was palpable. After a time of relatively smooth flying, my jangled nerves demanded rest. Exhausted sleep brought temporary relief from my ongoing nightmare.

* * *

Jarred awake by a blinding flash and a sickening roll, I could only gasp. The plane lurched like a wounded thing, groaning and whining. Tongues of fire appeared briefly, turning the night-blackened windows to a garish orange. The whine increased, but the rolling motion seemed to level out. There was a sinking, dropping sensation, like being on a rapidly descending elevator.

Cries of alarm from the cockpit.

A scream from Chevalier.

Just when I thought all was lost, the plane slowly leveled, pulling out of its sickening descent.

Too late.

We were skimming the surface of the water. Sea foam sprayed the windows.

The plane bumped along for terrifying minutes before the nose dipped under the foam, caught by a huge wave. The next instant was a mad scramble for escape. Dax unbuckled his seatbelt and struggled to release mine for desperate, anxious minutes as the plane slowly continued to sink. Water came pouring into the cabin. Somehow Dax managed to force the emergency exit to open.

I coughed and spewed out salt water, finding myself in the seas, surrounded by flotsam, grasping for anything that might float.

Walls of water washed over me, dragging me down before tossing me up again, sputtering and gasping for air. The storm-whipped swells were angry as a charging bull, the night blacker than a burial crypt and the seas completely disorienting.

"Dax! Where are you?" I gurgled, desperately trying to keep my head above water.

I heard an answering call before my head was submerged once more. Helplessly, I drifted with the wave, feeling myself swept along by its furious power, until there was something under my feet. Sand!

Straining my salt-burned eyes, I tried to see what I could only feel. We were near land! I could hear the surf pounding. The next swell caught me and cast my battered body onto a gently sloping, sandy beach. I managed to drag myself higher to escape the water's greedy grasp. If the tide had been going out, the undertow would never have allowed me to escape. Instead the waves deposited me safely in one piece.

"Dax!" I called again.

"Over here!" he answered from nearby.

* * *

We spent the remainder of the night huddled together under some leaves and scrubs, soaked by the wind and rain. Before morning, the squall line moved on, leaving the sea calm. At last, the sun beat down on us, wringing the moisture from our salt-laden clothes. Turquoise-colored swells rolled gently toward us, breaking frothy white against the sand.

"Where do you think we are?" I asked.

"My first guess would have been the island of Gonave, but I think we had already passed it when the plane went down. Haiti is only two hours' flight time from Miami, so it could be we're on one of the Turks and Caicos Islands. There's a whole chain of them around here. Depends how far off course we might have been." His voice sounded parched.

My next question was, "How are you feeling? Do you still have the antidote?"

Dax nodded and patted the zippered shirt pocket.

"Right here." He removed the precious life-saving vial and studied its contents, which were still a disheartening, orange color.

"Thank God!"

It would have been entirely too cruel to survive a plane crash in the ocean, wash up on a convenient island and then lose the vial that was meant to save his life.

"It's not red yet, but I am thanking God," he murmured. His eyes were still yellowish, and I knew he had to be suffering from thirst. My own lips felt parched and swollen.

"Come on," I said rising and extending a hand. "Let's find some fresh water."

We started walking along the beach on what appeared to be an uninhabitable desert island. I could see a stand of skinny trees atop a rocky ridge so we headed in that direction, stopping to drink fresh rain water that had pooled in the hollows of rocks.

"These islands can't be too far from the shipping lanes. We've got to start a signal fire with something," Dax noted, eyeing the scruffy brush dotting the sand. "You any good at rubbing sticks together?"

Before I could answer him, we saw it. Smoke curling up in a lazy spiral across the ridge. We ducked behind the trees and climbed to a higher vantage point overlooking the fire. Beside the flames stood Onyx Chevalier, braids hanging down his broad back. The white caftan was torn, revealing stocky legs from the knees down. He stood hunched over the blaze, a note of defeat somehow evident in his posture.

Dax put his finger to his lips, whispering, "Wait here. I'll scout around and see if Leroy is nearby."

A familiar voice spoke up.

"You will come with me."

Leroy stood behind us aiming a small silver revolver in our direction. I briefly wondered if the gun would fire after a dip in the ocean, but decided we couldn't risk it.

I wish I could say it was a glad reunion when the four of us met again beside the fire. Chevalier looked stricken, like someone who had just been told Hurricane Katrina had wiped him out and no FEMA trailers were available for the next year.

"So you survive," he spoke the words without gladness. "But not for long."

He turned and looked at the sea. In a flat voice, calm and devoid of emotion, he said, "The poison be working. The ocean has the book…and now the antidotes."

The antidotes? Then Chevalier's vial had gone down in the ocean! He hadn't remembered that Dax still had a vial inside his shirt pocket! I kept my eyes downcast, afraid of giving away my thoughts by a careless glance.

"*Ax* him to unzip his shirt pocket," Leroy spoke up.

Dismayed, I realized that Leroy knew where it was.

"You!" The voodoo priest hissed at Dax, a wickedly triumphant gleam replacing the hopelessness in his eyes. "Give it to me." He extended his hand.

I watched helplessly as Dax began unzipping his shirt pocket. He removed the vial.

"You mean this?" he held it carefully in one slightly extended hand.

So this was how it was going to end? Chevalier would drink the antidote prepared for Dax and live. Dax would die within hours. Certainly before any boat could find us.

I couldn't let this happen. Where was the cavalry? Cajun Jack? Anybody? Looking desperately around us for help, I saw only sand, rocks and trees. I had to do something, leap on Chevalier's back, grab the gun from Bad Leroy. But I was no match for either.

"But, there's only enough for one..." I stammered, "You have to share it."

"One. That be enough!" the she-male sputtered at me. "I had plans for you." He nodded toward the both of us. "But I want to live."

"*You* want to live," Dax began with a note of sarcasm in his voice. "Frankly Madame—I mean, *Sir*—I don't give a darn."

Only Dax didn't say "darn."

Before Chevalier could reach for the precious liquid, Dax tossed the vial high into the air. It sailed up into a sweeping arc, glimmering in the sunlight before plummeting toward the rocks.

Chevalier screeched like a wounded thing, racing after the life-saving container. Leroy followed close on his heels.

Too late. It hit with a splintering sound, shards of glass scattering and orange contents spilling out in tiny puddles and droplets over the rocky surface.

Dax grabbed my hand and we took off running in the opposite direction, leaving the pair of them scrabbling on their knees like giant crabs, Chevalier licking at the tiny droplets in a frantic attempt to save his life.

* * *

We hid among the rocks and trees, waiting and watching throughout the day and into the twilight. We found more rain water pooled in the rocky basins to slake our raging thirst. The light of Leroy's signal fire on the beach kept burning through the dark hours, and I wondered how Chevalier was feeling.

I watched Dax anxiously for signs that the poison was working in his body, bathing his forehead frequently with a cloth ripped from my green silk blouse.

Toward morning he seemed no worse, but I knew his allotted time was running out. Finally, I had to break our self-imposed silence.

"Dax, what have you done? You tossed away the vial with the only antidote left," I said miserably.

I kept thinking I should be praying for him but the words just wouldn't come.

"Does that mean you'll miss me when I'm gone?" he panted in a husky voice, turning over on his rocky bed to look up at me.

I choked back a sob, unable to answer.

He half-grinned.

"Why, Miss Flame, I think you've grown a woman's heart," he teased, then pointed to his cheek. "How about a little kiss for a dying man?"

I shoved my fist against my mouth and looked away. How could he tease me at a time like this? Steeling my emotions, I leaned forward and planted a brief kiss against his cheek.

"That was nice." He turned his head. "The other side?" and I dutifully kissed his other cheek.

"Equally nice. Now, how about a real kiss? One worth dying for?" He took my face in both his hands and looked up at me.

In a good imitation of Clark Gable's voice, Dax insisted, "Kiss me, Kaytie. Kiss me." Then he pulled me down for a gentle kiss, my parched lips against his.

With a sob, I pulled away. A hard lump closed my throat so that I couldn't speak.

"Maybe you will miss me," he teased. "And maybe when we get off this island, you'll have dinner with me at Antoine's in New Orleans."

"Stop it, Dax!"

I couldn't bear to hear him being flippant at a time like this. He must be going delirious on me, and I hadn't been able to pray for him yet.

"Say you will. I insist."

I could only manage to nod my head a little, and then lean my head against his chest. I could hear the strong, steady beating of his heart. It sounded healthy enough for the moment.

"Careful, darlin', careful," he cautioned, sitting upright and patting his shirt pocket.

I watched in amazement as he unzipped a second pocket on the other side of his khaki shirt and withdrew a small vial filled with liquid. He held it up to examine the contents. The color flamed bright scarlet in the morning sun.

That's when he grinned.

"I thought I might need *both* vials for a little bargaining leverage, so while Leroy was sleeping at Darcantel's cabin, I managed to slip my hand into his backpack and remove Chevalier's vial. They never missed it."

Hardly daring to believe what he just said, I gasped, "Dax, you're a genius!" and threw my arms around his neck. Then before anything else could happen, I turned my eyes on the vial. It was time.

"Dax, you can't wait another moment. Drink it," I urged and watched as he carefully removed the lid to peer inside at the blood-red liquid.

"It's ready. Drink it before something else happens. Now. Hurry!"

He lifted it slowly to his lips and drank. He coughed and a brief tremor coursed through his body. Then he lay back, pleasantly smiling at me before he closed his eyes.

Chapter 12

Not Today

Dax had guessed right.

It was one of the Turks and Caicos Islands where the waves had washed us up and spat us out on the sand. A scuba-diving boat captain saw the signal fire and pulled up near the beach. Captain Dan Johnson of Rockford, Illinois, welcomed us aboard.

As we pulled away, I saw a white fabric floating near the beach. Perhaps Chevalier had waded into the sea, preferring to drown rather than die from the horrible and painful poison in his blood. Leroy was nowhere to be seen, but Captain Johnson said he would notify the island authorities to be on the lookout.

With the help of Johnson, we were soon on a flight back to Miami and then on to New Orleans.

We contacted Detective Broussard as soon as we arrived and told him the entire story. He had already surmised that Madame Chevalier was actually Onyx, the brother of the twin sisters, after doing some research into the family's birth records. Broussard suspected that with his remarkable resemblance and comparable size, Onyx could easily assume the role of his sisters from time to time and probably had intended to take over the hotel business as well as declaring himself to be the voodoo priestess. The detective was glad to close the books on Emerald's murder.

That evening, we sat at a table in the famed Antoine's restaurant, where Dax ordered shrimp etouffe and I had a delicate seafood dish. Both of us sported sunburns from our island experience, but I thought my darkened skin contrasted nicely with the strappy white sundress I was wearing.

We congratulated ourselves for escaping at last from the threat of Chevalier and his evil book of sorcery.

"It's at the bottom of the Caribbean, no doubt already decomposed in the salty seas," said Dax as he raised a glass in a toast to our success. His eyes smiled into mine with admiration and something else, a hint of mischief.

I sipped sweet tea and smiled back, reminding myself to stay on guard against his strong, masculine charm. Every woman in the place had eyed him as he'd entered the room looking impossibly handsome in trim dark slacks, a pale yellow dress shirt and blue tie.

"I suppose Magnolia's book is still going to be used by that Darcantel woman," he muttered with a slight frown.

"I think not," I answered.

"What do you mean? You copied it for her word for word didn't you?" His expression changed to one of instant curiosity.

"Not exactly."

Dax placed his fork on the table and waited for me to explain.

"I copied it, but not word for word. Darcantel didn't bother to check every page. I changed a few ingredients in the recipes for the poisons, so they should be quite harmless now. There will be no more blood sacrifices, especially concerning the secrets of eternal youth. And I changed some words in the invocations to the *loas*. Those prayers are now remarkably Christian in their content. And not only that, I prayed over every page that it would do no harm."

Already chuckling, Dax burst into an outright guffaw.

"You little vixen! So the world is free at last from the sorceries of the African shaman."

I nodded. "Darcantel will be practicing Christianity before she knows it."

We laughed together, pleased at my deception. Then Dax reached across the table and took my hand.

"I have to tell you that I thought we weren't going to make it out of Haiti alive. At least not until you prayed that prayer at Darcantel's mountain cabin."

Aware of the warmth of his hand, my heart did a flip-flop.

"Dax, you bowed your head with me during that prayer. Tell me, did you pray too?"

He nodded.

"I did."

My heart leaped up. Did I dare hope that...?

"You prayed to Jesus?" I asked, my spirit ready to rejoice. A beginning smile on my lips.

"Yes."

My heart soared even higher.

"I prayed to Jesus," he nodded slowly, "and to Jehovah, and to Buddha and to Allah and Moroni," he added somewhat flippantly.

"What?" My heart hit the floor with a crashing thud.

"Well after all, we were in a tight spot, and I wanted to be sure I covered all the bases," he said still smiling.

I withdrew my hand.

"Ah, Kaytie, I can see you're disappointed. I know you'd like me better if I went to church. But come on. I'm not really an *un*believer. I'm just not certain yet that Jesus is the only way to God. You need to teach me more about Him. We're good together, you and I. You know that as well as I do."

I reached for my purse and stood up. "Sorry, Dax. Go to church if you like. Only don't go because you think it would please me. Do it for yourself. Now if you'll excuse me."

"Kaytie!" he called. I could hear his voice sounding in my heart, all the way back to Chicago.

* * *

Ed entered my office and waited till I looked up from my computer screen. He was holding a copy of the *Supernatural Seeker*. "Have you seen Larue's latest story on your island adventures?"

I nodded. Dax covered the story with a flare that left his readers hanging for more. My own series had drawn a nice audience as well, which pleased my editor greatly. Of course we had written from differing points of view. The verbal sparring between competitive journalists had worked to make our articles all the more appealing to readers. Chicago TV anchors and local radio talk-show hosts had begun inviting us to appear on their programs, separately or together.

I'd declined to do the joint interviews, thinking it best if I avoided Mr. Dax Larue and his charming grin.

"Well, he's on the phone asking for you again," said Ed. "That's about the tenth call he's made today. Will you please take this one?"

Ed knew very well why I'd been refusing to take calls from Dax. He could tell from our opposing points of view, clearly evident in our separate articles;

however, I suspected Ed was hoping I could straighten out the guy's misguided thinking. I knew that would have to happen before I consented to seeing him on any but the most professional basis. I also knew that I couldn't straighten out anyone's thinking. That would require conviction from the Holy Spirit.

The thing I have in common with the movie character, Flame, is that I'd rather postpone thinking about some things. I didn't want to make the decision to close the door on Mr. Dax Larue for good, although I knew it would be for my good to do so. *Be ye not unequally yoked together with unbelievers.* I dared not compromise my faith.

Oh, diddley squat. I had to think about it today. Glancing at the red light flashing to indicate a call waiting on my phone, I sighed and picked up the receiver.

"Hello, Dax."

"Am I speaking to the incomparable Miss Kaytie Flame O'Reilly at last?"

"That's me. Miss Incomparable."

Whatever he wants, you have to tell him *no*, I ordered myself.

This was the battleground between my flesh and my soul. Please myself or please my God.

"I've been reading your articles, and you're a very good writer. I especially liked the way you wrote about that prayer in Darcantel's cabin."

"Me too. But then I didn't think you took that part very seriously."

"Come on, Kaytie. I take prayer very seriously. As a matter of fact, I've been praying that you'll be interested in my next assignment. Interested enough to come with me and cover the story. We do a fantastic job together, you and I. Just look at the interest we've got going for our magazines right now. I bet your readership is up by two hundred percent."

"Three hundred percent."

I knew I should be making an excuse to hang up but he had my reporter's curiosity aroused.

"What kind of story?" I asked.

"Some guy in Missouri who claims he saw a UFO over a cow pasture where animals were mutilated. And get this. He's describing a garbage-can-shaped object hanging just above the tree tops. Does that sound familiar?"

Of course Dax knew very well that I couldn't pass up the chance to interview a guy who may have seen the exact same thing I saw and wrote about in *Beyond Fantasy*. How could I refuse?

Forget about the strong, masculine appeal of the man who would be there to cover that story alongside me.

I would not think about that today. Or tomorrow.

UFOs? Now that's another story.

Afterword

Because readers always want to know…

The story of the gypsy who wanted Kaytie to curse God so she could have occult power is based on an actual event in my own grandmother's life and a woman who could not tell my grandmother's future.

"You can have power to tell the future," she said to my grandmother, a young woman at the time.

"What must I do?" she asked.

The gypsy answered, "You have to curse God."

Needless to say, my grandmother refused.

The character of Sofronia is a composite of many who have turned away from seeking thrills or power in all the wrong places and received their healing from God.

The accounts of voodoo rituals are as accurate as possible, taken from eyewitness accounts as described in a 1938 book, *The French Quarter, an informal history of the New Orleans underworld*, by Herbert Asbury, Garden City Publishing Co., Inc., NY.

Butler the Beast and his infamous edict to thwart the women of New Orleans from their insulting practices is based on history found in the same book.

The interview with voodoo priestess Sally Ann Glassman is an actual interview which was posted on the Internet.

New Orleans' famed historical voodoo queen Marie LaVeau is surrounded by stories based on myth, legend and fact. I have attempted to portray her as accurately as possible, but some of the legends were too tempting to ignore.

All information regarding Haitian voodoo and the creation of zombies is taken from Internet sources. Senator Gutman and the Florida nursing home's story is from *Time Inc. Specials, Exploring The Unexplained*, 2006, New York, NY.

Vidya (not her real name) is an actual person who foretold the attack on the World Trade Centers as described in the book.

The scriptures which Kaytie alluded to regarding warnings against mediums, consorting with the dead, false prophets, witchcraft and sorcery are found in the following verses:

Deuteronomy 18:10, 11, 12
Jeremiah 23:16-40
Exodus 22:18
Galatians 5:19-21
Leviticus 20:27
Ephesians 6: 10-12
I Peter 3:15
I John 4:1
Acts 8:9; 13:6
I Samuel 28:11-16
Revelations 20:15

About the Author

H.L. Ford is a veteran news reporter, an award-winning writer, and the author of a long-running advice column. She writes stories of romantic suspense, including a touch of the supernatural, but with a sound biblical basis. It is her wish to expose the dangers inherent in paranormal activities, rather than to draw curious readers into deceitful mysteries beyond the realms of healthy fantasy.